DEAD CALM

AXEL BLAZE THRILLER
(BOOK EIGHT)

BILL RUNNER

RUNNER HOUSE BOOKS, LONDON
www.bill-runner.com

First paperback edition September 2024

978-1-7393196-8-7

www.bill-runner.com

From Soldier to Vigilante: Blaze's Path

Dear Readers,

First off, thank you for joining Axel Blaze on his journey. Whether you've been with him since *Blaze Returns* or are just diving in now, I'm thrilled to have you along for the ride.

When I first created Axel Blaze, I envisioned a man who couldn't stand by when innocent lives were at stake—a man who acts decisively, even when it means crossing dangerous lines. In his first adventure in *Blaze Returns*, he was still tethered to a semi-official role, stepping in to help his old boss at the U.S. Marshals track down a missing Deputy.

But as the series unfolded, Blaze began carving his own path, driven by his unwavering sense of justice and a deep disdain for the wrongs he saw around him. In the first seven books—*Blaze Returns*, *Lethal Force*, *Hard Target*, *Mean Streets*, *Unchained Fury*, *No Escape*, and *Fear City*—all set across different American cities, Blaze operates as a lone ranger. He steps into situations where innocent lives hang in the balance, doing what others can't—or won't.

Starting with *Dead Calm* (Book 8), the series takes a deeper dive into Blaze's past. In *Dead Calm*, we see him as a Captain in the U.S. Army Rangers, followed by his Delta Force missions in *No Mercy*, and the upcoming *Warpath* (April 2025) and

Crossfire (July 2025). These stories explore the intense operations and personal losses that forged Blaze into the man he is today.

The upcoming Book 12, *Nemesis* (November 2025), will be the final book exploring Blaze's military career. It's a deeply personal story where Blaze seeks justice for his brother Ryan—a U.S. Marine. This pivotal story will mark the turning point in Blaze's life, as he ultimately decides to leave the army. Disillusioned by the failures of the system, he becomes a man willing to cross lines to ensure justice prevails. Beginning in 2026, Blaze will be stepping fully into a world where the lines between right and wrong blur, and he's left to rely on his own moral compass to guide him.

In his words: You have to pay your dues. Period.

Your feedback and support have been instrumental in shaping this series. Blaze's journey has been as much yours as it has been mine, and I can't thank you enough for coming along for the ride.

Thank you for being part of Blaze's story.

Sincerely,

Bill Runner

CHAPTER 1

The night was dead calm, not a breath of wind. Every sound out there, even the smallest rustle, felt like it was cranked up to eleven. It was like the whole Afghan landscape was holding its breath. We moved down from our overwatch on the mountain, eyes locked on the village below. Nothing but shadows and silence, a cluster of mud huts in the dark, hiding at least thirty Taliban. We knew they were down there, just waiting for us.

The moonlight struggled to break through a thick canopy of clouds overhead, faint shadows that flickered like phantoms across the terrain. Even with our heavy rucks and gear, we moved like ghosts in those shadows, silent and deliberate, senses dialed in and sharp as a knife's edge.

"Hey Cowboy, what's with the ghost town vibe? Think the TB boys forgot to pay their electric bill?" Ninja Man's whispered words crackled over the radio, a stifled chuckle tagging along.

Ninja Man wasn't some wannabe martial arts dude. He was Sergeant Buck Conway, a tough-as-nails US Army Ranger and our official door kicker—the primary breacher of our five-man assault team from the 3rd Ranger Battalion. His call sign came from the ninja inked on his back and the 12-inch custom blade he never left behind.

"Maybe they're worried about their carbon footprint," Raptor's low growl of a response came back.

Raptor, or Sergeant Jackson Cole, was the third member of our assault team. Standing an inch taller than my six-foot-two frame and carrying 20 pounds more muscle than my 200, Raptor was a wrecking ball in close-quarters combat.

"Focus, boys. Save the comedy for the afterparty," I muttered, scanning the darkened village sprawled out below, eyes sharp for any sign of movement.

"Yes, sir, Captain sir," Ninja Man shot back with a chuckle, then fell silent.

Being the buzzkill wasn't my favorite role, but as team leader, it was part of the gig. We were neck-deep in Taliban territory, northern Kandahar Province—a hellhole where the TB, or Talis as we called them, had locked the region in a death grip. We were there to put a major dent in that.

The stakes were through the roof, and the threat level was off the charts. Ghorak District, nestled on the border of Helmand Province, wasn't exactly a tourist destination. It was the Taliban's nerve center in the region. The year was 2012, and coalition forces had barely made a dent, thanks to the unforgiving terrain—mountains and rugged hills that turned standard ops into a logistical nightmare.

But we weren't just any grunt squad. We were a handpicked team of Rangers, each one a battle-hardened warrior. Alongside Ninja Man and Raptor, we had Specialist Kevin "Echo" King handling comms and backing up on breaching. Staff Sergeant Robert "Hawkeye" Compton was our sniper, whose handle "Hawkeye" said everything you needed to know. You need targets taken out with surgical precision, well, Hawkeye was the man for it.

Then there was me, Captain Axel Blaze, the fifth piece of this puzzle. They called me Cowboy, not just because I grew up on a Colorado ranch and had a thing for cowboy boots. It was more about my knack for blazing my own trail and kicking against the system when needed.

Despite the banter, there was a weight hanging over us, one that wouldn't lift until this mission was a win. This wasn't just another op—it was personal. We had pulled strings and gathered the intel ourselves to get the brass to greenlight it. We were in this for keeps.

Our target was Bilal Mustafa, a high-ranking Taliban leader, and his right-hand man, Hamid Gul—an explosives mastermind. Just a week ago, Bilal and his squad mercilessly killed Omar Haq, our Afghan interpreter. They didn't stop there—Omar's wife and twin toddlers were slaughtered too. Bilal strapped a suicide vest on Omar's wife and blew her to bits. We swore we would make him pay, making sure he felt every second of his demise.

Omar wasn't just another interpreter. We had worked with plenty of terps over the years. But Omar was different. After a few missions together, he became our guy—reliable as hell. He wasn't just a terp; he was part of the unit. Always down for any op, no matter the risk, even when Tali psychos were blowing up his phone with threats. The Rangers he rolled with knew he had their six, and then some. We owed him big time.

Omar died holding my hand. Before he took his last breath, I promised him two things: Bilal and

Hamid would pay; and I would find his teenage son and daughter, Zara and Ayaan. Omar had managed to get them out of the village toward Kandahar just hours before Bilal's savage attack.

Now, it was a race against time to get them. Problem was, we didn't have a fix on the kids' location. All we had was a lead—a kid named Faraz Noor, Ayaan's best friend, who was helping them hide when the Taliban snatched him up. He was being held in the village by the Talis, lumped in with a group of other teenagers. They were being brainwashed, fed the usual bull about martyrdom and honor and eternal paradise. There was some twisted shit going on down there.

The clock was ticking, and we had to extract Faraz, but that wasn't official. What got us the green light was Hamid Gul—the explosives guru. He was our primary objective. Capturing him would be our ticket to Bilal. We would make Hamid talk, one way or another.

Hamid wasn't your average Taliban nutjob. He was a Brit, raised in England before he flipped and joined Al Qaeda. Turns out, the guy was a natural with explosives, quickly becoming the Taliban's go-to for suicide vests and IEDs. Every time I thought about the soldiers maimed or killed by his devices, my blood boiled. Hamid's mugshot made him look like a harmless geek with thick-rimmed glasses and a pudgy face, but he was pure evil. Before the night was over, he was going to answer for that.

As we descended the mountain, heading toward the village below, we knew the margin for error was non-existent. Stealth was our lifeline, surprise our only edge against a village full of armed Taliban fighters. One wrong move, one slip-up, and we would be staring down a hailstorm of AK-47 fire.

We had been air-dropped the night before by Black Hawk. Equipped with top-notch night vision tech, the helo skimmed the ground, low and fast. We fast-roped to a rocky ledge about four miles from our OP (observation post). It took us five grueling hours to hike through the mountain terrain before we finally set up camp beside a ridge at 0400 hours. The OP gave us a clean line of sight into the village. It was prime surveillance position.

We spent the day in overwatch, piecing together intel on TB movement. Our pre-mission intel was thin. The village was buried in a narrow valley, boxed in by steep, rugged mountains—natural barriers that limited visibility from above. Overhanging rocks and dense vegetation further made aerial recon a nightmare. No drones, no satellites could give us a clear look—this job required boots on the ground.

The village was a haphazard sprawl of mud-brick houses, twisting alleys weaving between them, like a maze built to confuse anyone not familiar. Strangely, most of the homes looked empty—no signs of life, no women. We realized this wasn't a village; it was a TB training camp for bomb makers.

In the middle of the chaos, four bigger houses stood out. One of them, with two guards posted outside, grabbed our attention. When a pudgy figure waddled out, we knew we had eyes on Hamid Gul. He stuck out like a sore thumb among the weathered faces and hardened physiques of the other villagers. Clad in traditional Afghan garb, his plump form lacked the ruggedness of a seasoned fighter. His soft round face and thick glasses made him look more like a geeky accountant than an explosives expert.

"Never seen a terrorist with a dad bod before," Ninja Man whispered, barely holding back a laugh.

"Yeah, looks like we stumbled upon the Chubby Jihadist prototype. Bet he's got a stash of Twinkies hidden under that robe," Echo shot back.

Of the remaining three houses, two served as barracks for Taliban fighters. The third, adjacent to Hamid's, housed a group of eight teenage boys. They looked terrified, almost broken. It didn't take a genius to figure out they were being groomed for suicide missions. A guard was stationed at the entrance, keeping a close eye on them, making it clear the Taliban didn't trust them to stay put.

Before we flew out, we had managed to catch a few grainy photos of Faraz Noor, the kid we were after. Peering through my binoculars, I honed in on a couple of boys who matched the description, but it was hard to be certain from such a distance.

"Well, boys, looks like we've hit the jackpot—a real Taliban summer camp down there. Teenage recruits on one side, bomb-making Brit on the other. Ain't that a heartwarming scene?" I said, lowering my binoculars.

"Who knew summer camp now includes Explosives 101," Raptor quipped.

"Never thought I'd see a Brit out here, teaching the Talis how to blow shit up," Hawkeye said, shaking his head.

"Yeah, talk about a career change—from fish and chips to grooming suicide bombers. Real step up, huh?" Ninja Man retorted.

"Dude must've been swayed by the great benefits package. You know, eternal paradise and shit," Echo chimed in.

"Must've been one hell of a mid-life crisis. Most guys just buy a sports car," Raptor said with a smirk.

"Probably sold them on the deluxe martyrdom package—one-way ticket, no refunds," Echo mused.

"And don't forget the virgins. How many do you get again? Fifty? A hundred?" Ninja Man asked.

"Seventy two," Raptor replied, not missing a beat.

"Whoa! Someone's done his research," Ninja Man came back.

"Those kids barely look old enough to shave," Echo muttered, his voice tinged with regret.

"Damn shame. Poor kids probably think they're signing up for some holy rollercoaster ride straight to paradise," Hawkeye added, shaking his head.

"Tonight we're ending this twisted little operation," I declared.

By the time night closed in and darkness shrouded the valley, our op plan was locked and loaded. Three tangos were on watch—one on the outskirts, one outside Hamid Gul's hideout, and another guarding the house with the teenage recruits. These sentries were our primary targets. Once they were neutralized, we would split into two fire teams to clear out the fighters in the two mud-brick houses flanking Hamid's place.

Stealth was everything. We had to keep enemy gunfire to an absolute minimum. The next village was five miles away. A couple of bursts of gunfire might slip under the radar, but a drawn-out firefight or an explosion would echo through the valley like a war drum. We didn't need a bunch of pissed-off Talis on our ass while we were still hauling up the mountain to the exfil point.

That was where it could get dicey. There wasn't a covert way to breach those structures. Maybe we would get lucky, and the doors would be unlocked, which is often the case in these villages. But with armed guards on watch, counting on that wasn't a smart move.

The windows were no-go—just small square slits for air and light, too tight to get through. From a tactical standpoint, not worth considering for ingress.

So, a door breach it would have to be. Normally, we would slap some breaching charges on the door and let the bang handle the entry for us. But those bad boys make a hell of a racket, something we were keen to avoid. The upside was that these mud-brick shanties had wooden doors that were a cinch to breach. No need for explosives—just a solid boot would do the trick.

That night, old-school door kicking was our go-to method. But even that makes a hell of a noise—not exactly ideal for a quiet takedown.

Once the door was breached, a couple of M67 frag grenades tossed inside would have done the job. This wasn't a hearts-and-minds mission where we were worried about collateral damage. Once we breached those doors with TB inside, we were looking for total destruction. But the M67s pack a mean punch, and the explosion is a real attention-getter.

An M84 stun grenade was our fallback option. Makes a loud bang and a blinding flash, but it would be mostly contained by the walls, and at least it wouldn't turn the whole place into rubble. But that was Plan B if things went sideways. Our preferred tactic was taking out individual targets with precision shots using our night scopes.

In the dead of night, kicking in the door would surely raise a ruckus. But once we were inside, clearing the house would be easy. These were two or three rooms max, mud-brick and bare bones houses. We would sweep through, neutralizing everything that moved. The key was surprise, speed and controlled violent action—that's CQB 101. And when it came to Close Quarters Battle, well, we were good at that.

With the house cleared, freeing the boys and grabbing Hamid would be the easy part, but the whole op hinged on nailing the first assault. We had about twenty tangos to drop, and it had to be surgical and swift.

"Time to move, boys. We've got doors to kick in. Weapons check!" I called out.

As each man went through his gear, the air filled with the familiar clicks and clinks of gear: magazines snapping into place, bolts sliding back, and the muted thud of rounds chambered. This was our pre-mission ritual, a silent promise that we were locked, loaded, and ready to raise hell.

We were geared up with MK 18 CQBR carbines as primary weapons. The MK 18 is a close-quarters version of the M4 carbine, with a 10.3-inch barrel compared to the M4's 14.5 inches. That 4.2-inch reduction in barrel length makes a world of difference in tight, confined spaces, making it perfect for close-quarters combat. The name CQBR—Close Quarters Battle Receiver—says it all.

Our CQBRs were kitted with suppressors, but we needed to be ghosts that night. So, we loaded subsonic rounds for the initial phase of the op—we had to take out the sentries with barely a whisper. Assault rifles fire rounds at speeds double or more the speed of sound. Suppressors cut down the muzzle blast, but they can't silence the supersonic crack of a bullet breaking the sound barrier. Subsonic ammo takes care of that. We were as close to silent as you can get.

"Subsonics in, suppressors on," I said, sliding a mag into place and securing extra mags of regular ammo into my vest.

"Roger that. This baby's all set. Those T-men won't hear a thing," Ninja Man shot back, his voice full of anticipation.

Raptor followed suit, snapping back his stripped carbine with practiced ease. "Yup, we know the drill... quiet as shadows till it's time to bring the thunder," he muttered, casting a glance at Mitchell. "Ready to work your magic, Hawkeye?"

Hawkeye was assembling his MK 12 Special Purpose Rifle, the weapon that could reach out and touch someone from 700 yards easy. He chambered a 5.56x45mm NATO round and checked the scope, ensuring everything was dialed in.

"Targets won't know what hit 'em," he murmured to himself, his fingers moving with well-honed precision.

Echo, perched on a rock, was meticulously checking his carbine. He glanced over at us, a smirk playing on his lips. "You boys ready to dance?" he grinned, slamming a mag into place with a satisfying click. "Don't worry, I've got your six."

Finally, we did a quick check of our SIG P320 sidearms, holstered them, and got ready to move out.

"Weapons hot, gentlemen. Let's go make some noise—quietly," I declared.

The soft clicks and clinks of our preparations faded into the night, leaving a focused silence as we strapped on our rucks, slung our rifles, and prepped to move out. The mountain descent in the pitch dark of the night was a bitch, but we were used to it. Each of us was hauling over 70 pounds of gear—weapons, ammo, armor, Claymores and enough firepower to light up the night.

Our mission was clear: infiltrate the village, take out the sentries, locate the targets, and extract them without alerting the rest of the valley. The time was 2300 hours. Exfil was set for 0100 hours. We had two hours to execute the op, haul ass back up the mountain, and hit the extraction point. No room for mistakes.

CHAPTER 2

We moved down that mountain with silent precision, every step in sync, every sense on high alert. The night was thick around us, broken only by the faint rustle of our gear and the hushed whispers of the wind. Each footfall upon the unforgiving ground was calculated, deliberate. In this kind of territory, a single misstep could turn a quiet op into a full-blown firefight.

Under the cover of darkness, we closed in on the village tucked in the narrow valley. The pitch-black night swallowed us whole as we navigated the rugged terrain, sticking to noise discipline, guided by the eerie green glow of our NVGs (night vision goggles). Ninja Man wasn't wrong when he called it a ghost town—an ominous silence blanketed the whole valley.

Just before we hit the ground, I signaled the team. Hawkeye broke off, setting up his MK 12 SPR about 300 yards out, ready to rain hell from his sniper perch.

With Hawkeye in position, the rest of us moved up, single file, MK 18s in low-ready, primed for action. With comms on whisper and weapons locked and loaded, we moved like shadows, closing in on our target. I signaled a halt fifty yards from the first sentry, perched on a boulder just outside the village.

I dropped to one knee, using the other as a brace to steady my shot. Pressing the rifle into my shoulder, I peered through the AN/PAS-13

Thermal Scope. It was set to "white hot" to detect the sentry's heat signature. Like an ethereal figure against the dark backdrop, he lit up in my sights, clear as day.

I gently squeezed the trigger, the subsonic round cutting through the air, almost silent. The shot was true to target, drilling into the side of the hostile's head. He jerked once, then crumpled into a heap. Scanning through the scope, I saw no movement. All clear.

We pushed deeper into the village, every sense dialed up, hyperaware of every shadow, every sound. We halted about forty yards from the two target houses. Each had a guard outside—one was out cold, slumped against the wall with his AK-47 propped up beside him. The other was barely awake, leaning against the wall, his rifle resting on the ground.

Raptor and I dropped to a knee, sights locked on the two targets. I gave Raptor a five-second countdown. On zero, we fired.

The suppressors and subsonic rounds did their job; each shot made nothing more than a soft "pfft." Both headshots were right on target. My guy jerked and dropped, lifeless. Raptor's target dropped like a sandbag, his rifle falling soundlessly onto his body, avoiding any clatter that could have betrayed our position.

I swept my scope across the village, checking for any signs of life. Nothing. The place was dead quiet.

Time to split up. Raptor and Echo would hit one barracks; Ninja Man and I would clear the other. Before the breach, each team circled their target house, checking the perimeter. That's when we spotted something we hadn't seen from the OP—a rear entrance on our target house. That changed the game.

"Raptor to Cowboy. Target house has a rear entry," Raptor's voice came through my earpiece just as Ninja and I made the same discovery at our target house.

"Copy that. Same situation here," I responded.

The other two houses—Hamid's and the one with the boys—didn't have a rear entry. Once we took out the hostiles in the first two houses, the rest would be straightforward.

We regrouped at the front door, prepping for a synchronized breach. The timing had to be dead-on. Ninja Man posted up beside the door, and I got set to kick it in. But then, I caught the sound of shuffling from inside and froze.

"Team two, hold the breach. Wait for my green light," I whispered into the mic, stepping back and hugging the wall, my senses on high alert.

Seconds later, the door creaked open. A half-asleep Taliban fighter stumbled out, leaving the door ajar behind him. He didn't notice us, two shadows pressed against the wall, as he shuffled toward the back of the house.

"Dude's going for a leak," Ninja Man's whisper crackled through my earpiece.

He was dead on. In Afghan villages, toilets are often separate from the main house, usually in small outhouses or makeshift structures in the yard.

"Copy that. Shadow him and drop him when you're clear of any other tangos," I ordered.

16

"Roger," he replied, slipping into the darkness like a ghost.

About thirty seconds later, Ninja Man's voice came back through. "Tango down," he confirmed, returning to my position.

We caught a break—the door was still open. We could slip in and clean house without alerting the rest of the compound.

"Cowboy to Team Two. Hold position while we breach."

"Roger that," Raptor responded.

I signaled to Ninja Man to prepare for entry. I hugged the wall by the door, paused to scan the inside, then slipped through the doorway low and fast, keeping my profile tight. I veered left while Ninja Man peeled right, both of us moving like shadows.

As I rounded the corner, my night scope lit up a figure, just starting to stand. He saw my shadowy outline in the doorway and reached for his gun, mouth opening to sound the alarm. I put him down before he could make a sound—a double tap to the chest. He hit the ground, choking, his gun clattering to the floor.

That sound woke the other five in the room. No time to waste. Ninja Man and I lit them up with precision shots. One tango managed to yell before going down, stirring up trouble in the next room. We could hear movement. No time for a tactical pause—we had to clear it, fast.

"I'm going full auto," I told Ninja Man, flipping my MK 18 to automatic mode as I charged toward the next room.

As a rule, we keep it semi-auto in most combat situations where accuracy and conserving ammo are critical. Full auto fire is reserved mainly for providing suppressive fire or dealing with multiple targets at close range. That's exactly what I needed to do as I stepped into the next room, blindly spraying bullets to take out as many as I could, clearing the way for Ninja Man to follow up with clean, precise shots.

As I moved left, staying low, my carbine spewed rounds in a deadly arc, catching the tangos by surprise. Ninja Man was right behind me, finishing the job.

"All targets down," he confirmed, while I slapped in a fresh mag.

"Copy. Team Two, prepare for breach. Team One, cover the rear door," I barked, sprinting to the back entrance of the adjacent house.

"Roger," Raptor replied, right as I heard the heavy thud of him kicking in the door.

"Hawkeye, keep eyes on the primary target. Don't let Hamid slip through," I instructed while on the move, making sure our high-value target stayed locked in.

"Copy," Hawkeye replied promptly.

A burst of AK-47 fire erupted from inside, followed by silence. I was just about to breach the rear door when it flew open, and two gunmen rushed out. Ninja Man didn't miss a beat, dropping them before they could pull the trigger.

"Friendlies coming in!" I called out as I stormed the room.

"Roger. All hostiles down," Echo's voice confirmed from the other end of the room.

"Give me a sitrep. You and Raptor good?" I asked as I moved in.

"Raptor caught a burst center mass, but his plates stopped it. His pride's hurt more than anything," Echo chuckled.

I found Raptor adjusting his vest. "How you holding up, big guy?"

He grumbled, "Bastard tagged me, but I'm good to go."

"Alright. Echo, keep an eye on Hamid's place. No one gets out unless they're crawling. Ninja and I will sweep the boys' house."

"Copy that," Echo acknowledged.

We stacked up outside the door, ready for a swift breach. Ninja Man took point, about to deliver a solid kick to the door when he noticed it was locked from the outside. No surprise—the boys inside were prisoners, not guests. He quickly undid the latch, pushed the door open, and slipped in first, pivoting left while I covered the right.

Inside, as expected, a group of boys was huddled in the corner, eyes wide with fear.

"*Per zameen wozhda!*" Ninja Man barked in Pashto, ordering them to hit the deck. It was one of the few local phrases we had drilled into our heads. The boys instantly obeyed, flattening themselves against the floor.

"Faraz Noor," I called out , scanning the faces. We were here to extract this one boy.

A kid, about sixteen, raised his head, locking eyes with me.

"Get up," I instructed, motioning for him to stand and extending my hand, not sure if he understood English.

He grabbed my hand, standing up with a mix of fear and relief in his eyes.

"Ta pa Angrezi poheegee?" I asked if he spoke English.

"A little. But my friend speaks good English," he replied, nodding toward the boy next to him.

"What's your name, kid?" I asked, crouching down to the boy beside him.

As he lifted his head and our eyes met, something clicked deep inside me. That face—it was familiar, but in the chaos of the moment, I couldn't place it right away. Then, it hit me like a ton of bricks. I had seen that face in a photo before, a picture Omar kept in his wallet—a memory of better days.

"Ayaan," the boy answered, his voice shaky but clear, confirming my suspicion.

"Ayaan Haq?" I pressed, needing to be sure, even though I already knew.

"Yes."

Well, I'll be damned! In this godforsaken corner of the world, surrounded by the chaos of war and despair, we had found a glimmer of hope. We had inadvertently crossed paths with Omar's son.

CHAPTER 3

"I'm Captain Axel Blaze," I stated, offering my hand.

"I know," he muttered, fighting back tears as he gripped my hand. "I recognized you from the photos."

I understood what he meant. Omar must have shown him that group shot we snapped after a successful mission.

"Is Zara safe?" I asked about his sister, hoping for an extended streak of luck.

"I don't know. Taliban grabbed us when we were on our way to her. I have to go find her."

"Give me a second," I said, before keying my radio: "Cowboy to Team 2, secure Hamid's house and detain him."

"Roger that, Echo, out," came the immediate response.

"Heading in for a quick debrief," I informed Ninja Man.

He nodded, his face mirroring my relief at locating Ayaan.

I took the boys into a side room to get the full picture. The intel we were rolling on came straight from Omar, who shared it with me just before taking his last breath. He had tasked his cousin Rafiq and Rafiq's son, Faraz, with getting Ayaan and Zara safely to the coalition-controlled sector in Kandahar. Omar planned to join them later, but time ran out on him. Bilal and his men stormed in before Omar and the rest of his family could escape.

I burned through every asset trying to trace the kids. They seemed to have vanished without a trace—until two nights ago, when credible intel came in from Rafiq's village. Word was that Faraz had been captured by the Taliban and was being held at this camp, with Hamid Gul running the show. That intel got me the green light for this mission.

Ayaan filled in the blanks. They had avoided main roads, but the rough terrain left them with few choices. When Rafiq caught wind of a Taliban checkpoint, he told Ayaan and Faraz to double back on foot to the village and lay low while he and Zara posed as a father-daughter pair to pass through.

"We were lying low, waiting for Uncle Rafiq, when the Taliban suddenly stormed the village," Ayaan recounted.

"Was it just bad luck, or were they hunting for you?" I asked.

"I think it was just bad luck. If they were after me, I'd be dead by now," he replied matter-of-factly.

"Our source told us that only Faraz was taken and that he'd hidden you somewhere. Isn't that what happened?"

"That's how it started. Faraz hid me in a secluded hut outside the village and went back to get some food. That's when they caught him. But Faraz didn't tell them about me. They just did a sweep of the area around the village and eventually found me."

"What happened next?" I enquired.

"The Taliban were forcibly recruiting all adult males as soldiers. They do that in a lot of villages. As for us teenagers, they brought us here to study the Holy Quran—their version of it, anyway."

"Their version, huh?"

"Yes. They kept preaching about martyrdom being the highest honor for a true Muslim. They showed us videos of western atrocities and talked about how true believers are fighting back. They said it's our duty to support their cause in any way we can."

"What do you boys think about that?"

"They killed my family. The only duty I feel is to kill them all and save my sister," Ayaan declared, his voice steely.

"And what about you, Faraz?" I asked, turning to him.

"Ayaan is my brother," he replied simply, but with a depth that spoke volumes.

"And the boys outside?" I pressed further.

"All they want is to go back home. These men are monsters, especially Hamid. He... does terrible things to Abdul," Faraz answered.

"Who's Abdul?"

"One of the boys. He's in Hamid's house," Ayaan cut in, stopping short of elaborating, his tone implying more than he said.

"Hamid will get what's coming to him. You know your father was part of our team, right?"

"Yes," Ayaan replied, struggling to hold back tears.

"How'd you manage to stay off their radar? I take it they had no clue who you really were?" I quickly redirected, trying to shift his focus.

"I gave them a fake name, and Faraz backed me up right away. They didn't dig any deeper after that. But I wasn't too worried about that. All we wanted was to get out of here and find Zara."

"Do you have any idea where Rafiq was taking her?"

"Uncle said he was taking her to a women's aid organization in Kandahar called New Beginnings. He planned to leave her there, where she'd be safe until he could contact you. Didn't he reach out to you?"

"No, he didn't. I've been trying to track him down, but no luck. We'll figure it out and check on New Beginnings. Are you sure that's the name?"

"Yes. It's run by an American woman named Madison Blake."

"Madison Blake. You sure of the name?"

"Yes, uncle told me that. I won't forget these names until I find Zara."

"Got it. You boys stay put. We'll be leaving soon. I need to have a word with Hamid Gul before we move."

As I walked out, I saw that Ninja Man had got the boys to line up against the wall, and was handing out gummy bears he had somehow managed to dig up.

"Brit jihadist's place is secure," Ninja Man reported. "But you might wanna check on Raptor and Echo. They were just about ready to throttle him."

"Tell me about it. I'd like to do the same. This isn't chubby boy's lucky night. Be ready to roll in fifteen," I said as I headed out.

I found Raptor posted up outside Hamid's house.

"All good, big guy?" I asked him.

"Yeah, but Brit boy inside ain't just into blowing stuff up. Sick fuck's got a kid in the back room, totally out of it. Echo's trying to talk to him, but I doubt anyone's gonna get through," Raptor said, struggling to keep his anger in check.

"I know. I got the lowdown from Ayaan. Can you believe we just stumbled on to Omar's kid?"

"Yeah, heard about that. Real stroke of luck," Raptor replied, a brief smile crossing his face before it vanished. "You sure you wanna drag this perv back to civilization?"

"The only thing I'm sure of is that we're getting Bilal's location out of him, even if it means sticking my arm up his ass to pull it out."

"That's all I needed to hear. First thing he squealed when I grabbed him was 'British citizen'," Raptor said , disgust dripping from his voice.

"Yeah, I bet the Brits are just lining up to welcome him back. Did he bring up the Geneva Convention yet?" I asked, knowing it would be next on Hamid's list.

"Yep, right after I slammed him down and hogtied him."

"Good work. He should be ready to crack. I'll send Echo to stand guard while we get him talking. Let's make sure he spills everything."

"Roger that."

When I walked in, I realized Raptor hadn't been exaggerating. Hamid was literally hogtied—hands and feet bound tight behind his back, lying helpless in a corner.

"I'm a British cit—" he started as I entered.

"Shut the fuck up," I snarled, my voice dripping with menace.

He clammed up quick, realizing that uttering another word might not be in his best interest. I moved to check on the kid in the back room. He was around fifteen, dazed, mumbling to himself like he was doped up. Echo had thrown a sheet over his shoulders, but the look on Echo's face told me everything. We didn't need to say a word.

"Kid's not going anywhere. Take Raptor's post and send him in. Time to put the fear of God into this sick bastard," I told Echo.

He nodded, and we left the room together. I dragged two chairs over to the corner where Hamid was trussed up, eyes wide with fear, sweat dripping down his face. I sat down, and Raptor took the other chair. Hamid squirmed, trying to get away from Raptor's reach.

"Let's talk. Here's the deal: your explosives have killed and maimed American soldiers, good men. That suicide vest you built took the life of Omar Haq's wife. Omar was family to us. And now we know you're a pedophile. So, tell me why we should let you keep breathing."

"Uh, that's not true. That, in there, it was consensual. That's a grown adult..."

I lunged, grabbing him by the throat, fingers digging into his flesh as I lifted him off the ground, our faces inches apart, my fury burning through my eyes.

"That's a kid in there, you sick fuck. You even think about going there again, and I'll crush your windpipe. End of story," I hissed through clenched teeth.

Hamid gasped for air, struggling as I threw him back to the floor. He lay there, coughing and wheezing.

"What were you saying?" I demanded, my tone ice-cold.

"Bilal killed Omar and his family," Hamid whimpered, terror etched on his face, tears ready to spill. "I'm a victim here! You have to take me as a prisoner under the Geneva—"

"You bring up 'Geneva' one more time, and I'll leave you to explain the Convention to Raptor. If you think hogtying's the worst he can do, think again. There's a reason he's called Raptor. Got it?"

"Yes," Hamid stammered.

"Good. Here's the deal, Hammy boy. We were ordered to wipe out everyone in this camp. Twenty-four of your fighters are dead around this hellhole. The only reason you're not one of them is because you might have intel. If it's worth our time, you might make it up that mountain to our exfil point. Raptor doesn't think you're worth it. Convince me otherwise, or you're getting a bullet now. We're not leaving you for the Talis to rescue."

Even though our orders were to extract Hamid and bring him back to base, I wasn't about to do that until I had squeezed Bilal's confirmed location out of him. Hamid was a murderer, and now we knew he was a pedophile. As it was, I would have a hard time explaining to my team why we couldn't just toss him off a cliff. The only reason to keep him breathing was if he led us to Bilal. As far as we were concerned, Bilal was a dead man walking.

I had no doubt Hamid would talk. I was ready to carve him up if that's what it took, but it didn't look like it would come to that. I had encountered many wannabes like him—half-baked jihadist converts who are quick to lose their new-found fervor and very willing to reconvert when shit around them gets too hot to handle. A hardcore Tali fighter would have been impossible to break, especially in the time frame we had.

But Hamid wasn't a zealot. With his Tali buddies dead, he was scared shitless. He knew we wouldn't hesitate to kill him. That fear would make him talk. But before getting Bilal's location, I wanted to see if he had anything else worth spilling. This was our only shot—once he was back at base, he would be out of our reach.

"I, uh, don't have much information..." Hamid stammered, scrambling for something to say.

"Then we're wasting time," I snapped. "Raptor, take care of it. We're moving out," I said as I stood up from my chair.

Raptor swiftly pulled out a knife, grabbed a handful of Hamid's hair, and yanked his head back, exposing his neck.

"No, no, wait!" Hamid pleaded, sheer terror in his eyes. "I have something. There's a lead in Tangi Shahbaz that'll interest you."

"Where's Tangi Shahbaz?" I demanded.

"About eight miles north down the valley. They're holding two hostages —an American and a Brit."

"What hostages?" I asked, suddenly intrigued.

"A woman and a man. They run a women's center in Kandahar. The woman's American, supposedly the daughter of some big shot in Washington, D.C. They haven't confirmed her identity yet, which is why they're keeping her alive until they do."

"And the guy?"

"He's just a regular Joe, some academic."

28

"How do I know you're not just making this up?"

"You can verify it. Check with your base. There was an attack yesterday. They grabbed them along with some Afghan girls."

"What are their names?"

"The man's called John Hughes. The woman's name is Madison Blake."

I was stunned. Madison Blake was the same woman Ayaan had mentioned moments ago—the one who might hold answers about Zara.

CHAPTER 4

I had to lock it down, keep my face like stone, not letting on that what Hamid just dropped was big.

"Raptor, get Echo to verify that with base. What were those names? John Hughes and Madison something?" I said, playing it cool.

"Madison Blake. She ran some place called New Beginnings," Hamid replied.

That sealed it. New Beginnings was the name I had just heard from Ayaan. The hostage was the same woman Zara and her uncle were trying to reach. I looked at Raptor. He nodded and headed out.

"Alright, Hamid, keep talking," I ordered.

"That's it. That's all I know," he stammered, trying to convince me.

"Where's Bilal?"

"I don't know," he shot back, a little too quickly.

"You ready to die for him? 'Cause we'll find him eventually. But if you want to live, you'd better speak up now."

"I swear I don't—"

"You don't get it, do you? We're here for revenge. If you don't give us Bilal, you're forfeiting your life. I'm the only thing stopping my men from tearing you apart, just like Bilal did to Omar's family. Once I'm out that door, it's their call how you go. You're smart enough to know that unless you're of use, and it makes sense for us to take you back to base with us, we're not leaving you alive."

"How do I know you won't kill me after I tell you about Bilal?" Hamid's question told me he was close, just trying to cut a deal.

"Here's the deal: I don't give a fuck about you. I want Bilal. You give us the location, and we'll take you with us. You'll have to lead us to him so he doesn't bolt. If you make it happen, you get to live. Your call."

"Uh, can you at least untie me? Let me sit up and think? I can't feel my limbs."

"Consider yourself lucky you still have them. We don't have time for bullshit. We need to move out. You had your chance, and you blew it," I said, standing up like I was done with him.

"No, wait! I'll tell you. Bilal's set to meet an arms dealer in Quetta in five days."

"In Pakistan?" I needed to be sure.

"Yes. He goes there for deals."

That checked out. Quetta was a known Taliban hub, just over the border from Kandahar. The city was a critical nexus for Taliban operatives, who frequently crossed the border to conduct their deals. It was a stronghold, a place where they got their guns, ammo, and plenty of support. It wasn't just the physical proximity. The strong Pashtun cultural and tribal connections facilitated easy movement. Quetta had an extensive network of Taliban sympathizers providing logistical support, shelter, and intelligence. Taliban ops move through Quetta like it was their backyard.

"Where exactly in Quetta? I need exact coordinates," I asked.

"I'll give them to you once you take me to base."

"You think you've suddenly got leverage?"

"No, I'm just trying to ensure I stay alive."

"The only reason you're still breathing is to lead us to that meet without spooking anyone. You do that, we grab Bilal, and you get a shot at negotiating your sorry ass back to England. But for that to happen, you've got to leave this place alive. Prove to me you're worth the trouble, or you're getting a bullet, and we'll call it mission accomplished. Dead or alive, it doesn't matter to my superiors."

Raptor walked in at that moment.

"The intel checks out. There was a Tali raid in Kandahar yesterday. The man and woman were taken, along with some girls," Raptor confirmed. "So, we dragging this piece of shit with us or what?"

"Not yet. Give me a minute. If he plays ball, we take him back. If not, he's all yours."

"I still say he's full of shit."

"Sixty seconds, Raptor. Then I'll make the call," I said, letting Hamid hear that time was running out.

Raptor shrugged and left. I pulled out my knife and cut the cord binding Hamid's hands and feet together. He was still restrained, but not hogtied anymore. The relief on his face was clear, but I didn't let him get comfortable. I had thrown him a bone; now it was time for him to deliver. Basic negotiation tactics.

"You heard that? Sixty seconds. I need the location of Bilal and the hostages, or else, I'll have a mutiny on my hands if I keep you alive. I'm not about to let that happen."

"The coordinates are in my phone," he said, a note of resignation in his voice.

"You're shitting me? There's no signal out here."

"I went to Khakrez yesterday. Forty miles from here. That place has connectivity."

"Where's the phone? Clock's ticking."

"Under my pillow. The code is 7860. It's saved in the contacts as Khan's Dry Fruits."

I found the phone, unlocked it, and scrolled through the contacts. There it was: Khan's Dry Fruits, with coordinates listed under a phone number.

"Whose number is this?"

"Arif Khan. He's the dealer."

"How do I know you're not bluffing?"

"I can't prove it from here. You can run a recon. You'll see I'm not lying."

"Not good enough."

"Uh, check the maps on the phone. The location is tagged. There are photos too."

"What about the hostages? Where are they hidden in that village?" I pressed, scrolling through the photos, trying to squeeze every last bit of intel.

"They're high-value targets. They don't keep them in the village. They're being held in caves in the mountains behind it, guarded round-the-clock. There's a narrow path from the village to the caves. It's not much of a path—more like a goat trail—but these fighters move on it like it's a highway."

I stopped at a photo showing a big shop with a sign that read "Khan's Dry Fruits", and a bunch of Urdu scribbled all over it. The place looked legit— full of dried fruits and nuts stacked high in burlap sacks, people bustling around like it was any other day. No surprise there—no one's stupid enough to hang AK-47s and RPGs out in the open.

The next photo, however, made my blood boil. It showed three men in a room: Hamid, a second guy I didn't know, and a third figure that had burned into my brain from all the intel photos we had gone over the past week. A menacing presence, tall and imposing, with a gaunt face framed by a thick, unruly beard. Eyes that could freeze a man in his tracks. His expression was a deep, perpetual scowl. That was Bilal Mustafa.

Behind them were wooden crates, piled up haphazardly and marked with black stenciled labels that screamed danger—AK-47s, rocket launchers, enough ammo to start a war. The whole place looked like a makeshift armory, ready to supply death at a moment's notice. I zoomed in on the unknown guy's face, but the dim light and shadows didn't help much.

"Who is this?" I asked.

"Arif Khan."

"Right. We'll confirm it on the move. If it doesn't check out, you're finished. Think long and hard about that," I warned, then walked out.

I joined Raptor and Echo outside.

"We've got a location on Bilal. He's meeting an arms dealer in Quetta."

"You trust him?" Raptor asked.

"It's not about trust. I think we've scared him enough not to lie. And the photos on his phone back it up," I said, showing them the photo.

Both men swore when they saw Bilal.

"It's 2350 hours. Rendezvous is at 0100. Let's get moving in five. We're taking all the kids. Echo, make sure they're ready to roll."

"On it," he said, already moving.

"Raptor, same goes for Hamid. We're dragging him up that mountain."

"Copy that. Let's hope he's in better shape than he looks," Raptor replied, not exactly sounding kicked about it.

Raptor headed toward the hut but froze in his tracks at the door. He motioned for me, eyes locked on something inside. When I got there, the reason for his sudden paralysis was clear as day. The boy was sitting right next to a terrified Hamid, their hands cuffed together. Wrapped around the kid's torso was a suicide vest, and the digital timer was ticking down—21 seconds, 20 seconds. The boy's glazed eyes were fixed on Hamid, as he muttered something in a language we couldn't make out.

CHAPTER 5

I dashed inside the house, my mind racing for a solution to somehow disarm the vest. My fingers scrabbled at the mechanism, searching for any way to remove it. No such luck. The vest was fastened with a thick chain and a sturdy lock. That lock wasn't coming off without a key. There was none in sight, and the boy, barely coherent, was the only one who knew where it was.

"Help me! Get him away from me!" Hamid's voice was a shriek of raw terror, each word trembling with desperation.

15 seconds to detonation.

I scanned the room for anything, anything at all to cut the chain or disable the bomb. But there was nothing. That lock might as well have been a tank. The kid kept mumbling, lost in his own world, completely unaware of the ticking death strapped to his chest.

12 seconds.

Desperation crystallized into a sharp, cold clarity. Every heartbeat was a countdown, each second a fragile lifetime. It hit me—this thing was going to blow, and there was no stopping it. More hidden explosives throughout the house was also a grim certainty.

No time to free Hamid, no time to drag him out even if I wanted to save him. There was only one move—get everyone clear of the blast radius and brace for impact.

"Cowboy to all teams, fall back and hit the dirt! Ten seconds to detonation in Hamid's house. I repeat, ten seconds! Move, move, move!" I barked into my radio, my voice sharp with urgency, as I bolted out with Raptor on my heels.

We sprinted toward the boys' house. Echo and Ninja Man were already on it, hustling the kids out, pushing them toward the edge of the village, trying to put as much distance as possible between them and the incoming blast.

Two seconds before detonation, I shouted, "Hit the ground! Now!"

My order was instantly relayed by Ayaan to the boys. Eleven bodies—four Rangers and seven boys—hit the dirt in sync. We had managed to get some open ground and some cover between us and Hamid's place —mud-brick houses, just enough to break the worst of it.

A second after we hit the deck, the stillness of the night was shattered by a sudden, bone-rattling crack. It echoed through the air, a grim prelude that sent a chill down our spines. For a split second, there was an eerie silence, an almost surreal calm before the storm.

The night shattered as the first explosion ripped through the air, a deafening roar that rattled our bones. The ground beneath us trembled violently as the shockwave burst outward, racing toward us with a roaring force. A searing light pierced the darkness, a blinding flash that turned night into day for an instant. Flames shot up from the house, sending a column of fire and smoke into the sky.

Silence followed, like the world held its breath.

We were mostly unscathed, thanks to the houses that we were able to put between ourselves and the explosion site. But I knew more was to come.

"Stay down. Don't move yet. Keep your heads down and cover them with your hands," I shouted.

A second later, another, more ferocious explosion followed, as the hidden explosives within the house detonated in a devastating chain reaction. The sound was a rolling, concussive boom that shook the ground once again. The shockwave from the second blast tore through the night with renewed fury, hurling debris and shrapnel over the houses that had shielded us, crashing into walls and scattering across the open ground.

The force of the explosion hit us almost like a physical blow, pressing us hard against the earth. Dust and debris rained down, pattering on our backs. The air was filled with the acrid stench of burning materials and the thick, suffocating cloud of pulverized mud bricks.

The light from the blast lit up the night like a fiery sunrise, casting long shadows and revealing the devastation in stark relief. As the echoes of the explosions died away, the silence that followed was almost as shocking as the blasts themselves. The night once again became still, save for the crackling of flames.

"Alright, time to get up. Everyone OK?" I shouted, coughing and shaking my head to clear the ringing in my ears.

The acrid smell of burnt earth and shattered stone hung heavy in the air as we slowly pushed ourselves up from the ground. Dust and debris coated our uniforms and faces, making us look like ghosts emerging from the wreckage of the blast.

Echo, closest to me, rose to his feet and brushed himself off, patting his gear to check for any damage. "I'm solid," he declared.

Raptor, still on one knee, quickly scanned the area before nodding. "All good, just shook up," he said, sweeping a layer of dust from his helmet.

Ninja Man emerged from behind a collapsed wall, his face streaked with grime. "Clear and intact," he confirmed, checking his rifle and gear.

I moved toward the boys, huddled together near the edge of the village, wide-eyed and visibly shaken but miraculously unharmed. "You guys good?" I directed my question to Ayaan.

He nodded. "Yes, we're all OK," he replied, his voice trembling but firm.

Ninja Man broke the tense silence. "So, who's up for not doing that again anytime soon?" he quipped, dusting off his gear.

Echo replied: "Well, that was one way to clear out the neighborhood. Think we overdid it with the redecorating?"

Raptor shook his head, a smirk tugging at his lips. "Remind me to bring earplugs next time we crash a party like this."

Just then, Hawkeye's voice crackled through the radio from his sniper perch: "Did you guys forget this was supposed to be a stealth mission, or did I miss the memo?"

I shook my head and replied with a weary sigh, "Stealth's overrated, Hawkeye. Besides, nothing like a little fireworks show to liven up the night."

Ninja Man smirked and added, "Guess we can scratch 'subtlety' off the mission checklist."

"I'd say that ship's sailed. Hawkeye, keep your eyes on the horizon and let us know if there's any trouble heading our way," I told him.

"Roger that," he replied.

None of us mentioned the kid back at Hamid's. That image—the bomb-strapped, drugged-out boy—was something that would stick with us, but we weren't dwelling on it then. The kid didn't deserve such a fate, but Hamid? He got exactly what was coming to him.

The clock was ticking, and I was acutely aware of it. The massive explosions wouldn't go unnoticed for long. They would surely draw Taliban fighters from nearby villages. The time was 2355 hours. We barely had enough time to make it to the exfil point by 0100, especially with the kids in tow.

"Hawkeye, got any movement in your sights?" I radioed in.

"Negative. All clear," he responded.

"Roger. Pack up your rifle and start moving up the mountain path. Find higher ground so you can get eyes on the valley. We're rolling out in five."

"Roger that. Moving out," came his swift reply.

"Alright, guys, we need to haul ass," I addressed the team. "That explosion's gonna have the Talis on our six."

"No shit, that blast is a beacon," Raptor chimed in.

I motioned Ayaan over.

"You're in charge of the boys now. Tell them we're headed up the mountain and over the other side. We've got a helicopter coming in to pick us up from there. Got it?"

"Yes," he replied, and turned to go.

"Hang on. That's going to be a grueling climb. Make sure everyone's had some water. If you can find any bottles, grab them. OK?"

"Got it, I'll do that now," he replied, heading to brief the group.

"Ninja, Echo, you're on point. Echo, fall in behind Ninja. I'll take the rear with Raptor."

"Roger that," they replied in unison and walked off . I signaled Raptor to hang back.

"We'll rig a couple of Claymores to keep the Talis off our backs, in case they pick up our trail and try to follow us. Gotta slow them down and give them second thoughts about chasing us in the dark," I said.

This was Taliban territory. I had zero illusions about how deadly a well-armed pursuit team could be. We were all in peak shape, but we had the boys to consider. A few might be naturals on the mountain paths, but I doubted every one of them had the mountain goat agility that TB fighters usually boasted. In the pitch dark, those Claymore mines would be a nasty surprise.

"Good call," Raptor agreed. "What's the play for the hostages Hamid mentioned?" he asked.

"Priority one is getting the boys to the helo. After that, we're extending the mission for a hostage rescue. It's going to be optional—anyone's free to tap out."

"You know nobody's gonna tap out. You really think any of these guys will bail unless you knock them out and strap them to the bird."

"True, but I gotta ask for the record."

"Yeah, sure. But we're all in this together. That hostage is the key to Omar's daughter. The boys won't find peace until she's safe. And getting Bilal is part of that. We still good on that intel?"

"Yup, I'm holding on to Hamid's phone. I've got a feeling the intel's solid. That guy in Quetta is Bilal's go-to arms dealer. The meeting's a lock—I don't think Hamid had any influence over it. Bilal won't suspect a thing. Those guys own the turf in Quetta; an attack's the last thing they'd expect."

"You think we'll get the green light for that?"

"No idea. We'll play it by ear. For now, I'm keeping this intel close to the chest. Not sharing it with command."

"Smart move. I'm in."

"But I'll need to radio HQ for clearance on a new mission plan for the hostage rescue. We'll decide once we're on high ground and out of the Talis' reach. The guys coming to check this place are going to be heavily armed, likely packing RPGs. We don't want them lighting us up during our climb."

"Copy that. On the upside, they might think it was one of Hamid's screw-ups and not start a manhunt right away."

"Yeah, that's our edge. It could buy us the time we need. Hide the sentry's body we took out first. He was outside the blast zone. The other two were right by the house; that area's flattened. TB won't get any clues from them."

"Roger," Raptor said and moved off.

Three minutes later, our squad—four Rangers and seven boys—was climbing the mountain, moving fast and quiet, knowing we were racing the clock and the enemy.

CHAPTER 6

We set off on the steep, rocky path up the mountain. Calling it a "path" was generous—it was more like a series of sketchy footholds cut into the rock, barely wide enough for a boot. Some stretches forced us to hug narrow ledges that clung precariously to the mountain, where one wrong move could send us crashing down the mountainside. That path was more suited for mountain goats than men. Not a place for the faint-hearted.

That's why I had Ninja Man on point. Guy grew up in the Appalachians, scrambling around mountains like a pro. As for me, I cut my teeth in the Colorado Rockies—so this wasn't new ground for either of us. Ninja moved with the kind of sure-footed confidence you need up here, guiding the group through the treacherous climb. Echo followed close behind, moving like a man on a mission, with the seven boys right behind him. The air was crisp, with a faint whiff of burning from the explosions we left behind.

The boys weren't exactly thrilled about the climb, but they were young, fit, and used to this kind of rugged terrain—better than some city kid, for sure. They pushed on, driven by survival and the trust they had placed in their newfound protectors. Raptor and I took the rear, scanning our six for any sign of movement. We weren't out of the woods yet.

Ten minutes in, Hawkeye's voice crackled over comms. "Hawkeye to Cowboy. I've got eyes on two vehicles coming in from the east. About two miles out. They'll hit the village in around four minutes."

"Cowboy here. Copy that. What's your position? Do you see us coming toward you?"

"Affirmative. You'll reach me in two minutes."

"Copy. Hold your position but be ready to move."

"Ninja Man to Cowboy. Three of the boys are struggling. What's your take on easing the pace once we hit Hawkeye's position?"

Ninja had set a punishing pace for good reason—we needed distance. The AK-47's effective range is 400 yards. On flat terrain, maybe we could cover four miles an hour, but on this climb, with the steep and rugged terrain, we would be lucky to make one mile an hour. With our rucks and the boys in tow, 400 yards would take us about 14 minutes. To be safe, we needed to keep up the pace for another five minutes to get out of AK range.

"Cowboy here. That's a negative," I replied. "We can't slow down. We need to keep moving for five more minutes to get out of AK range. After that, we'll take a 60-second water break. I'll be setting a Claymore near Hawkeye's spot. If it comes to it, you, me, and Raptor will each carry a boy."

"Ninja Man here. Copy that. Just as long as the boys don't start calling me Dad."

"Don't worry, Ninja Man. You'd make a lousy role model anyway," Echo cut in.

"Man, I can handle Talis with AKs, but that... really stings," Ninja Man chuckled.

Ninja Man got why I was playing hardball. He probably made the slow-down request more for the boys' morale. With a clear timeframe to catch a breather, they would dig deep and push through. That's how you keep folks moving under pressure. We soon reached a narrow bend where the path squeezed tight, cliffs on one side and a sheer drop on the other.

"Looks like a good spot," I said to Raptor, nodding toward a crevice in the rock.

I dropped to a knee, pulling a Claymore from my pack. Setting it against the rock face, I camouflaged it with loose stones and dirt, rigging the tripwire to a jagged outcrop.

"That'll ruin someone's day," Raptor quipped as we picked up the pace, moving to catch the others.

About 200 yards up ahead, where the path leveled out briefly before splitting into two steep inclines, a lone figure stood watch. Hawkeye, with his eagle eyes and steady hand, had set up a lookout position. His MK 12 SPR was perched on a rocky ledge, its scope fixed on the village below.

As we approached, Hawkeye turned, his expression calm but alert. "Two vehicles inbound, two minutes out," he reported, voice low but tense.

From our vantage point halfway up the mountain, we had a clear view of the village below. It was a wreck—flattened, charred, smoke still twisting into the night sky from the explosions. Beyond the smoldering ruins, two sets of headlights cut through the darkness, their eerie beams sweeping across the scorched ground.

Hawkeye, still glued to his scope, whispered urgently into the radio, "We've got another vehicle about a mile out. Moving fast. They're coming in hot."

"Time to move. Pack the rifle while I set up another Claymore," I replied.

Hawkeye gave a curt nod and began to break down his rifle with practiced precision. He secured it in its case, his movements quick and efficient, before slinging the rifle case over his shoulder.

Meanwhile, I set up another Claymore in the shadow of a protruding boulder. If this one went off, it would make them think twice about charging up the mountain.

With my night-vision binoculars, I took a quick look down at the village. The two vehicles had stopped at the edge of the ruins. About fifteen fighters, armed with AK-47s, had jumped out and were now staring in disbelief at the flattened, smoldering houses.

"Ninja Man to Cowboy. Proceeding with a 60-second water break," he informed me.

That told me they had been climbing for 15 minutes. The main group was 100 yards ahead of us, well out of firing range, but we weren't out of the woods yet. Those Talis could move fast, and if they zeroed in on our position, they would close that gap quicker than we liked. We couldn't let up.

"Cowboy here. Copy. 60 seconds it is," I replied.

Just as I said the words, I spotted two Taliban fighters. "Shit," I muttered. Each had an RPG-7 rocket launcher slung across his back. That suddenly changed the equation. We were no longer in the safe range. The RPG had a range of about 360 yards, but its max range was twice that. They might not have pinpoint accuracy at that distance, but a lucky shot could still reach us. With grenades, you don't wait around for fate to decide.

We couldn't just hope that it wasn't the Talis' lucky night.

We had about 15 minutes of climbing left before hitting the peak. From there, we would have to cross the ridge and get to the other side where the LZ (landing zone) was waiting. That meant 20 more minutes of staying exposed.

I checked my watch. The 60 seconds were almost up. Right on cue, Ninja Man's voice crackled through the radio, "Break's over. On the move again. Boys are still holding up."

"Cowboy here. Copy that."

We pressed on, the team moving cautiously, every step deliberate. The mountain's path was unforgiving—narrow, winding, and rugged. But with each step, we put more ground between us and the village, improving our chances of making it to the exfil point unscathed.

Ten minutes passed, and we were closing in on the peak. Just as we neared the top, a sudden flare shot up from the village below, lighting up the sky. It exploded, casting harsh shadows against the rocky cliffs, turning night into day for a brief, blinding moment.

"Down! Everyone, hit the ground and close your eyes!" I ordered, keeping my voice low but urgent.

Immediately, everyone complied, dropping low and shielding their eyes from the harsh glare. The Rangers, seasoned and responsive to commands, quickly pulled the boys down with them. Each Ranger wore AN/PVS-15 dual-tube night vision goggles, which adjusted swiftly to the sudden burst of light. But I was worried about the boys. The flare's intensity could ruin their night vision, and without the goggles, they would struggle to see.

"Ayaan, tell the boys to keep their eyes shut. We can't risk them losing their night vision," I called out.

"OK," Ayaan replied, before saying something in Pashto to the boys.

The flare hung in the sky for about 30 seconds, casting an eerie glow over the mountainside. We could hear distant voices echoing up the slope. The light from the flare gradually dimmed before darkness reclaimed the night, plunging the mountain back into blackness. I could see the boys blinking rapidly, their eyes struggling to readjust to the dark.

"Alright, let's move. Careful steps," I ordered, my voice low but firm.

The group rose cautiously, their movements deliberate as they resumed the steep and narrow climb. The path ahead was treacherous. Each step was a calculated risk, but we pressed on, driven by the urgency of our situation.

Barely a minute later, another flare shot into the sky, followed by the unmistakable staccato of AK-47 fire. The sharp, crackling sounds echoed up the mountain. I knew we were out of range, but that wasn't the concern. The real issue was that the Talis now had a good fix on our location.

"They've got our position," Raptor muttered, his voice grim.

"Yeah, stealth's blown. We're hauling ass to the LZ. Double time, move, move!" I ordered, urgency creeping into my voice.

With the enemy hot on our trail, there was no point in trying to hide anymore. The focus was now on speed. We needed to reach the LZ as quickly as possible. The team picked up the pace, the boys struggling to keep up, but driven by the fear of what lay behind them. Every second counted.

The staccato chatter of AK-47 fire from below became a constant backdrop, but we ignored it, knowing we were out of range. We were almost 700 yards away, although I knew the Talis would set off in pursuit and try to close the gap. Suddenly, a different sound cut through the air—a sharp hiss, followed by the unmistakable thump of an RPG launcher.

"RPG incoming!" I shouted, my voice barely carrying over the chaotic symphony of gunfire and heavy breathing.

We instinctively ducked, eyes scanning the horizon for the incoming projectile. The rocket's bright, fiery trail streaked across the dark sky, cutting through the night like a blazing comet. Its ominous whistling crescendoed as it approached. But it quickly became clear that the shot was wildly off-target, with the RPG whizzing past us and slamming into the mountainside far away. The explosion echoed through the valley, a dull roar followed by the distant rumble of debris cascading down the rocky slope.

A few seconds later, there was another whoosh as another grenade made its way up. But the result was the same—it exploded somewhere far below us.

Hawkeye's voice crackled over the radio, cool and collected amidst the chaos. "Hawkeye to Cowboy, should I engage? I've got a clear shot."

I glanced up the path, the mountain's peak tantalizingly close. We didn't have time to get bogged down in a firefight. "Negative, Hawkeye.

They're too far below, and we're just five minutes from the top. Keep moving."

We pressed on, legs burning, lungs straining against the thin mountain air. The boys struggled to maintain the pace, but fear drove them forward, their youthful energy fueled by adrenaline and sheer survival instinct.

Suddenly, the night was split by a different kind of explosion—shorter and sharper. The unmistakable crack of a Claymore mine echoed off the mountain walls, followed by the muffled screams and shouts from below. I realized with a grim satisfaction that our precautionary measures had worked.

The enemy was persistent, but we had the advantage of the high ground. With renewed urgency, we quickened our pace, the LZ and safety now within reach. In a few minutes, we arrived at the summit. The village and the vast expanse of the valley was far below. Ahead, a narrow ridge beckoned, its rocky spine stretching precariously across the mountain's crest.

The time was 1235 hours. Twenty five minutes remained until exfil. But once we crossed the ridge, we would be in a commanding defensive position. Everyone in the team was struggling to breathe from the arduous trek. Even though I wanted to cross the ridge immediately and move to safety, I was worried about the boys. They would need to be completely focused while crossing the ridge. It was quite exposed and a little lack of focus could send one of them tumbling down the sheer face of the mountain. I decided to give them a short breather.

"One-minute breather before we cross the ridge. Have a few sips of water and catch your breaths.

We're still not safe until we're on the other side," I told the group.

As if to emphasize what I said, a distant, muffled explosion echoed up from the valley—the second Claymore mine going off. The sound reverberated off the rocky walls, a grim confirmation that the Taliban were still hot on our trail, but at least we had slowed them down. The LZ was about a five-minute simple walk beyond the ridge. But we would need to set up a defensive position as soon as were on the other side.

"Hawkeye, Echo, you'll take point. Hawkeye, find a good spot and set up your overwatch. Need you to cover our six."

"Roger that," he replied.

"Echo, as soon as you touch ground, prep the radio. I'll need to talk to command."

"Roger that," he echoed Hawkeye's response.

As soon as sixty seconds were over, I got everyone moving. We walked out single file, moving cautiously as we navigated the rocky outcrop. The wind howled, whipping around us as we crossed the narrow ridge, a precarious pathway with sheer drops on either side.

As soon as we crossed the ridge, we paused at a small clearing, the mountain's rugged terrain giving way to a narrow plateau. The boys' faces were etched with the exhaustion of the climb. It was time for them to sit down and take a breather.

"Ayaan, tell the boys to take a breather. Rest up for a bit," I told him.

The boys didn't need Ayaan to translate what I said. They had already sunk to the ground, taking grateful gulps of water. By then, Hawkeye had moved to a rocky outcrop that offered a clear view down the mountain and had already begun setting up his MK 12 SPR rifle with the practiced efficiency of a seasoned sniper. Meanwhile, Echo pulled out the PRC-152 tactical radio from his pack. He keyed up, adjusting the frequency to reach command.

I signaled Raptor and Ninja Man to gather around us. It was time to break the news to the team about an extension to our current mission. We would be sending off the boys on the helicopter while we made another eight-mile trek to attempt a hostage rescue.

CHAPTER 7

"Alright, listen up. Here's the deal. We've got a helo inbound to extract the boys. Once they're safe, I plan to extend the mission. We're heading to Tangi Shahbaz, eight clicks down the valley. Got intel on two hostages—an American woman and a Brit guy. This isn't just a hostage rescue mission. The woman's the only lead we've got on Omar's daughter, Zara. We leave her behind, and we might never find Zara."

The team exchanged glances, the gravity of the mission sinking in as I continued speaking.

"This mission's gonna be extremely high-risk. More Talis, and they'll be on high alert. We'll be deep in hostile territory, dodging patrols and possibly fighting our way in and out. We'll have to make it to the village, grab the hostages, and get out clean. It's gonna be a rough ride. The threat level's gonna be off the charts, way beyond what we've dealt with tonight."

I scanned their faces, looking for any sign of hesitation.

Ninja Man was quick with a quip: "Just another day in paradise, huh?"

"More like a stroll through hell, but yeah, something like that," I replied. "The only upside is we're making this trek deep in the night when we won't be spotted by any TB patrols. We stay dark and hit the village before daylight. If this was a daytime trek, we wouldn't have had a chance in hell. But I'm not gonna sugarcoat it. The threat level's through the roof. The mission is optional. If anyone's had enough, you can hop on the helo with the boys. No shame in it."

The Rangers glanced at each other. They had faced death together more times than they could count, and backing down wasn't in their DNA. It wasn't just that. I had spoken for each one of them when I made the promise to Omar.

Raptor was the first to break the silence. He grinned, his eyes gleaming with a fierce light. "Skip the speech, Cowboy. I'd miss your pep talks too much if I don't go on this ride. Besides, I haven't had a good fight in days. You know I'm in."

Hawkeye, busy setting up his rifle, didn't even look up as he muttered, "Hell, I didn't crawl through the mud and eat MREs for a year to pass up a chance to dance with the Talis. I'm in."

Hawkeye had never made any secret of his dislike for MREs (Meals, Ready-to-eat), which were our lifelines on such extended missions.

Echo, still working on the radio, looked up with a smirk. "Ain't no way I'm missing out on this. You think I'm gonna let you have all the fun? Not a chance, boss."

Ninja Man, always cool and collected, chuckled softly. "Someone's gotta keep you guys out of trouble. Might as well be me."

I couldn't help smiling. "Alright, you crazy bastards. Let's get this done. We get those hostages, and show them why you don't mess with the Rangers."

The next step was to radio HQ for clearance on the new hostage rescue mission plan. It was time to call Battalion Commander Lt. Colonel Seamus Flynn.

Flynn was a seasoned warrior, one of those officers who didn't turn into unempathetic desk jockeys when they went up the chain of command. He was a fair man who never forgot the human element in the battlefield equation. He understood the genuine struggles soldiers faced, whether it was the suffocating heat of the Afghan mountains or the crushing weight of impossible decisions. He was the kind of commander who balanced the cold calculus of war with a deep, abiding care for his men, always ready to support them in their most desperate hours.

By then, Echo had the radio up and running. The connection crackled to life, the line hissing with static.

"Sierra One to Lightning, do you read?" he said, his voice calm but deliberate, as the radio's display flickered with the signal lock.

Sierra One was the call sign of our unit while Lightning was the command unit.

There was a brief pause before a reply came through: "Lightning to Sierra One. I read you. Over."

"Sierra one to Lightning. Requesting immediate comms with Lightning Actual. Over."

Lightning Actual referred to the commander, Lt. Colonel Flynn. There was a brief pause, then a crackle of static followed by Flynn's calm voice, "This is Lightning Actual. Go ahead."

"This is Sierra One Actual," I said, getting on the line. "Do you copy?"

"Solid copy, Sierra One Actual. Go ahead."

"Lightning Actual, be advised. Target Hammerhead has been neutralized. Target was not viable for capture due to extenuating circumstances. Additionally, 25 tangos KIA. We've reached the exfil point but have another armed group tailing us. Over."

"Copy that. Understood about Hammerhead. Any casualties on your side?"

"Negative, just a few scrapes and bruises. We've secured intel on two hostages, one American, one British, located at Tangi Shahbaz, approximately eight miles out. One HVT confirmed, linked to CIA. Intel is reliable, repeat, reliable. Over."

I knew the magical words—HVT (high-value target) and CIA—would give Flynn more than enough justification to give us the green light.

There was a pause, then Flynn's voice came back: "Copy that. What's your status?"

"Currently at the LZ, awaiting exfil in twenty mikes. Requesting a priority update on mission parameters. Permission to extract rescued personnel only—seven teenagers—and extend mission to include hostage rescue at Tangi Shahbaz. Time is critical. Over."

There was another brief silence before Flynn responded. "Sierra One Actual, you have a go for the extended mission. Be advised, helos are about to be wheels up from FOB Ramrod. ETA to your location, 20 mikes. Any resupply requests? Over."

FOB Ramrod was a military base located in Maiwand, due south from our location—a flight time of about 15 minutes. The Black Hawk must be ready to take off any moment. Despite my last-minute request, Flynn offered to pack some extra supplies before the bird took off. Well, I had my list ready.

"Roger that, Lightning Actual. We could use some extra MREs and water, and a resupply on ammo—5.56x45mm NATO mags, Claymores, and frag grenades. And basic climbing gear—two lengths of 60-meter rope, carabiners and belay devices. Over."

"Copy that, Sierra One. We'll get those loaded on the bird. Over."

"Also requesting satellite and drone photos of Tangi Shahbaz, particularly the caves in the mountains behind the village. Need detailed layout for OP setup and potential nightfall assault. Over."

"Copy that, Sierra One. I'll get the intel teams on it. Photos will be relayed via SATCOM. Stand by for transmission. ETA for intel, 15 mikes. Over."

"Copy, Lightning. Over."

"Stand by for extraction in twenty. Get your team ready. Good hunting. Lightning Actual out."

I handed the radio back to Echo.

"Alright, we've got the green light. Let's get these boys on the bird and then head out."

"Roger that, but why the climbing gear? You figure we'll need it?" Ninja Man asked.

"All I know is the hostages are being held in some caves on a mountain. Can't be sure until we've seen the layout. And we've got this trek in front of us… unknown terrain… we just might get stuck on some cliff and need a way out. But we might end up not needing the stuff at all," I replied.

"But best be prepared. Makes sense."

"I guess. Hawkeye, you see anything?" I asked him.

"Negative. It's quiet. For now."

"Good. Maintain overwatch. Ninja Man, head back over the ridge and set up one more Claymore at the end of the path leading to the ridge. We've got almost a 30-minute head start on the Talis. It should be safe enough, but better give them a little more disincentive in case any fast climbers make it up early."

"Roger," he replied and headed back toward the ridge.

I called Ayaan and explained the situation to him.

"We'll put all you boys on the helicopter. It'll take you to Kandahar Airfield. The rest of us will meet you there tomorrow."

"You won't come back with us?"

"No, we've got to finish off something else first," I replied, not wanting to tell him about the hostages and the link to Zara.

"Can I go out to look for Zara once we're back in Kandahar?" Ayaan asked.

"No, you'll have to stay at the base to be debriefed. It's not up to me. But Zara's my top priority. I give you my word."

"I believe you. Thanks."

"No worries. I know both of you have had a harrowing time. But you're going to be fine. Just a matter of time."

Ninja Man was soon back after planting the mine on the other end of the ridge. But it turned out to be more of a precaution. The first couple of Claymores had made the TB men extra cautious and slowed them down.

Meanwhile, Echo had begun receiving information on his SATCOM terminal. It was beeping softly, indicating the incoming transmission. He tapped the small screen and it flickered to life. A series of high-resolution satellite and drone images began to load, detailing the layout of Tangi Shahbaz and the caves behind the village. The photos captured the village and its surrounding terrain in crisp detail, highlighting the narrow streets winding between mud-brick houses, and more importantly, the cave systems in the mountains behind the village, their dark mouths gaping like ominous portals against the rocky landscape.

I gathered the guys for a quick brief.

"This is the plan. The village is eight miles north. We'll move along this ridge line here," I said, pointing to a path leading north, "It looks a little steep, so when we get a chance, we'll navigate around it and use the lower trail. It's a bit longer, but we avoid any open exposure until we descend into the valley. Keeps us out of sight and gives us some cover. We go dark and keep it quiet. No lights, no noise."

"Roger. And when we hit the village?" Raptor asked.

"We'll circle around to these higher rocks here," I replied, pointing to a vantage point overlooking the village, "and set up the OP. We'll be there by 0400, just before dawn. We hunker down, observe all day, pinpoint the hostages' location, and make our move once it's dark. Stealth will be key. We can't risk a firefight in those tight quarters."

"What's the extraction plan once we have the hostages?" Hawkeye asked.

"We'll figure that out based on what we find. Could be a hot exfil, so be ready for anything. Any questions?"

"Just one," Ninja Man cut in. "Who's making breakfast?"

"We make it to the OP without a firefight, I'll whip up some top of the line MREs for you," I shot back. "Anything else?"

"Nope, sounds like a solid plan. Let's get moving and make this happen."

"Alright, gear up. We roll out at 0100, as soon as the helo takes off with the boys. Speaking of which..."

I stopped as we caught the low hum of the Black Hawk's rotor blades, giving us the first indication of its approach.

CHAPTER 8

The night was inky black as the helo approached the designated LZ at precisely 0100 hours. It was flying dark, its skilled pilots relying solely on advanced avionics and night vision to guide the helicopter through the night. No external lights revealed its approach, keeping it invisible against the starless sky.

Inside the Black Hawk were two men. Major Jack "Viper" Reed, the pilot, a seasoned aviator with a reputation for executing the impossible, and Chief Warrant Officer Mike "Gator" Harris, the co-pilot, known for his razor-sharp focus and unmatched aerial gunnery skills.

Both were part of the elite 160th Special Operations Aviation Regiment (SOAR). Also known as the Night Stalkers, the 160th dudes were the epitome of military aviation badassery. Whether it was flying into the most dangerous territories or extracting teams under heavy fire, the Night Stalkers were the ones who got the job done.

As the Black Hawk descended, the sound of its rotors grew louder, the air thrumming with the power of its twin engines. The helicopter hovered just above the ground, a disciplined display of control and expertise, before settling gently onto the rough terrain. The backwash of the rotors kicked up dust and small rocks, but the LZ was secure.

While Raptor and the guys helped the boys get on board and buckle up, I approached the open door where Viper was waiting. Viper and I went some way back—it wasn't the first time he had come to get our team on an exfil.

"Viper, good to see you, pal," I said, raising my voice over the noise.

"Always ready for a wild ride, Cowboy," Viper replied, his eyes hidden behind night-vision goggles but his confident grin clearly visible.

"You sure you didn't get lost on the way here? Thought you might've taken a wrong turn at Kabul," I said, raising my voice over the noise.

"Ha! You know I'd have found you in a snowstorm in hell, Cowboy. Just had to stop for a kebab on the way," Viper shot back.

"Figures. I've seen your flying. Hope you didn't spill any on the controls," I laughed, patting the helicopter.

"Just keeping you on your toes. And hey, I brought extra napkins," Viper chuckled, giving me a friendly punch on the arm. "So, what's the plan?"

"We need a little show. Strafe the area beyond the ridge when we lift off. There are Talis making their way up the mountain. Make them think we're headed out of here. We're actually going to haul ass down the other side of the mountain and head to another village. But we need those Talis to think we've gone," I explained.

Gator, listening in from the co-pilot's seat, chuckled. "You boys always up to some crazy shit, huh?"

"Just another day at the office, Gator. We just need that cover to get out clean."

Viper gave a thumbs-up. "Consider it done. We'll give them a show they won't forget. You just make sure to keep your heads down."

"Thanks. You guys are the best."

"Damn straight," Viper replied with a smirk. "Night Stalkers don't quit. We've got some goodies for you back there. Make sure you get them," he signaled to the back, where the extra supplies I had requested were stashed.

"Can't get our fill of MREs and ammo," I quipped.

As the Rangers began unloading the supplies, Viper gave a final nod. "Stay safe out there, Cowboy. We'll keep their heads down for you."

"Thanks, Viper. We'll see you on the other side."

The Black Hawk lifted off, its rotors slicing through the air as it ascended rapidly. Moments later, the sound of machine-gun fire erupted, strafing the area beyond the ridge with a display of firepower that echoed through the night. It was time for us to move.

Time: 0100 hours.

As the helicopter flew off, we began our rapid descent down the opposite side of the mountain, heading toward our next objective, the village of Tangi Shahbaz. After the fireworks at the ridge, the Talis didn't have any doubt that we had flown away with the boys after a successful mission. It never entered their consciousness that we had voluntarily missed the flight to stay back and take in the scenery. We had a long trek ahead of us, but at least running and hiding from pursuing gunmen firing at us wasn't part of the equation.

The night was pitch-black, the mere sliver of a moon hidden behind thick clouds, but the NVGs painted the landscape in eerie shades of green. We moved carefully down the rugged terrain.

"Alright, team, keep it tight. We got three hours to cover eight miles. Let's make it count," I whispered, trying to get them in the right frame of mind.

"Yes, boss. These night hikes always remind me why I joined the Army. Nothing like a midnight stroll in enemy territory to get the blood pumping," Hawkeye replied, panting slightly.

"C'mon, Hawkeye, it beats the treadmill at the gym any day. Just hope we don't run into any mountain goats. They always have the right of way."

"Or worse, those goats with a grudge. Last thing I need is to get headbutted off a cliff," Hawkeye grumbled.

"Don't worry, Hawkeye. I'll put in a good word with the goats for you," Raptor chimed in.

We carried on in silence for a while. The air was cold, the silence broken only by the occasional crunch of gravel under our boots and a little bit of grumbling every now and then. Every so often, we would halt, scanning the surroundings with our NVGs to ensure we were not being followed or observed.

Time: 0130 Hours.

It wasn't easy going, especially after the rapid ascent we had made along with the boys. After the initial descent, we were faced with another climb to get to the ridge. The trail steepened, winding up through the craggy mountainside. Ninja Man, in the lead, signaled a halt to evaluate the path ahead. The team paused, taking a moment to catch their breath.

"Welcome to the scenic route, folks. Watch your step, unless you're into free-falling," he cautioned as we began moving again.

"I didn't sign up for base jumping, Ninja Man," Echo replied, sounding a little nervous.

"No worries, Echo. I'll make sure to go first and check if it's safe," Raptor muttered.

Time: 0200 Hours.

The path narrowed, clinging to the mountainside with a sheer drop to the right. Moving in single file, each Ranger treaded carefully, the wind carrying faint sounds from the valley below.

"Anyone else feel like a mountain goat on a tightrope?" Echo muttered.

"You mean with these fancy hooves? Totally," Hawkeye replied.

"Just don't start chewing grass, and we'll be fine," Raptor added.

Time: 0230 Hours.

The landscape opened up into a flat, barren stretch. We picked up pace, moving swiftly across the valley floor.

"Alright, let's clock some distance now that we've got it nice and level," I urged the team.

"Roger that, Cowboy. Just don't complain if I outpace you," Echo cut in.

"You outpace him?" Raptor snorted. "Last I checked, you were the one eating dust on the last run."

"Hey, that was tactical dust ingestion. Builds character."

"Yeah, keep telling yourself that."

Time: 0300 Hours.

The valley narrowed again, guiding us toward the final ascent before the village. It was a brutal, relentless climb that tested our endurance and resolve. But we pressed on, our muscles burning from the relentless climb, each step drawing us closer to our destination. Sweat trickled down our brows despite the cool night air.

"This mountain better come with a free drink at the top," Hawkeye said, panting.

"Yeah, right. I'll take mine with a little umbrella, please," Echo chimed in.

Time: 0330 Hours.

The ridge loomed ahead, a jagged silhouette against the dim pre-dawn sky. The team clambered over the rocks, muscles burning with the effort. I checked my watch; we were right on schedule. The village was just over the next rise.

"Alright, team. We're on the home stretch. Let's keep it tight and quiet," I said.

"I'm saving my noise for when we hit the village," Ninja Man replied.

"I just hope they've got some coffee ready for us," Raptor chimed in.

"No promises, Raptor. But I'll see what I can do," I replied.

Time: 0400 Hours.

As the first light of dawn began to tint the sky, we reached the ridge overlooking Tangi Shahbaz. The village lay below, quiet and deceptively peaceful. It was still shrouded in shadows, but I knew the daylight would soon reveal its secrets.

"Alright, team. We're setting up the OP here. Hawkeye, you're on overwatch. Echo, get the comms ready. Let's get a clear view of the village."

"Copy that, Cowboy. I'll get the gear set up."

"Anyone fancy a morning jog after this?" Ninja Man asked.

"Only if it's downhill, Ninja, and comes with breakfast," Raptor replied, propping himself against a rock.

We swiftly set up our observation post, melding into the rocky landscape with practiced precision. From our concealed position, we commanded a clear, unobstructed view of the village and the treacherous terrain surrounding it, ready to gather intel and plan our next move.

"Good job, team," I said. "Let's get our intel and be ready for whatever comes next. And remember, no cliff diving until I say so."

"Roger that. I'll keep my wings clipped," Hawkeye replied.

"Next time, how about a beach mission? Sand, sun, and no mountains," Echo suggested.

"I second that," Raptor replied. "Mountains are overrated."

Despite the grueling trek and the peril that loomed like a dark specter, our focus was razor-sharp. We had a singular, non-negotiable goal—to extract the hostages from Taliban captivity.

Ayaan had been saved. Rescuing Zara was next on our list. Before we squeezed the life out of Bilal. Each of us had promises to keep. The stakes were deadly high, and we were ready to face the firestorm.

CHAPTER 9

Tangi Shahbaz, a secluded village with a headcount of around 600 locals, was precariously perched within a narrow gorge deep in the heart of an unforgiving landscape. Encircled by towering, rugged cliffs and sheer, hostile terrain, the only way in and out of the isolated settlement was by a single, serpentine path that twisted and turned its way up the treacherous slopes. This trail, carved into the cliffside, served as a natural fortification, effectively isolating the settlement from the outside world.

The village looked like it was clinging to the sides of the gorge, with its mud-brick houses huddled together as if for collective protection against the looming cliffs. The atmosphere was one of constant vigilance, with a palpable tension that underscored every movement and conversation. It looked like life in Tangi Shahbaz was lived under the oppressive shadow of the Taliban, who had turned the secluded hamlet into a stronghold of fear and control.

An unpaved path snaked out from the village, lined by steep cliffs on one side and a sheer drop on the other. Six battered pickup trucks were lined up haphazardly along the side of the path. The vehicles were a mix of old Toyota Hiluxes and slightly newer models, all bearing Taliban insignia—black flags with white Arabic script— fluttering from antennas, and makeshift racks on their roofs carrying spare tires, jerry cans, and various supplies.

The trucks had seen better days—none of them looked like they had come into existence in the recent past. Dust and dirt caked their exteriors, giving them a uniform, grimy look. One of the pickups stood out—a white Toyota Hilux with a rusted mount on its bed, supporting a DShK, a Soviet era heavy machine gun. The gun's muzzle pointed skyward, its worn barrel a grim reminder of its lethal capability.

High above the village, hidden among the crags and crevices of the mountains, were a series of dark, foreboding caves. These caves served as the Taliban's secret lair. In one of those caves were the hostages we had come in search for. Trapped within these stone prisons, they would be living under the ever-watchful gaze of their captors—mean, battle-hardened fighters whose eyes never ceased their search for any hint of escape or intrusion.

The Taliban's control over access to these hideouts was absolute. The guards, armed and ruthless, ensured that no one but their own men ever set foot near these hidden chambers. The threat of violence hung in the air like a dark, suffocating cloud.

By that time, we had received intel on the two hostages on the SATCOM terminal. The woman, Madison Blake, was actually going by a different last name. Her real name was Madison Davis. Her old man, James Davis, was Deputy Director of Operations at the CIA. Madison had been using her mother's name for good reason. If the Talis found out about her CIA connection, she would never see the light of day again. No negotiations, no deals—she would be taken out in the most ruthless way. Madison was 26, five foot five, and according to the mug shot that came with the intel, she was quite striking to look at.

Why she decided to risk her neck saving young women in Kandahar was anyone's guess. There were plenty of downtrodden women in relatively safer places. I was getting the feeling she used her mother's name not just to hide her relationship with the CIA big shot. She was doing it to make some kind of a point. James Davis clearly didn't have much say over how she lived her life.

The other hostage, John Hughes, wasn't based in Kandahar. He was officially just a consultant who had dropped in for a short visit. Talk about tough luck. The guy was Oxford-educated, some kind of expert on global affairs, and looked like a professor who would much rather be buried in books than out trudging the Afghan landscape.

We spent the whole morning scouring every inch of the village and the caves with our binoculars. We hadn't spotted the hostages, but we zeroed in on one cave, which stood out due to the constant presence of two armed guards.

"Looks like they're serious about that cave. You think the hostages are in there?" I asked Raptor, peering through my binos.

Raptor, lying next to me with his own binos trained on the same spot, replied, "I'd bet on it. No reason to have two guys guarding a cave otherwise."

Late in the morning, three Taliban fighters approached the cave, stayed inside for about twenty minutes and then left. Their faces had scowls when they went in, and there wasn't any change in their disposition on the way out.

It was the trio's second visit during late afternoon that confirmed our suspicions. When they ascended the tricky path from the village, their demeanor was more aggressive, their movements charged with a sense of purpose as they went inside the cave.

A couple of minutes passed before two of the Taliban emerged from the cave, each dragging a captive before him. The captives, hands bound tightly behind their backs, stumbled awkwardly, their heads hung low. Initially, they offered no resistance, resigned to their fate, until they began to realize the direction they were being forced to move in. Panic set in as they neared the cliff's edge, and the terror on their faces became palpable. It was at that moment, when the men raised their heads, that I realized that one of them was the British hostage, John Hughes.

Both captives tried to dig in their heels, feet scraping against the rocky ground in a desperate attempt to resist. But their efforts were in vain. The Taliban, fueled by grim purpose and superior strength, pushed them closer to the precipice. The men teetered on the brink, their breath coming in ragged, panicked gasps, eyes wide with fear.

As we watched, the third man appeared at the cave entrance, his grip firm on a struggling woman. I recognized her instantly. It was Madison Davis. Her hands were tied behind her back, but she fought fiercely, kicking and thrashing against her captor. Her efforts only seemed to amuse him. He tightened his grip, grabbed her by the hair, and forced her to witness the scene unfolding before them. Madison's face twisted in anguish and fury as she watched the other captives.

The two men stood at the edge, a mere heartbeat away from a fatal plunge. They cried out, their voices a chilling symphony of terror that echoed through the gorge. Without warning, one of the captors gave his prisoner a slight push and released his hold. The man's scream was bloodcurdling, getting abruptly silenced as his body struck the jagged rocks far below.

"Goddamn it," muttered Raptor, unable to contain his horror. "That's just pure evil."

Hawkeye's eyes narrowed as he watched the scene through his scope. "Cowboy, I can take a shot. Just give the word, and I'll drop them right now."

Every fiber in my being wanted Hawkeye to blast those guys to hell and back. But we knew we couldn't do it.

"Negative, Hawkeye. Too risky. Both remaining hostages will die if we do."

"Son of a bitch," growled Ninja Man. "I can't believe they just did that."

The man they had thrown off the cliff was an unknown entity. The Brit was still alive and in the clutches of the other guy. His struggle had ceased, replaced by a blank, numbing dread, as he teetered over the abyss. His captor seemed to relish his fear, holding him there for what felt like an eternity before yanking him back to safety and throwing him roughly inside the cave. Madison was dragged back inside after him.

"Damn bastards," Raptor growled softly, his fists clenching. "We need to get them out of there."

"We will. But we need to know more. We can't rush in blind," I replied.

We knew the stakes were sky-high and the threat level was way beyond the rescue op we had just wrapped up with the boys. Tangi Shahbaz was crawling with TB fighters. It was difficult to make an accurate estimate, but from the number of men carrying rifles, the minimum number was 50 active fighters. But if it came to it, they could easily increase their numbers to three or four times that. It wouldn't take much to hand AK-47s to village folk scared about their families' safety and ask them to pursue us and fire in our general direction.

We couldn't hope to outgun that many tangos armed with AK-47s, even though most of them couldn't hit the broad side of a barn. But with that many of them spraying rounds on full-auto in our general direction, the odds of catching a few stray shots were not in our favor. And if some of those clowns had RPGs in the mix, we would be out of luck in a straight-up firefight, especially with two civilian hostages in tow.

A beat-up pickup pulling into the village a little while later suddenly upped the stakes.

"Check out this pickup that just rolled in. Six not-so-friendly Talis onboard," Ninja Man spoke up, signaling me to join him.

I zoomed in on the truck, its body battered and rusty, tires caked with dust from countless treks over rugged terrain, which had just pulled up. Six Taliban fighters climbed out, their movements purposeful and alert.

"Looks like they're up to something," I muttered as they began unloading gear from the truck bed.

One fighter reached into the back of the truck and pulled out a long, cylindrical object. He hoisted it onto his shoulder and started walking toward a nearby house.

"Hold on. Is that what I think it is?" I whispered as I adjusted the binoculars for a better view.

"Looks like a MANPAD," Ninja Man confirmed, his voice tinged with concern. "Can't be sure, though. We need a closer look."

Man-portable air-defense systems (MANPADS) like the Stingers are infrared homing surface-to-air missiles (SAM). That introduced a whole new element of danger into the mission. We shifted positions slightly to get a clearer view. The long cylindrical tube the fighter was carrying was unwieldy and required both hands to balance, but the way he handled it with practiced ease suggested familiarity with its weight and shape.

"That's definitely a SAM. No way he's handling it like that if it's just a mortar tube," I said, the cylindrical shape and the way the fighter handled it leaving no doubt in my mind.

The realization hit us like a cold wind. The Talis had SAMs—the stakes had just escalated dramatically. Extracting the hostages without detection was now a matter of life and death. Any hint of our presence, and the Taliban would unleash a barrage of rockets, potentially sealing off our escape route with landslides or, worse, bringing down our extraction bird.

"We'll need to be ghosts. No noise, no light, just in and out," Ninja Man muttered, his eyes still glued to the man.

"Roger. If they realize their guards are down and the hostages are gone, they'll light up the mountainside with everything they've got," I agreed.

One wrong move could turn this into a bloodbath. We would have to plan our approach down to the last detail and strike with surgical precision if we had any hope of rescuing the hostages and making it back in one piece.

From the layout of the caves and the heavy hardware the Talis had, it was becoming clear this rescue mission wouldn't be a cakewalk. We had four guards to neutralize quietly before reaching the hostages. Two were stationed at the cave entrance, and two more were perched on a ridge with a direct line of sight to the caves. We couldn't make a move on the cave guards until the ridge guards were down.

The only way to handle those guys was with long-range sniper shots. Luckily, we had Hawkeye behind the scope of the suppressed rifle, so that wouldn't be an issue. But we needed to ensure the shots were positioned so the bodies didn't tumble forward and land on a house in the village. They had to fall backward.

"I'll shift my perch once it gets dark. Need to get a line of fire so the bullet pushes them back and they collapse against the rock face," Hawkeye laid out his plan.

"What about ammo? Can you manage a subsonic load at that distance?" I asked.

I was worried that in the dead of night, despite the muzzle suppressor, the supersonic crack of the bullet breaking the sound barrier would alert the guards at the cave.

"That's a negative," Hawkeye replied. "The distance is about three hundred yards. Subsonics don't work well at those ranges. The bullets are heavier and way too slow. Increased bullet drop and wind drift mess up accuracy. About 150 yards is the max they'll be true to target. Are you worried about the sonic crack?"

"Yeah, that's what I was thinking about."

"No worries. It matters only when the bullet passes by a person—that's when you hear the crack. From that perch, those cave guards won't be anywhere near the bullet's flight path. With the suppressor on, they won't hear a thing."

"Well, we've got nothing to worry about then. As soon as you've taken out the ridge guards, you'll head back to the OP for a wider view. Our view down there will be limited. Take out any hostiles you see moving from the village."

"Roger."

"Well, that settles the first part of our assault. Any questions?" I asked.

"Yeah, how do we fly out to those cave guards to take them out," Raptor pointed out, smirking.

He had a point. Dropping the two ridge guards was just the beginning. Taking out the cave guards was the tricky part. The caves were only accessible via a steep path leading up from the village. Beyond the caves, it was all sheer rock face—no escape routes. We couldn't just walk up to the guards. And Hawkeye's perch for taking out the ridge guards didn't have a line of sight to the cave guards. We couldn't wait for him to hoof it out for twenty minutes to get a clear line of sight to them.

"I was coming to that. Any ideas?" I asked, looking around the group.

"I guess the only option would be the two of you doing your Spiderman routine," Echo said, glancing at Ninja Man and me.

He was right. The only way to take out the cave guards silently was by dropping onto them from the mountain above. Ninja Man and I were the best climbers in the team. We would have to be the ones to do it.

"That does seem to be the only option," I agreed.

"So, the climbing gear's going to come in handy after all. I was cursing you on the trek for making me lug the rope," Ninja Man grumbled.

"I had the other one on me, Ninja. And you know what, I was wondering all the way if we shouldn't just chuck it somewhere."

"Well, good thing we didn't. But, man, setting up that anchor in the dark and rappelling down without making a sound ain't going to be easy."

"That's why they call you Ninja Man. Time to live up to your name. It's the only way to catch the guards by surprise."

"Yeah, sure. So, what's the plan once we neutralize the guards? Looks like we've got no choice but to take a stroll through the village."

"Affirmative," I replied, scanning the terrain. "There's no exit from the cave except through the village. Here's the plan: we secure the hostages, head to the village, then hike back up to the exfil point. Echo, once all four guards are down, your task is to rig those six clapped-out pickups with C-4 for remote detonation. Just enough to blow up the trucks, not the whole village. If our luck holds, we exfil back to the OP without stirring up the Talis. Then, we give them a wake-up call minutes before we fly out. If they catch on and we get them on our tail, the fireworks will keep them busy."

"Roger that," Echo responded, grinning. "I'll make sure it's a wake-up call they won't forget."

"Once you've set the charges, Raptor, Echo, you'll take position along this path up from the village. Use your carbines with subsonic rounds. You see any movement in the village as we exfil, neutralize on sight."

"Copy that," Raptor and Echo affirmed together.

"What about the SAMs? Do we make a move to take them out?" Ninja Man asked.

"Negative. They've got the MANPADS stowed in a house in the middle of the village. We try to get them, we might wake up the whole neighborhood. It has to be absolute stealth. We move in and get out like ghosts. If that village wakes up before we're within touching distance of this post, we'll be swarmed. No way we're fending off a mob of Talis once the alarm's raised."

"Copy," everyone replied.

"LZ is half a mile northeast on that flat patch behind that ridge. Exfil is at 0100. Miss that bus, and there won't be another one to catch—the Talis will be on us with RPGs and mortars faster than you can say 'clusterfuck'. So, gentlemen, let's make sure this goes like clockwork," I cautioned.

"Don't worry, Cowboy," Raptor chimed in with a grin. "You know we love working under pressure. Makes the coffee taste better in the morning."

"Speak for yourself," Ninja Man added, "I prefer my coffee without a side of shrapnel."

It was going to be one hell of a night, but we were ready for whatever hell was about to throw our way.

CHAPTER 10

We locked in our final weapons and gear check at 2200 hours. Next, it was time for war paint—thick streaks of black camo slathered across our faces. And then, we played the waiting game.

At 2230 hours, we moved out. Hawkeye went solo to set up his new perch. Raptor and Echo looped around to drop down to the village level. They would stay cloaked in the shadows, just minutes away from their final spot near the village entrance, waiting for the green light once the four guards were neutralized.

Ninja Man and I took the scenic route to the mountain face above the cave. We started our slow descent, using our NVGs to pick out each hand and foothold with surgical precision, heading for an anchor point about forty meters above the cave mouth. We set up the anchor at 2300, rigged ourselves up with the rope and belay device, and held tight.

One thing working in our favor was that while the cave was lit from the inside by a lamp, the entire mountain wall above and below the cave was shrouded in complete darkness. From our anchor point, we could clearly see the ridge guards, silhouetted against the mountain by the faint lamp light from the village below them. The crucial thing was that they couldn't see us as long as we stayed clear of the cave entrance.

At 2320 hours, Ninja Man and I began a methodical, controlled descent down the rock face, moving horizontally with deliberate, quiet steps. We navigated down to just above the cave entrance, our primary weapons securely fastened to our backs to avoid any accidental noise from contact with the rock. Each of us had a suppressed SIG P320 and a combat knife within quick reach, ready to neutralize any threats based on proximity.

We hung there, suspended against the mountain, feet braced horizontally against the rock while the ropes held our weight. Only one guard was visible outside the cave.

A few seconds past 2330 hours, Hawkeye's voice whispered through our earpieces: "Hawkeye to Sierra One. Both ridge targets down."

"Raptor to Hawkeye. Copy," came the confirmation from Raptor.

Ninja Man and I maintained radio silence but confirmed the message receipt by double-clicking the PTT (Push-to-Talk) button. The brief radio clicks were followed by Hawkeye's confirmation: "Copy." Hawkeye immediately began making the ascent back to the observation post up on the ridge.

It was go-time. We descended further until our feet touched down on top of the cave entrance. One target was directly beneath me. I could have simply drawn my SIG and put a round through the top of his head. But we had no idea how deep that cave was and where the second guard was positioned. For all we knew, he could be taking a nap. But until we knew for sure, we couldn't make a move. One hasty takedown, one guy shouting out a warning, and we would have a small army down on us.

We remained in position, vigilant and patient. Five minutes elapsed without any movement.

However, in the sixth minute, the guard below me got up, stretched lazily, and sauntered to the edge to take a leak. It was the perfect moment. I drew my SIG, aligned the sights, and fired a double tap into the back of his head. The man crumpled silently and vanished from sight over the edge.

I signaled Ninja Man, and we descended swiftly and quietly, landing with practiced precision on the hard ground on either side of the cave entrance, cloaked in the darkness. I peered inside the cave, dimly illuminated by a single, flickering lamp hanging from a rusty hook, casting long, wavering shadows across the rocky interior.

About ten yards in, a Taliban fighter sat cross-legged on the ground, smoking a cigarette, his gaze fixed on the woman hostage in a lecherous stare. I instantly recognized her as Madison.

She was seated on the cold stone floor, her hands bound tightly behind her back, visibly shaken but striving to maintain her composure. Despite her disheveled appearance and the loose, dusty clothes she wore, she was strikingly attractive, with rebellious blonde curls peeking out from beneath her headscarf, catching the dim light. Her body was tense with fear, and she desperately avoided making eye contact with the guard.

Beside her sat a middle-aged man, the second hostage, his head bowed in despair. I recognized him as John Hughes. His hands were also tied behind his back, and he seemed to be whispering words of comfort to Madison, though his own terror was evident in his every movement.

The guard took a long drag from his cigarette, exhaling smoke through a sneer that twisted his face into a grotesque mask of menace. His rifle lay casually across his lap, fingers twitching near the trigger guard as he leered at the woman, absorbed in his sadistic amusement. No wonder he wasn't outside pulling guard duty as he should have been.

Not that it would have made any difference to what was about to happen. I nodded to Ninja Man, who stayed vigilant outside the cave. With quick, silent steps, I moved inside, my SIG drawn and ready. The guard, assuming it was his partner, didn't bother to look up immediately. He never saw my face. I shot him twice in the head before I had taken my second step.

"Cowboy to Sierra One. Both cave guards neutralized. Hostages secure," I spoke into my mic, then moved inside to free the hostages.

My eyes landed on Madison first. Despite the fear and exhaustion etched into her features, her vivid green eyes were captivating. She looked to be in her mid-20s. A fit and athletic woman who had somehow gotten it into her head that running a women's education center in Taliban-infested territory was a good idea.

Next, I glanced at John Hughes. He had a tall, lean frame with thick, slightly unruly salt-and-pepper hair, looking every bit the quintessential absent-minded professor who had somehow managed to get himself kidnapped by the Taliban. His outfit confirmed my impression: a crumpled light blue dress shirt, dirt-streaked beige slacks, and leather sandals—the kind that flapped with every step. He was taken hostage straight from his workplace in Kandahar, and he still wore the same clothes, which were now wholly inappropriate for the rugged mountainous terrain.

Those flimsy sandals, with thin leather straps and soles about as tough as cardboard offered little protection from the sharp rocks and uneven ground. I wondered how the hell we would get him to walk out of that rock-strewn terrain in those.

As I approached the mismatched pair, their expressions were far from relieved. It wasn't hard to figure out why. I had holstered my SIG and drawn a knife as I walked toward them, intending to cut the ropes that tied them. That, and the way I had black camo paint streaked across my face, plus the fact that I had just blew the brains out of a man sitting a few feet from them, I realized that I didn't exactly present a picture that inspired their instant confidence.

"We're US Army Rangers. You're safe for now," I said as I bent down to free her. "You're Madison Davis, right?" I asked, aiming to put her at ease.

"Yes. Uh, I mean, I'm Madison Blake," she replied, her voice soft and a bit shaky, doing her best to keep her eyes on me and away from the dead guard.

I understood what was going on. She was still trying to stick to using her mother's surname so she couldn't be tied to her CIA dad.

"Yeah, I know you're using your mom's name. You don't have to hide anymore. You're gonna be fine," I said, cutting through the ropes binding her hands.

She looked surprised I had been able to crack her real identity. Before she could respond, I turned toward the other hostage, who too was trying his best to keep his gaze averted from the dead Tali.

"John Hughes?" I asked, slicing through the rope binding his hands.

"Yes, indeed. Thank you ever so much," he replied in a classic British accent, bringing his freed hands forward and rubbing his wrists with a sigh of relief.

"No sweat."

"May I have the pleasure of making your acquaintance?" Hughes asked, extending his hand with impeccable politeness.

I looked at him, barely believing I had stumbled across such a prim and proper Englishman in the badlands of Kandahar. But formalities would have to wait.

"Just call me Cowboy for now. The Ranger at the entrance is Ninja Man. We're sticking to call signs for simplicity. We'll do proper introductions once we're clear of this mess."

"Understood, Cowboy."

"Good," I said, turning to Madison. "Are you alright? Did these men hurt you physically in any way?" I asked her.

"No, I'm fine. And, uh, sorry, I haven't thanked you for coming for us," Madison cut in, her voice tinged with a mix of relief and disbelief. "I'm still processing this. How did you even know we were here? Not that I'm complaining, but..."

"We got lucky," I replied. "I'll explain later. We're not out of the woods yet. We still need to get you guys out of here safely."

"Oh! You mean those other ghastly fellows are still out there?" Hughes asked, looking alarmed.

"Yes. The only silver lining is those ghastly fellows are asleep. We aim to keep it that way if we're going to get you out in one piece. But where are the other hostages? Our intel said a group of girls was taken as well when these guys grabbed you," I said, looking at both in turn.

"They aren't here," Madison replied, her voice tinged with apology. "We were separated and brought to this place. I have no idea where they've taken the girls. It's my fault—I was supposed to be looking out for them," she added, on the verge of tears, looking guilty as hell.

That was a setback. I was banking on Madison being our lead to find Zara. Suddenly, it felt like we were back to square one.

"Was there a teenager called Zara Haq with you?" I pressed, hoping for a lead.

"Yes. Sweet girl. Intelligent and articulate," she replied, looking surprised. "But... I don't understand. How do you know her?"

"I promised her dying father I'd get her to safety. We rescued her brother last night. Once we're out of here, can you help us track her down?"

Madison's demeanor shifted, her eyes locking onto mine with a newfound resolve. "Yes, of course I will," she replied, her voice steady and full of conviction, a stark contrast to the hesitant tone she had been using. It was clear she was deeply committed to the cause she had dedicated herself to. "Just give me some time once we're back in the civilized world. I'll get those girls back if it's the last thing I do."

Those were the words I needed to hear. They spoke of stubborn determination and unwavering resolve. I had found her fascinating before I met her, but those words sealed it for me. However, time was not on our side. We needed to get the hell out of there. Fast.

"That's all I needed to hear. Now, both of you need to get up, get your circulation going. We've got a long trek ahead," I said firmly, scanning their faces for signs of readiness.

"Oh," Hughes muttered, looking more perplexed than mobilized. Madison seemed lost in thought, probably still grappling with the fate of the girls. They both looked shell-shocked, understandable given the ordeal they had been through, but time wasn't on our side.

"I meant now. As in this very second. Get up. We need to vanish from this place fast. We're hitting the trail in sixty seconds," I emphasized, extending my hands and pulling them to their feet without waiting for any more hesitation.

"I don't get it. Didn't you say you were US Army Rangers?" Madison asked as she stood up, confusion etched across her face.

"Yeah, that's right. But we didn't roll in with a full platoon. This is a deep-into-Taliban-territory stealth op. Small team. Got it?"

"Yes," she replied, still looking unsure. "Uh, how small are we talking?"

"Five of us."

"Five? That's it?" she asked, eyes widening in disbelief.

"Yup."

"Against that whole village full of Taliban?"

"Not the whole village. Most are just regular folks scared stiff of the Taliban maniacs. The actual fighters are a lot fewer."

"How many fewer?"

"Maybe 50. Definitely under 100."

"Good heavens!" Hughes exclaimed, his voice rising before he caught my look and realized he needed to keep it down. "My apologies. I shall endeavor to keep my voice down."

"Yeah, do that. And once we're out of this cave, no talking. If you've got any questions, ask them in the next sixty seconds."

They couldn't immediately come up with anything, too busy processing the complexities of being freed from their immediate captors but still being under a truckload of danger. The realization of their freedom and the risky escape ahead was slowly dawning on them, but we didn't have the luxury of time for them to mull it over. I was waiting for Echo's signal, which I received a minute later.

"Echo to Sierra One, six packages are in place. We're hot and ready for remote detonation. Over," Echo whispered into the radio.

That was Echo's confirmation that he had rigged the six Tali pickups parked at the edge of the village with C-4 for remote detonation. That was our back up plan. A single press of the remote switch would light up the night, crippling the enemy's mobility.

"Cowboy to Echo. Good work. Let me know when you're in position at the extract route. Over."

Raptor's confirmation came a minute later. "Raptor to Sierra One. We're in position," came the message through my earpiece.

That was the signal. Raptor and Echo had taken cover behind some rocks on the road out of the village, ready to engage if necessary.

"Cowboy here. Copy that. Ninja, all clear?" I asked.

"All clear," Ninja Man confirmed.

"Copy. Join me inside. Cowboy to Raptor. Moving hostages for extraction. ETA at your position two mikes. Over."

Madison looked geared up to make a run for it, but Hughes was doing calf and hamstring stretches like he was prepping for a marathon. I didn't mind as long as those stretches got him ready for the climb ahead. But in those sandals? We would end up carrying him halfway, no question. When Ninja Man walked in, his first comment echoed my thoughts.

"Whoa, dude, those sandals are a one-way ticket to disaster. You'll be toast out there no matter how much you stretch," Ninja spoke up.

"I know," Hughes said apologetically. "They were quite the dandy in the office, but not exactly expedition material, I must say," he added, glancing down at his feet and sighing like a man resigned to his fate.

I signaled to Ninja Man, bringing his focus to the dead Tali fighter's sneakers. The Taliban seemed to have a thing for white sneakers. If they could scramble around these mountains in them, Hughes could surely manage without needing a medevac to save his toes.

"We've got a grueling trek ahead. These are your new kicks if you want to keep those feet intact," I said, yanking the sneakers off the dead guy and thrusting them at a wide-eyed Hughes. "You've got fifteen seconds. Move it," I ordered, leaving no room for debate.

"Yes, John, makes sense. Do it now," Madison added, pushing the urgency.

"Good heavens. Under any other circumstances, I wouldn't have touched these with a barge pole.

God help me if I catch something incurable," he said in a whiny voice, but he quickly ditched his sandals and slipped into the sneakers.

"That's more like it," Ninja Man said with all seriousness. "Now just grab that guy's turban too, and you'll be ready to hit the slopes."

"Turban? Really?" Hughes asked, incredulous.

"Cut it out, Ninja," I said, barely restraining a chuckle. "Time to move out."

"Roger that, Cowboy. I was just going for full Tali chic," he chuckled as he walked to the entrance for a quick scan.

"Ha ha, I get the joke now. Lead the way, chaps," Hughes said sportingly.

"Remember, once we step out, absolute silence. You won't say a thing unless we ask you to. Ninja Man's in the lead. Keep your eyes on the ground and follow in his footsteps. One noisy stumble and we might wake up the village. That's something we don't want to do. Got it?" I confirmed.

"Yes," both replied, their faces telling me they were hanging on to every word I said.

"Alright, let's move," I said, leading them out into the night.

CHAPTER 11

We emerged from the cave and began to descend the narrow path toward the village. We moved carefully, each step deliberate and cautious. The ground was uneven, strewn with loose gravel and rocks, which could easily give us away. Each footfall was a delicate balance between speed and silence, every rustle of clothing or shift in the dirt a potential alarm bell in the quiet night. Madison and Hughes were heeding directions meticulously, following in Ninja Man's footsteps like shadows.

Raptor and Echo were already in position, hidden behind some rocks on the path leading out from the village. Their eyes were sharp, scanning the village for any signs of movement. The flicker of a distant lamp and the soft murmur of night sounds were the only indications that life still stirred in the village below.

We moved cautiously, finally making it to the position where Raptor and Echo were stationed. The ascent to the OP where Hawkeye had resumed his position was about 30 minutes up a steep incline.

"Ninja Man, take the lead. Madison and Hughes will follow you. Raptor and Echo, stick close behind them. I'll cover the rear," I said.

We began the ascent. Madison didn't seem to have much of a problem following Ninja Man. Hughes stumbled slightly at times but kept up, driven by a mix of fear and determination. Raptor and Echo fell in behind them.

Ten minutes into the climb, Hawkeye's voice crackled through our earpieces: "Hawkeye to Sierra One. I see headlights. Three vehicles incoming. ETA five minutes."

The situation had just escalated to Defcon 1! I heard Raptor, Echo and Ninja Man going "Fuck!" under their breath simultaneously. That was one message none of us wanted to hear.

The incoming Talis would certainly notice the guards were missing. It wouldn't take much deduction for them to figure out the hostages had gone missing as well. They would light up the mountain with flares and get out the RPGs and SAMs. Even a near miss could bring down a rain of rocks, sealing off the escape route or worse, trapping us under tons of debris.

It was time to move to Plan B. The problem was, I didn't have a plan B. The entire operation depended on stealth. But with the incoming vehicles, stealth would soon go out the window when they discovered the dead guards. We would have to improvise—do the opposite, make a bang and create a diversion. I made a quick decision.

"Cowboy to Hawkeye. Copy that. We're in a tight spot. Keep your eyes peeled but do not engage. We don't want to reveal our escape route."

"Roger," Hawkeye replied.

"Raptor, take point from Ninja Man. Ninja, fall back and regroup with me at the rear. Raptor, Echo, maintain speed, don't slack off. Echo, get ready to light up the trucks parked in the village in about six minutes. Stand by for my signal. Copy?" I confirmed.

"Echo here. Copy that. What's the play?"

"Ninja and I are heading back down. All of us moving up isn't feasible anymore. Once the Talis have eyes on us, they'll turn us into mountain rubble. We'll draw their attention and absorb the heat. Once you're at the OP, you're in the clear. Ninja and I will navigate a different route to the OP. Everyone, move fast and stay low."

"Copy," they all responded in unison.

"What's happening?" Madison whispered to the group.

"We need silence, Madison. Stay quiet. Follow Raptor. Minor tweak to the plan, but we're good. Details later," I whispered back.

As the team pressed on with their climb, Ninja Man and I rapidly descended back to ground level. The mission was straightforward but risky—divert the Taliban's focus to us and away from the ascending team. This wasn't a death wish. We would strike at the right moment to steer them away. We still had a trick up our sleeve—the C-4 rigged to the trucks parked outside the village.

"Do we have an actual plan, or are we just flying by the seat of our pants here?" Ninja Man asked as we descended.

"There's a plan, alright. Once those trucks roll in, we're borrowing one and making some noise on the way out. I want the Talis scrambling for their rides, probably toting that MANPAD with them. We'll get one truck to tail us, keeping their eyes glued to us, while Raptor moves the group to the OP. Once the first truck is on our tail, Echo will light up the rest. The MANPADS should go sky-high with the trucks."

"You missed one crucial detail."

"What's that?"

"The part about saying 'Hail Mary' and crossing our fingers. Doesn't exactly sound like a solid plan, Cowboy."

"I know, pal. We're winging it a bit," I replied, chuckling. "But if we keep the Talis distracted long enough for Raptor to get to the OP, we'll be good. I've scoped out the mountains. There's a hidden trail on the far side, completely out of sight from the village. We can still hit exfil on time. Just gear up for a little uphill sprint."

"Got it. Now I see why you didn't pick Raptor for this. He'd be whining and dragging his feet the whole way."

"Exactly. At least you won't bellyache about eating my dust on the climb."

"You wish. Dream on, Cowboy."

We took up position behind some rocks near the parked trucks, blending into the shadows. The engines of the three approaching trucks broke the silence of the night, their low rumble echoing through the gorge. As they rolled into the village, they parked close to the other battered pickups already there. About fifteen Taliban fighters disembarked. Four stayed near the trucks, while the rest moved toward the village, where a few lights flickered on in the mud-brick houses.

Once the majority of the fighters had moved a reasonable distance away, I signaled to Ninja Man. We moved swiftly, switching our suppressed carbines to semi-automatic. We took down the four remaining guards with precise headshots—they were dead before they hit the ground.

The keys were still dangling in the ignitions of all three trucks that had just arrived. We targeted the one parked furthest from the village, leaving the keys in the truck next to it. For the third truck, we removed the keys, effectively blocking the path for the other six parked vehicles.

I slid into the pickup's driver's seat, while Ninja Man hopped into the open bed. We waited, biding our time to give our team heading for the OP every possible second. A faint commotion from the direction of the houses indicated that the Taliban had discovered the missing guards. A larger group of fighters emerged, a few heading quickly toward the cave where the hostages had been held.

"Shouldn't we be flooring the gas pedal right about now? Unless you're planning a heart-to-heart with the Talis," Ninja Man whispered through the rear window.

"Hold on. We're buying our guys as much time as we can. The Talis need to see us making a run for it. They'll come after us with AKs blazing, but I'm banking on someone grabbing RPGs and MANPADs before they do," I replied.

"Got it, boss, but it still feels like we're winging it," Ninja Man muttered.

We had managed to buy our team about five extra minutes since taking up our positions inside the truck. Overall, they had been on the move for twenty minutes, with about ten minutes left to reach the OP. It was time to signal Echo to halt and establish a direct line of sight to the trucks to detonate the C-4. With the path winding up the mountain, there would be moments when Echo couldn't maintain visual contact with the trucks. Although remote detonators using RF signals can penetrate obstacles like walls and light vegetation, they are limited by range and signal strength. We couldn't afford any chances—those trucks needed to go sky high.

"Cowboy to Sierra One. Raptor, keep ascending with the hostages. Echo, get eyes on the trucks and stand by for detonation. Wait until you confirm the MANPADS being loaded into a vehicle," I relayed over the comms.

"Echo to Cowboy. Copy that," came Echo's steady reply.

The Taliban fighters had finally discovered the hostages were missing. I turned the ignition as soon as I saw a few of them rush out. The sudden roar of the engine startled them, and they froze for a moment, unsure if it was one of their own men inside the vehicle. When I gunned the engine, shifted gears, and floored the gas pedal, they figured it out. The truck's roar shattered the night's silence as we sped down the path away from the village, dirt and rocks flying from beneath the tires. Shouts erupted, followed by the staccato rattle of AK-47s firing wildly.

"Keep your head down, Ninja! We're getting the hell out of here. Do not engage. Let them come after us," I yelled through the rear window.

"Echo to Cowboy. I've got visual on the targets. Standing by for detonation upon confirming MANPADS," Echo's voice crackled over the radio.

"Cowboy here. Copy that," I acknowledged.

After a few hundred yards, once we were out of the effective range of the AKs, I eased off the throttle. I deliberately began grinding the gears, making it sound like the truck was having mechanical trouble, hoping to bait them into thinking the escape was botched. This would hopefully encourage them to load up their RPGs and SAMs while they still had a visual on us.

"Please tell me this is part of the plan and the damn thing isn't dying on us," Ninja Man hollered through the back window, crouching low.

"All part of the master plan, Ninja. Just keep your head down and be ready," I replied.

By that time, a group of five had piled into a truck and were barreling down the road after us, closing the gap. That was my cue to floor the gas pedal again. The truck bounced along the rough, narrow road, with the mountains on one side and a perilous drop on the other.

I gripped the steering wheel tightly as Ninja Man stood in the open bed, bracing against the jolts. He ducked as three men in the trailing truck emptied their AKs in our direction. But their shots went wild. As it is, most Talis weren't crack shots. And shooting an AK in automatic mode from a moving vehicle? Well, not a chance in hell.

"Echo to Cowboy. MANPADS are in sight. Ready for fireworks," Echo reported.

"Copy that. Give 'em hell, Echo," I shouted into the mic.

"Roger. Fire in the hole," Echo responded, hitting the detonator.

A few seconds later, the night sky lit up with a series of fiery explosions ripping through the trucks. Each blast sent a wave of heat and light across the valley. The initial flash was blinding, illuminating the rugged landscape for miles. The sound followed—a deafening roar that shattered the silence and reverberated off the mountains like a monstrous growl. The ground shook as shockwaves pulsed through the village, turning the night into chaos.

"Echo to Cowboy. All trucks, hostiles in proximity, and MANPADS neutralized. Heading to OP," Echo's voice came through, a hint of satisfaction evident.

"Good job, Echo. See you at the rally point," I responded.

In my rearview mirror, I saw the trucks transformed into towering infernos, flames licking up into the sky, silhouetting the village against the backdrop of destruction. Shocked by the sudden explosions, the driver of the truck following us momentarily lost control and the truck swerved dangerously close to the edge, barely avoiding a deadly plunge into the ravine below. The driver narrowly regained control at the last moment. Meanwhile, I pressed the accelerator harder to increase the gap between us, our truck lurching forward with a surge of speed.

"Looks like our friends back there almost took a scenic dive," Ninja Man shouted over the roar of the wind and the engine, his voice tinged with amusement.

"Guess they didn't get the memo about the 'no swimming' zone down there," I replied with a chuckle, my eyes locked on the treacherous road ahead.

"Next time, we should charge for the thrill ride. I'd say that near-miss was worth at least fifty bucks a head."

"Alright, Ninja. After the next bend, I'm stopping this rig. Get ready to bail and take cover behind those rocks. We're gonna deal with these jokers."

"Roger that, Cowboy. I'm ready to rock 'n' roll."

I maneuvered the truck around a sharp bend, then abruptly hit the brakes, executing a controlled swerve that spun the vehicle around to face our pursuers. The truck skidded to a halt, tires screeching on the gravel as it completed a perfect U-turn. Ninja Man leapt from the bed, hitting the ground running and diving behind a cluster of rocks on the side of the road. I quickly reversed the truck fifty yards, then jumped out, taking cover behind it and using its body as a makeshift shield.

I steadied my carbine on the truck's hood, my eyes locked on the bend in the road. Moments later, the Taliban truck roared around the corner, its headlights piercing the darkness. I didn't hesitate, squeezing the trigger, sending a volley of precise rounds that shattered the windshield. The driver slumped over the wheel as the truck veered wildly.

AK-47 fire erupted from the remaining Taliban fighters, forcing me to duck behind the truck for cover. Bullets pinged off the metal, sending sparks flying into the night.

Meanwhile, Ninja Man, from his position, watched the Taliban truck approach his ambush point. With practiced ease, he pulled the pin on an M-67 frag grenade and lobbed it into the open bed of the truck. The grenade bounced once before settling amongst the fighters. At the same time, he raised his weapon and fired at the occupants, forcing them to dive for cover just as the grenade detonated.

The explosion was devastating. A fiery blast ripped through the truck, sending a fireball and debris into the night air. The vehicle lurched violently before teetering on the edge and then tumbling down the ravine, engulfed in flames and twisted metal.

"Nice toss, Ninja. Think they'll want a refund for that ride?" I called out, rising from my cover to survey the wreckage.

"Nah, that was the grand finale. Can't top that kind of exit," Ninja Man replied, a grin spreading across his face as he brushed the dust from his hands.

"Alright, let's get the hell out of here before more of their buddies show up. We've got a long hike back to the exfil point."

"Roger that," Ninja Man agreed.

But a moment later, we realized we had celebrated too soon. There were more Talis coming for us. And these guys were toting RPGs.

CHAPTER 12

Hawkeye's voice crackled through my earpiece: "Hawkeye to Sierra One. We've got two pairs of Taliban fighters leaving the village on motorbikes. They've navigated around the burning trucks and are heading your way. Both passengers are packing RPGs. Should I engage?"

"Negative, Hawkeye. We can't give away your position. Stand by," I responded, my mind racing through the next steps.

"Roger that, Sierra One. I'll keep eyes on them," Hawkeye confirmed.

"Back to same positions?" Ninja Man queried.

"Yup. They've got RPGs. Let's take them out."

I moved back behind the truck, which we had parked strategically in the middle of the narrow road. The rocky mountain rose sharply on one side, while the other side dropped away into a sheer cliff.

Ninja Man took cover behind the same rocks off to the side, his eyes scanning the bend in the road where the motorbikes would soon appear. The sound of engines grew louder, reverberating off the cliffs. I tensed, my MK-18 carbine trained on the bend.

The first motorbike roared into view, its headlight cutting through the darkness as it rounded the bend. I took aim and fired, my rounds finding their mark and taking out the driver. The bike swerved violently as the driver slumped forward, but the passenger, already with his finger on the RPG trigger, inadvertently fired as he fell. The rocket streaked through the night toward Ninja Man's position. He ducked just in time as the rocket exploded against the rocks behind him, sending shards of stone and debris raining down.

There was no time to check on him as the second motorbike roared into view. I quickly fired a burst, hitting both the driver and passenger. The bike careened off the road, tumbling into the ravine below. The RPG the passenger had been gripping fired off harmlessly into the dark void, exploding far below.

"You good, Ninja?" I shouted as I sprinted toward him.

"Yeah, just had my world rocked. Literally," he replied as he shook off the dust, a wry grin spreading across his face.

He seemed uninjured, but the blast had clearly left him a bit rattled.

"Well, look on the bright side. Now you know what it's like to be on the receiving end of your own fireworks," I chuckled, feeling a wave of relief.

"I guess I can cross 'Getting blown up by an RPG' off my bucket list. What's next, a vacation in Kabul?" he laughed, still catching his breath.

"I was thinking more like a nice, quiet stroll through this lovely mountainside. I'll try to take it easy—you've ingested enough dust for one night."

"Dream on, Cowboy. RPG be damned, you're gonna get a run for your money," he retorted, his spirit undiminished despite the close call.

We climbed back into the truck and drove another half mile before stopping. This was the point where we could take an alternate route to climb to the OP. But before beginning yet another ascent, I got the news I had been waiting for from Raptor.

"Raptor to Cowboy, we've reached the OP with the hostages. Both secure," his voice crackled through the static on the radio.

"Copy that, Raptor. Ninja and I are taking an alternate route. ETA to your position is twenty mikes. We'll be there by 0030 hours. Hold tight," I responded.

"Roger that, Cowboy. We're in position and watching the perimeter. Raptor out."

I glanced at Ninja Man, who nodded back. We moved swiftly through the rugged terrain, navigating the alternate route up the mountain. The night air was cool, and the burning wreckage below served as a stark reminder of our narrow escape.

When we arrived at the OP at 0030 hours, Raptor and Echo, were waiting for us, their silhouettes blending with the dark landscape.

"How are you holding up, boys? Ready to roll to the exfil point," I called out.

"Looks like you guys had a close call. Glad to see you both in one piece," Raptor replied, relief evident in his tone.

"Thanks. Let's get the hell out of here before more party crashers show up," Ninja Man quipped.

My eyes then fell on Madison. Despite the exhaustion and the trauma of being held hostage for two days, she still had a spark in her eyes. She had been sitting with Hughes but stood up and walked over when she saw us arrive.

"You holding up alright, Madison?" I asked her gently.

Madison had a way about her—a natural ease in connecting with people. Whatever drove her to risk her life running her charitable outfit in Kandahar, it wasn't a death wish—she was a genuinely caring soul.

She took mine and Ninja's hands in hers, and with a gentle smile, said: "Thank you. Raptor told me how you two drew the Taliban after you so we would be safe. I can't believe you risked so much to get us out of there."

"Don't worry about it. Just another day in the office," I replied, shrugging it off.

"Yeah, can't do without a daily adrenaline rush. Though next time, maybe opt for a less adventurous spot," Ninja Man chuckled, lightening the mood.

"Speaking of which, we need to move to the exfil spot," I added, turning my gaze toward Hughes, who was sitting on the ground, still trying to catch his breath. He looked like a fish out of water in the harsh environment.

"How's the Tali chic going, Hughes? Did those sneakers make you float on air?" Ninja Man asked as we walked over to him.

"I don't know about floating, old chap, but they did keep me alive. I never thought I could climb this mountain in the time we did," Hughes replied.

"We're almost out of this mess. Just another twenty minutes to the exfil point. Come on, we need to get moving," I said, extending my hand to help him up.

"Lead on, Captain. Let's make this last leg a dash less eventful, if you don't mind," he replied, taking my hand with a weary but appreciative smile.

At 0100 hours, the helo appeared in the distance, flying dark to avoid detection. The rotors were barely audible over the sound of the wind, and the craft descended with precise control. At the controls were Viper and Gator, back to exfil us once again.

"Cowboy, I see you're still finding ways to keep us on our toes," Viper called out with a grin.

"Just trying to keep things interesting, Viper. Can't let you flyboys get bored, can we?" I shouted back.

Gator chimed in: "Heard you took care of those SAMs. Saves us from having to pull any fancy moves tonight."

"Figured you'd appreciate a straightforward extraction for once. No need to make your life more complicated," I replied.

"You can say that again. Dodging rockets is fun and all, but I'd rather avoid the whole 'getting shot down' part of the job," Gator shot back with a laugh.

The rotors of the Black Hawk cut through the cool Afghan night air as we all climbed aboard. Inside, the helicopter was dimly lit with red lights, casting an eerie glow over the cabin. We settled Madison and Hughes into the bench seats, strapping them in for the journey. The rest of us quickly followed suit, securing ourselves in the jump seats along the sides of the cabin.

The helo soon lifted off, and the landscape below quickly became a patchwork of shadows and faint outlines as the helicopter gained altitude. Through the open side doors, we could see the rugged Afghan terrain slipping away, a landscape both beautiful and perilous.

The Black Hawk touched down at Kandahar Airfield at precisely 0200 hours. As we disembarked, the vastness of the base became apparent. Floodlights illuminated the tarmac, casting long shadows across the expanse of concrete and revealing a sprawling complex of buildings, hangars, and vehicles. The base was a bustling hub of activity, even at this late hour. Soldiers moved with purpose, and the hum of machinery and aircraft engines filled the air.

We escorted Madison and Hughes toward the base's main area, where they would receive medical checkups and a chance to rest. As we walked, my attention kept returning to Madison. Despite the grime and exhaustion, there was something captivating about her. She had been remarkably composed throughout the ordeal.

"Madison," I said softly, matching my pace to hers, "I know you've been through a lot. Being kidnapped by the Talis must've been terrifying. But we had to keep moving, keep pushing forward. That area was deep inside Taliban territory, and our priority was getting you out of there safely and quickly. You get that, right?"

Madison glanced up at me, her eyes heavy with fatigue but still gleaming with a quiet resilience. A hint of a smile played on her lips despite her weariness.

"I understand why you had to do it. I'll never forget how you guys risked your lives for us. You pulled us out of a nightmare," she replied, gently touching my arm.

Her voice was soft, almost tender, and for a moment, the chaos of the airfield faded into the background.

"Just doing our job," I said, giving her a reassuring smile. "For now, just focus on getting some sleep. You've earned it. We'll talk details tomorrow."

We handed Madison and Hughes over to the medical staff, who were about to guide them toward the infirmary. But before they walked away, Madison paused and looked back.

"You think it's time for formal introductions yet?" she asked, her voice laced with a hint of teasing curiosity as she looked around at all our faces.

I realized we hadn't had proper introductions. Back in the caves, formalities had been a luxury we couldn't afford. I had told them to stick to call signs due to the urgency.

"Oh, yes, of course. Let's fix that. I'm Captain Axel Blaze," I began, extending my hand. "This sneaky guy here is Ninja Man. His formal handle is Sergeant Buck Conway. He's the guy you want if you need someone to sneak up on a fly and swat it without making a sound."

Ninja Man gave a mock salute, adding with a smirk, "Except, of course, for the days when the fly wins."

I moved on to the towering figure next to him, who looked like he could bench press a tank. "This bear of a man is Sergeant Jackson Cole. We call him Raptor. He's a big, cuddly teddy bear—if your idea of a teddy bear is something that could rip your head off and feed it to a dog."

Raptor grinned, his eyes twinkling. "Only on Tuesdays."

"And over here we've got Hawkeye," I said. "Staff Sergeant Robert Compton. He can shoot the wings off a fly at a hundred yards, and he's got more eagle in him than most birds."

Hawkeye gave a modest shrug. "I only missed once," he said with a smirk. "It was a windy day."

"Hawkeye also tends to be very modest most of the time," Echo chipped in.

"Yup, You got it right, Echo," I added, before introducing him. "This tech wizard here is Specialist Kevin King, better known as Echo. If it beeps, whirs, or can be blown up, he's the one to talk to. Just don't ask him about his video game collection—it's disturbing."

Echo gave a quick wave, flashing a boyish grin. "Hey, they're all educational, I swear."

Madison and Hughes took turns shaking hands with each Ranger as I introduced them. Finally, Madison looked at me with a curious tilt of her head.

"And what's the story behind the call sign 'Cowboy'?" she asked, a hint of mischief in her voice.

"Well, I did grow up on a ranch...," I began, not wanting to go into too much detail. But the other guys weren't about to miss the chance.

"And he still can't go to sleep unless he's wearing his cowboy boots," Ninja Man cut in with a grin. "True story. We once had to wait an extra hour for a mission because he couldn't find them."

"And he has a mind of his own, especially when it comes to following orders," Raptor chipped in. "You know what they say about cowboys—always riding off into the sunset their own way."

"Hey now," I protested with a mock frown, "I like to think I just have a healthy respect for creative problem-solving."

Hawkeye, who had been quietly observing, finally spoke up. "Creative, sure. Just remember that time you insisted on rappelling down that cliff face with a broken harness because you didn't want to wait for a replacement?"

"Hey, we got the job done, didn't we?" I retorted.

Madison shook her head, amusement dancing in her eyes. "Sounds like you keep things interesting, Cowboy."

"That's one way to put it," Echo remarked dryly, drawing a grin from Madison.

"Gotta keep the Wild West spirit alive," I said, tipping an imaginary hat. "And it helps to have a little charm out here in the wilds of Afghanistan."

"Quite the adventure, gentlemen. I'll have to write a book about this one day," Hughes said, a broad smile spreading across his face.

"Make sure you get my good side, Hughes," Ninja Man chuckled, giving a sly wink. "But leave out the part where I almost got taken out by a dead Tali's RPG. That's classified."

"And don't forget to add a few extra inches to his height," Echo quipped. "Makes for a better action hero."

Madison chuckled, the tension of the past few days easing a bit. "Thank you, all of you. I promise, no embellishments necessary—you guys are already larger than life."

We finally made our way to our assigned quarters in the barracks. It wasn't luxury, but it was a welcome sight after the mission. We hadn't had a proper sleep in three nights. As soon as we hit the sack, it was lights out for all of us.

CHAPTER 13

Kandahar Airfield, or KAF as we called it, was a sprawling epicenter of military operations, laid out against the unforgiving expanse of southern Afghanistan. At the peak of coalition presence, it housed nearly 20,000 personnel, including soldiers, contractors, and support staff.

KAF was the largest base in the region, a buzzing microcosm of war effort and logistics. It was a melting pot of military personnel, including soldiers, marines, airmen, and contractors from across the U.S. branches. KAF was also an international hub, with NATO contingents from over a dozen countries operating shoulder to shoulder with American troops.

When I stepped out of the barracks in the morning, KAF was a flurry of activity, a bustling mini-city where the rumble of jet engines merged with the hum of daily life. The main drag, bordered by rows of utilitarian tan and green structures, was dominated by the massive airstrip, a stretch of tarmac that constantly saw Black Hawks, Apache helicopters, and the occasional lumbering C-130 cargo planes bringing in supplies or taking out personnel. Enormous hangars and maintenance bays flanked the airstrip. Nearby, clusters of prefabricated buildings and converted shipping containers served as offices, barracks, and makeshift stores.

After a debrief with my commanding officer, Lt. Colonel Flynn, at 1000 hours the next morning, I was in another debriefing room at 1100 hours, sitting across a table from Madison and Hughes. The room was windowless, stark, and efficient, designed for focus. A large table dominated the center, surrounded by functional chairs. A whiteboard on one side was cluttered with maps and notes. A projector screen hung from the ceiling, ready for briefings.

Madison and Hughes looked much more refreshed than the night before. I had arranged for them to have fresh clothes from the quartermaster. Madison wore a military-issued olive drab T-shirt, snugly tucked into khaki cargo pants, paired with sturdy tan army boots. Her golden blonde hair, which had been tangled and matted last night, now fell in soft waves over her shoulders, framing her face. She looked radiant, her green eyes bright with new life. As she sat down, she gave me a warm smile, the kind that could light up a room.

"Thanks for ensuring we had fresh clothes. It's nice to feel human again," she said, her voice carrying a note of relief.

"I guess that's the least we could do. Glad to see you looking all perked up. Those quarters aren't exactly the Hilton, but sure beat a Taliban cave, huh?" I responded, trying to lighten the mood.

"You bet they do," she replied.

Hughes, meanwhile, was sporting a similar outfit—a gray T-shirt that highlighted his wiry frame, and a pair of military cargo pants that were a bit too large but functional. His clean, sturdy boots were a far cry from the filthy sneakers he detested with a passion.

"How are those boots treating you? Missing the Tali sneakers yet?" I asked Hughes, trying to restrain a smile.

"Oh, those wretched things? Quite the abomination, if you ask me. I wouldn't wear those filthy sneakers again even if they were the last shoes on Earth. These boots, though a bit military for my taste, are a welcome improvement any day," Hughes replied with a wry smile.

"Well, I'm glad to hear you're not longing for a fashion statement from the Talis," I quipped back, feeling the tension ease just a bit.

Once we broke the ice, Madison and Hughes began recounting their harrowing experience of abduction. They were taken from the compound where Madison ran her charity.

"We were at the New Beginnings compound. It's in the coalition-controlled part of Kandahar—you don't hear about Taliban attacks there. I wasn't deliberately trying to put myself and everyone in danger," Madison started, her voice tinged with a defensive edge.

"No one's saying that. You're doing an incredible job. Takes guts to do that," I reassured her, hoping to put her at ease.

I didn't truly believe it was wise for her to be there, but it was clear that she was driven by a deep-rooted conviction. It took real guts to champion women's rights and education in what was one of the most dangerous places on the planet for such causes. My words seemed to have the intended effect, and she continued.

"I guess we got a little too comfortable," she admitted. "You know how it is... you start out being super careful, but then routine sets in, and you let your guard down."

"I know. I get it. We've had too many good men lost to IEDs and snipers when patrols start becoming a little too routine. Go on."

"That day, a group of four—two men and two women—came by. They said they wanted to set up similar projects in Kabul. Seemed genuinely interested, scheduled an appointment a couple of days earlier, and everything seemed legit. It felt like a routine visit, so I didn't inform the patrols that check in on us daily. It was pure chance that James happened to be visiting that same day," she said, glancing at Hughes.

"I was only there for the day," Hughes explained. "I'm in Afghanistan for five days on a think tank-funded tour, doing research on the status of women under the Taliban and local empowerment initiatives. I thought it would be a valuable experience. I was supposed to fly back to London yesterday."

I kept my thoughts to myself. Expressing my skepticism wouldn't help the conversation. While I was against Madison's risky endeavors, she at least had spent time in Afghanistan and understood the inherent dangers. It was another matter that she got too comfortable and got caught off guard. But Hughes struck me as a man who didn't know his ass from his head when it came to conflict zones—as out of place there as a penguin in a desert.

"During the meeting, everything changed," Madison's voice quivered as she continued. "They suddenly pulled out handguns and AK-47s and started barking orders. They herded us through the back entrance and forced us into two waiting vehicles."

"Was that you and Hughes in one vehicle and the girls in the other?" I asked.

"Yes. Zara was with the other girls," Madison replied, looking guilty as hell.

"How did Zara come to your place?"

"Her uncle, a man named Rafiq, brought her to the center. She spoke English remarkably well. Rafiq told me the Taliban was after her because her father had worked as an interpreter for the U.S. Army and because her English was excellent. For an Afghan girl, that alone can be a death sentence. Rafiq said he'd contact her dad's unit, and they'd help her get to safety. I guess he meant you guys."

"Yes," I confirmed, then briefly told her how Zara's family had been wiped out by Bilal's men, without really going into the grisly details.

"Oh my God, that's horrible," Hughes exclaimed before Madison could respond. "Did you manage to catch the men responsible?"

"We're working on that. That guy is a dead man walking; he just doesn't know it yet. A week tops, and he'll get what he deserves," I said, my voice turning ice cold, which visibly affected Madison and Hughes.

I quickly shifted the conversation to keep it moving. "But the crucial thing now is, we've managed to rescue her brother, Ayaan. I won't rest until we find her and bring her back. It's not just me, but every Ranger you met yesterday feels the same."

"I don't know where they took the girls. All I know are they are in a very bad place. I would gladly switch places with them if I could," Madison replied, her voice heavy with guilt and self-recrimination.

"It's not your fault. Let's focus on how we could get to them. Let's take it from the start. Think about any clues you might have. Who were those guys who captured you? Why did they come for you? Did they mention anything?"

"Only one of them spoke English. A scary man—tall, gaunt, with a harsh face and piercing eyes. He didn't hide his contempt for me and my mission, calling me an agent of the West, cursing me for teaching Afghan girls my infidel ways, poisoning their minds with lies and corruption," Madison replied, shuddering at the memory.

"That's their usual spiel. What else did he say?"

"He said he'd make an example of us," Hughes chimed in, an involuntary shudder running through him. "He claimed they'd show the world that the Taliban won't tolerate the corruption of their daughters and traditions. He promised we'd pay for our crimes. Madison was brave enough to point out that I was just an outsider and had nothing to do with it," he added, glancing gratefully at Madison.

"It didn't really help," Madison quickly interjected. "In fact, it had the opposite effect. He said we were both agents of the West... and that we'd die in the darkness of the caves with no one to hear our screams. He even got one of his men to throw someone off a cliff."

"Who was the man they killed?" I asked, not wanting to reveal that we had witnessed the execution. I didn't want to disrupt their chain of thought.

"He was just some scared man, already being held there as a prisoner when we arrived. Didn't speak English, so we didn't know who he was. But the way they casually threw him off the cliff..."

"That's how these guys operate. I'm sorry you had to see that. But I'm trying to understand why they went to all the trouble of dragging you to that village. Killing you wasn't their primary motive. Did they mention anything about your background?"

"I know what you're getting at... it's about my father, right? You know my background, right?" Madison asked.

"I know about your dad. That's about it. It looks like Hughes was just in the wrong place at the wrong time. You were the main target. But did they know about your dad?"

"No. They had a suspicion I was connected to someone important in D.C., but they didn't know who. They kept asking about my family, my parents, my siblings... But I made up an elaborate background story when I began working in Kandahar and I've got that story down pat. I stuck to it, no matter how much he tried to scare us."

"Good thing you didn't break."

"Or they'd have killed me sooner, right?" Madison said matter-of-factly, looking me straight in the eye.

"I believe so," I replied, avoiding the details. But she was smart enough to understand that if they knew she was connected to a CIA big shot, they would have really made an example of her.

"We clung to the hope of being rescued, although I didn't think either of us believed it would happen. That's why we were so dumbstruck when you suddenly walked in there looking like the angel of death," Hughes said.

"But how did that happen? How did you find us out there in the middle of nowhere? Were you actually sent to look for us?" Madison asked.

"No. It was sheer luck, thanks to Ayaan's rescue. We had raided another village the previous night and interrogated a guy who told us there were two hostages in a village eight miles away—an American woman and a Brit guy."

"And you decided to come rescue us? Just like that?" Madison asked, looking amazed.

"As I said, you had a streak of luck going for you. The village was eight miles away from where we were, which meant we could hoof it overnight. And my CO happens to be a hell of a guy who trusts my word and is willing to cut through the red tape if needed. Otherwise, we'd have had to fly back, and then bureaucracy would have taken over. We'd have to wait for more conclusive intel before getting the green light for a rescue mission."

"And you didn't have any idea about my, uh, connections... my dad?"

"By the time we got to that place, we did. Once we asked HQ for more intel on the hostages the Talis had taken."

"Thanks. I just needed to know. I can't quite explain why. It's a little complicated."

I could see she made it a point to go out of her way to ensure her dad's connections didn't make things easier for her. I couldn't figure out why, but it didn't really matter. I had more pressing things on my mind.

"I don't need to know," I replied. "But getting back to the abduction of the girls, you don't have any clue about what happened to them?"

"Unfortunately, no. What I do know is that the man was gloating that he had sent the girls to a fate worse than death. He was talking a lot of nonsense... like they didn't deserve to breathe the air of this pure land and so he's sent them to the worst sewers of the world. I did ask him what he meant, but he just laughed and told me I needn't be worried as I'm not going to be alive for long."

I waited for her to go on, not wanting to interrupt the chain of thought.

"But I've got this strong feeling that I kind of know what he meant," Madison continued, a look of deep anguish crossing her face when she said: "I hate to say it, but I've heard that some Taliban factions are involved in sex trafficking."

"Sex trafficking? The Talis? Are you sure?" I asked, genuinely surprised.

I knew the Taliban were deeply entrenched in the drug trade, which was their main source of revenue. But sex trafficking didn't fit their usual image of forcing women to stay behind veils.

"I know it seems contradictory, but it's just a few factions of the Taliban doing it on the side," Hughes explained. "They justify it by claiming they're sending women who disgrace Islam to a fate worse than hell."

"You know this for a fact?" I asked, surprised by his certainty.

"Not the exact details, but I've heard it with a fair degree of certainty. I got the lead during interviews with women who escaped the Taliban. I traveled to the Europol offices at The Hague to dig deeper. I confirmed that some Taliban factions are working with the Bulgarian mafia as part of a big drug and sex trafficking network. They're using land routes from Afghanistan to reach Bulgaria, from where they're sent to various places. These women just disappear, never heard from again. The women I talked with had a lucky escape. That's about all I know for now."

What Hughes had revealed made sense. The Taliban wasn't a monolithic entity. It was a complex coalition of factions, each with its own leadership, objectives, and methods. While united by the goal of expelling foreign forces and establishing their version of an Islamic state, their secondary goals and methods could differ significantly. Many of these factions were involved in the opium trade. Afghanistan's vast poppy fields and the lucrative European drug market made it a tempting proposition to fund their operations. Now it seemed they were into sex trafficking as well.

These latest revelations had just reduced the chances of finding Zara. The guys at Europol were completely clued into every police network in Europe. If they had confirmed Hughes's lead, there wasn't any reason to doubt his theory that Afghan girls were being sent to the Bulgarian mafia.

A sense of urgency had begun to gnaw at me. If we didn't act fast, Zara would disappear into a network of human trafficking. But we would need very specific information to have any chance of rescuing her.

CHAPTER 14

"If what you're saying is true, the chances of finding the girls just plummeted," I said to Hughes. "The search area has expanded massively. Is there any way we can confirm this and get more specific intel, like which factions are involved?"

"I can reach out to my Europol contact, pull some strings, try to get actionable intelligence," he replied.

"That'll be good. Do you have any idea about the English-speaking Tali guy at the cave?" I asked Madison.

"Well, it's not like he ever introduced himself, but I know his name is Yousuf. They were talking among themselves in Pashto, thinking we couldn't understand them. But I do. Can't speak too fluently but can understand pretty well."

"That's good. Do you think you can identify him if we show you photos?"

Military intelligence had enough information to pinpoint the most active factions in specific areas. While banning girls' education was a common Taliban agenda, some factions had made it their primary mission. Identifying those factions and key players would narrow the search.

"If I see his photo... absolutely," Madison replied with conviction.

"Me too," Hughes echoed.

Madison looked like she was about to say something else, but appeared hesitant, like she was struggling with something.

"Is there anything else? Any lead that could help us?" I asked.

She took a moment before replying: "There's one person who can confirm all this and give us really specific intel much sooner than we could gather on our own. I've been told he'll be landing at KAF in about an hour."

I knew she was talking about her dad. During my morning sitrep, Flynn had already briefed me that Davis was inbound and had radioed ahead, requesting a face-to-face with me as soon as wheels hit the tarmac. But sensing there might be some friction between Madison and her old man, I hadn't relayed that to her yet, figuring I would drop that intel at the end of our debrief.

"Who are we talking about?" I asked, playing dumb.

"He's... in intelligence. Deputy Director of Operations at the CIA," she replied.

"Go on. What's his name?" I asked, suppressing a smile as I saw her grappling with the idea of seeking help from her father.

She finally met my gaze and, with slight reluctance, said: "James Davis."

"I'm sure he has access to intel we can't get otherwise," I agreed. "The question is, how much of it will he be willing to share."

"I'll make sure he's ready and willing to give us what we need. Leave that to me," Madison replied in a determined tone.

Madison getting her old man to share the intelligence was our best hope of rescuing the girls. In his role as the Deputy Director of Operations at the CIA, James Davis oversaw a vast network of field operatives and intelligence analysts, directing covert operations ranging from high-stakes espionage to delicate negotiations with foreign powers.

But before Davis arrived and Madison had her talk with him, we needed to get a jump on identifying the Talis who had kidnapped her. I reached for the comm device and asked Echo to come in.

A few moments later, the door swung open, and Echo strode in carrying a laptop. He moved quickly but deliberately, setting the laptop on the table, his fingers working expertly as he connected cables to the equipment set up in the room, synchronizing the laptop with the large screen on the wall. The screen flickered to life, the laptop's display mirrored in magnified detail for everyone to see.

"Alright, let's get this show on the road," Echo declared. "We'll start with Taliban figures operating in Kandahar. That should give us a manageable pool to work with."

The large screen flashed and began displaying rows of images, each showing various men in traditional Afghan garb.

As the images loaded, Echo spoke, his voice steady and precise. "We're focusing on Taliban factions based in Kandahar. These images are filtered for known leaders and significant members."

The screen filled with the grim, weathered faces of numerous insurgents, many with their faces partly obscured by turbans, all sporting thick beards. The sheer number of images was daunting.

Madison leaned forward, scrutinizing each face intently, while Hughes did his best to keep up, his eyes darting between the photos. "It's hard to tell,"

Madison admitted, frustration creeping into her voice. "They all look the same with those beards and head coverings."

"Echo, narrow it down to factions particularly notorious for targeting schools and punishing women for seeking education."

"Roger that," he replied.

The screen flickered as the database filtered through the parameters, highlighting a smaller, yet still substantial collection of faces. The narrowed selection featured individuals from three factions: Sharia Righteous Brigade, known for its brutal enforcement of bans on female education; Al-Madrasa Harakat, infamous for their draconian punishments against women deemed to have violated Islamic principles; and Jihad Purifiers, a group that took particular pride in rooting out what they called "Western corruption" from Afghan society.

Madison and Hughes continued to sift through the faces, their frustration growing as the subtle nuances of the faces blurred together. "It's like trying to pick out a needle in a stack of identical needles," Hughes muttered.

"Echo, try filtering the list by the name Yousuf. Let's see if that tightens our focus," I suggested.

Echo keyed it in the parameters, and the screen immediately responded, showing seven photos. Madison and Hughes leaned in, their eyes scanning each face more carefully now.

"There! That's him!" Madison's voice was filled with certainty as she pointed to one of the photos.

Hughes immediately nodded in agreement. The image showed a tall, gaunt man with a piercing gaze. The name beneath it was Yousuf Rashid.

Associated with the faction called Sharia Righteous Brigade. Echo and I exchanged glances when the faction's name popped up. It was a familiar name, one we had been researching for a few days.

My face hardened as Echo brought up the associated profiles and additional images of Rashid's faction members. The screen displayed a series of profiles, each face more sinister than the last, until our eyes homed in on one image. A face that made our blood boil.

"Bilal Mustafa," Echo's voice was tight with controlled fury despite his usually calm demeanor, each syllable heavy with loathing. The room seemed to have grown colder.

"Zara is in serious danger. She's likely already en route through that hellish network," I said, my voice low and urgent, my expression grim.

"Why? Who is this Bilal? What do your mean she's in serious danger?" Madison asked.

"Bilal Mustafa is the one who murdered Zara's parents and her entire family. He's got a history of brutality that's almost unmatched. If he's involved, it's likely that Zara's facing the worst fate imaginable."

"Oh my God!" Madison whispered, the reality of the situation hitting her with full force.

Just then, the intercom on the desk buzzed. Echo answered the call, then looked at me and handed me the receiver.

"Captain Blaze here," I spoke into the phone.

"Captain, this is Staff Sergeant Watson calling from the front desk. I'm under orders to confirm this call isn't on speaker. The message is for your ears only," came a crisp voice.

"Roger that. Go ahead," I replied, keeping my tone level.

"CIA Deputy Director of Operations James Davis has just touched down at the compound. He's requesting to meet with you before he sees his daughter."

My gaze flicked over to Madison and then back to the screen. I quickly assessed the situation, deciding against telling her about her father's arrival just yet. I didn't want to complicate things or shift her focus at this critical juncture.

"Copy that. I'll be there in a few," I confirmed, ending the call.

I turned to Echo, my demeanor all business. "I'll be back in a few minutes. Echo, keep running the drill with Madison and Hughes. Go through the other Sharia Righteous Brigade members. See if they can ID any more of these targets."

"Copy that," Echo replied as I headed out.

I walked down the corridor to another wing of the building and entered a slightly larger briefing room. The room had only one occupant—a man in his mid-fifties with blond hair touched with gray, rugged features, and piercing green eyes. He was standing beside a chair, having just tossed the jacket of his tailored navy suit over its back. As he stood rolling up the sleeves of his shirt, his gaze was fixed intently on his laptop screen.

Even without the eyes and features that bore a striking resemblance to Madison's, it wasn't hard to ID him. The air of quiet authority he exuded made it clear that this civilian who seemed to own that space like it was his area of operations was none other than James Davis, Deputy Director of Operations at the CIA.

CHAPTER 15

Davis looked up as I pushed the door open and scanned the room. His eyes flicked to the laptop screen, then back to me with a look of recognition. I got the distinct feeling he had my file opened up on the screen.

"Captain Blaze?" he inquired, stepping around the table and extending his hand.

"Affirmative. Deputy Director Davis, I presume," I responded, taking his hand.

"I owe you a great deal of gratitude for rescuing Madison, Captain," Davis said, his handshake firm and his eyes showing a glimmer of sincerity.

"Just doing my duty, sir," I replied. "And it wasn't just me—took the effort of my entire team of five to pull it off."

Davis nodded, his expression thoughtful, as we took our seats.

"Tell me, Captain, how did you come across the intel about Madison? By the time I received word about it in D.C. and had begun scrambling about in desperation trying to think straight about how to even locate her, I was informed she had been located and a rescue operation underway. You can imagine my absolute amazement. It's not often that these things happen by sheer coincidence."

I leaned back slightly, crossing my arms. "Funny you ask. It was purely by accident. We were on a different mission, a rescue op targeting another compound. One of our Tali targets spilled the beans. Tried to save his own skin by giving up information about two hostages, who turned out to be Madison and Hughes. Once he gave us the intel, we moved fast."

I gave him a quick recap of all that had happened.

"You've done far more than just your duty, Captain," Davis said. "If there's anything I can do for you or your team... I'd be more than happy to assist in any way I can."

"I'll keep that in mind," I replied, nodding. "Right now, we're focused on the next steps. You must have received the intel that when the Talis abducted Madison, they also took a group of girls from her center."

"Yes, I did. The girls gone missing... that's not good. But what next steps are you talking about?"

"We're trying to get clues to where they might have been taken. We've got some leads, but still a long way from getting anywhere. And the clock's ticking."

I was curious to see how he would react. Davis paused, looked at his laptop screen for a couple of seconds before looking me over with a keen eye.

"I hope you don't take this the wrong way, but I'm wondering why you're on the case of the missing girls. I mean, young girls getting abducted, that's really fucked up, but would the army get involved in this?"

The man was smart. He wasn't a CIA big shot for nothing. I decided to lay my cards on the table. Davis did say he owed me one. It was time to see if he really meant it. And how far was he prepared to go beyond mere words.

"I know what you mean. And you're right, it doesn't fall under our mandate to go looking for kidnapped local girls. I'll be frank with you, I don't even know at this point if I'll get clearance from the brass for a rescue mission. I've got a great CO who goes out of his way to be accommodating, but this will be pushing it a bit. I might have to eventually go on a couple of days of leave and do it on my own time, as a civilian."

"I thought so. And I appreciate you being frank about it. But I still don't get why you're doing it. I know Madison can be persuasive as hell, but is that the only reason?"

"No, it isn't," I replied, before telling him about what happened to Omar and the promise I made to him.

"Hmm... I see now. This isn't something you can back out of. And from what I know of Madison, she's not just going to give up on the girls. But I'm not sure if you realize that it's a bit of a lost cause. Those girls haven't gone on a school vacation. Once they disappear down that rabbit hole, the chances of finding any of those girls are pretty much zero. It all just might be a wasted effort."

That comment did raise my heckles a bit, but I had a feeling he was testing me and not just being a condescending prick.

"I'd think they're still better than the chances we had of finding Madison. In this case, we at least know some of the key players involved. But in Madison's case, it was a blank slate," I replied pointedly, knowing I might piss off the guy but willing to take the chance before he went too far on the patronizing road he had just embarked upon. "And yet we did find her. I'm not denying that dumb luck played a part in it, but the more you follow leads systematically, you increase the likelihood of encountering that dumb luck. That's what we're trying to do."

The man was a seasoned pro. He didn't take offence. Rather, I think he took things a little more seriously.

"You've got a point. I've been in the field long enough to understand you need to work hard and work intelligently to get lucky. You must be wondering why I asked to meet you before I meet Madison," Davis asked, suddenly shifting the conversation.

I didn't really need to be a rocket scientist to figure out the reason for that. No matter how much sway the guy seated across from me held in global power politics, Davis didn't have a clue how to deal with his daughter. From my interaction with the dad and the daughter, I had got the distinct impression that most of the time, Madison wouldn't even give him the time of the day unless she happened to be in the right mood. I didn't try to guess if it was the old man's fault or just the downside of a job that required long absences and maintaining secrecy about his work. That often comes at a personal cost. He might care deeply for her, but he couldn't do shit if she chose to keep him at arm's length.

"Well, can't say I've had the leisure to dwell on it, but my guess would be that you don't expect her to be super communicative, so you're getting the full story before you meet her."

"Yeah, that about sums it up," Davis replied, letting out a sigh. "How is she? Did she have a hard time?"

"She must have, without a doubt. Getting kidnapped by Talis, being held captive in a cave guarded by scary guys wouldn't have been a picnic. But she was lucky the Talis didn't have a clue about her relation to you. All they suspected was she was connected to someone powerful in D.C. But she stuck to her story. She's tough that way and handled it better than I would've expected under the circumstances. She's had a good night's sleep and when I debriefed her this morning, she was over most of the exhaustion of the ordeal."

"Thanks. That's mostly what I wanted to know. I guess I'm ready to meet her now. But before that, when I asked if there's anything I can do for you, those weren't just empty words. I'll dig up as much intel as I can to help you find the girls before those bastards make them end up in a shitty brothel in some filthy godforsaken hole. But other than that, what else can I do to help you get the greenlight for this mission?" Davis asked, an earnest look on his face.

I knew this was a golden opportunity I couldn't pass. For Lt. Colonel Flynn to give it a go, he would have to jump through a few hoops. For a special mission like the one I wanted to embark on, he would need approval from the appropriate combatant command. That would mean authorization from the U.S. European Command (EUCOM). Not just that, it would need diplomatic engagement with Bulgaria to ensure the mission was sanctioned.

The easiest way out was to secure covert approval to give the mission a go without formal public acknowledgment. The man I was looking at—CIA's Deputy Director of Operations—was just the guy for such a covert approval. I explained the situation to him.

"I see. Leave this with me. I'll figure it out. Before I meet Maddie, I want you to meet someone," Davis said, pressing a speed dial button on his cellphone.

"Nate, I need you in here," he spoke into the phone before turning to me. "The guy who's about to come in is the most brilliant analyst on my team. An expert on everything to do with the Taliban and all the bullshit they've been up to ever since Uncle Sam decided it was a good idea to sell the dream of democracy in a place where they'd much rather live in the Middle Ages."

The door soon opened to reveal a guy in his late 20s, nerdy-looking with neatly combed brown hair even though he wasn't wearing specs, which are almost like a mandatory accessory for a nerd. But the guy also had an air of confidence that set him apart from the typical stereotype. His demeanor exuded quiet confidence rather than awkwardness. A high-functioning nerd was the phrase that came to mind.

His lean frame suggested a life spent more in front of books and computer screens than in the gym, although there was a subtle athleticism in his movements, hinting at a regular habit of morning runs or weekend hikes. Dressed in a crisp white dress shirt, navy chinos, and polished loafers, he embodied the blend of formality and practicality necessary for his role.

"Meet Dr. Nathaniel Foster. This is Captain Blaze," Davis introduced us.

"Thanks for rescuing Maddie, Captain."

"Just doing our job. Call me Blaze. Let's dispense with the formalities."

"Sure thing, Blaze. I'm Nate."

"Nate, the Captain is here to pick your brains. Set up your stuff and let's get started," Davis addressed Nate before bringing him up to speed with what I had conveyed to him.

Davis wasn't kidding when he said Nate was an expert on the Taliban. Nate started talking about the faction Davis mentioned like he had come prepared to give a lecture on the subject.

"Sharia Righteous Brigade is bad news," Nate began. "Those guys are brutal and ruthless. Maddie's lucky she was rescued, or else..." he trailed off.

"You think they were targeting her specifically?" Davis asked.

"I don't think so. Not specifically targeting her as the daughter of a CIA Deputy Director. They just have a thing for terrorizing women. My guess is the abduction was meant as a signal they could strike even in a coalition-controlled zone and that no one is safe from them. The fact that Maddie was running her center there must've indicated she wasn't scared because she knew someone influential. But we got a good cover story for her, and she must've stuck to it. That's what kept her alive until you got her out."

"Are you familiar with the name Yousuf Rashid? He was one of the men who abducted her and the only one who spoke English," I asked.

"Yeah. He went to college in Kabul, that's how he speaks English. But then he chucked it all and decided to join the Taliban. He's a mid-level player. Not very bright, would be my guess, or else, with his knowledge of the language, he would've risen up the ranks."

"Is that man still alive?" Davis asked me.

"Can't say for sure," I replied. "We took out a bunch of them back at the village, but it was pitch black in the dead of night. We can't ID even a single one with certainty."

"I see. Well, go on Nate. What else about these guys?" Davis asked.

"Yeah, sure. I'll start with their beliefs. Sharia Righteous Brigade's ideology comes from a hardline cleric known for his unyielding stance on women staying invisible behind veils. These guys believe that educating women is an affront to their interpretation of Islam and a Western conspiracy to undermine their traditional values. One of their primary agendas is to ensure women do not receive any form of education. They dole out harsh punishments to girls and women who defy their edicts, ranging from public beatings to more severe penalties like stoning or execution."

"Sounds like a lovely bunch. What else?" Davis asked.

"Like many other factions, they're heavily involved in the opium trade. They cultivate vast fields of poppies in the Kandahar region, process them into raw opium, and then traffic it to a Bulgarian mafia. The mafia has established sophisticated networks for processing the raw product into heroin, which is then distributed across Europe, generating significant revenue for the faction and funding their militant activities."

"The Bulgarian mafia's involvement matches with the intel I received from Hughes as well," I said.

"Right. But it isn't just about drugs. These guys are also involved in sex trafficking. Under the guise of punishing women who 'disgrace' Islam, they abduct Afghan women and girls and sell them into sexual slavery. They justify these actions by claiming these women are being sent to a fate worse than hell as a divine punishment. Sharia Righteous Brigade is bad news. If they abducted the girls, they're on a one-way ticket to a really bad place. But there's still hope for a rescue."

"Go on."

"The human smuggling takes place through a treacherous land route that passes through Iran and Turkey, eventually leading to Bulgaria. It's not easy even for the Talis as they aren't best buddies with the Iranians. The most straightforward land route from here to Bulgaria is about 3,000 miles, with a big part of it being mountainous."

"So, even if you factor in short sleep breaks, that means at least a four-day drive," I estimated.

"I'd think so. And this is the best-case scenario, without any hiccups on the way. But realistically, these guys will have to take major detours close to the big cities with checkpoints."

"That means five days is a more realistic timeframe. Could even be more, but certainly not less, given the route."

"I'd agree. But let me open the maps on my laptop and give you a more accurate estimate," Nate replied, digging out his laptop from a leather satchel bag he had slung over his shoulders.

"When were the girls taken?" Davis asked.

"Three days ago. They were taken the same time as Madison," I replied.

"That gives us a good two-day window," Davis interjected.

"It sure does," I replied, my spirits lifting at the realization of a realistic possibility of a rescue.

"But once the girls reach Bulgaria, they effectively fall into a rabbit hole from which it is almost impossible to escape. They are sold off and quickly moved to different destinations across Europe and the Middle East, making it exceedingly difficult to trace or rescue them," Nate cautioned.

"Keep digging, Nate. I'll go meet Maddie and get her here," Davis said. "Captain, mind taking me to her?"

"Sure thing," I replied, leading him out.

CHAPTER 16

We walked down the corridor toward the debriefing room where I had left Madison with Echo and Hughes. As we approached, I glanced at Davis, noting a mix of anticipation and concern on his face. I could see this reunion was going to be complicated for him.

Opening the door, I stepped inside first, followed by Davis. Madison looked up from the table, her eyes initially surprised, but soon softening at the sight of her father. She rose, took a couple of steps toward us, but then stopped short. Her expression shifted to one of guarded defensiveness, as if unsure whether she wanted to let her father see her in a vulnerable state.

Davis moved forward, his eyes locked on his daughter. "How're you, Maddie?" he asked, his voice soft but strained.

Madison's reply was cool and measured. "Not too bad, James."

James? Man, this was going to be awkward. I looked at Echo, who managed to keep a neutral expression. But then I saw Davis's face soften, and he closed the remaining distance between them, pulling Madison into a hug. She remained a little stiff at first, but she didn't pull away, allowing herself to be held for a moment.

"We'll wait for you two in the other room," I said, sensing their need for privacy, and signaling Echo and Hughes to join me.

"Wait," Davis said, turning his gaze to Echo. "Specialist Kevin King, correct."

"Yes," Echo replied, looking a little surprised that Davis knew his name.

"Thanks for being part of the rescue op. I know it was a dicey mission," Davis said, extending his hand.

"Time for introductions," I interjected. "This is CIA Deputy Director of Operations, James Davis. Specialist King is our comms whiz kid. We call him Echo."

"Just doing my duty, sir," Echo replied, shaking Davis's hand as realization dawned on him about how the apparent stranger knew his name.

"It was more than that. I mentioned this to Captain Blaze as well. Acting on the intel as fast as you Rangers did was above and beyond."

"No big deal, sir," Echo said, looking a little embarrassed.

"And you must be John Hughes," Davis said, turning to Hughes. "Glad you made it out in one piece."

"Relieved to be out, thanks to these lads. And Madison was a rock through the entire ordeal."

"I know. She can be a real tough cookie," Davis beamed.

"We'll catch up on what Nate has dug up. Join us there?" I intervened again, wanting to give Davis and Madison a chance at some privacy to navigate their complicated reunion.

I signaled Echo and Hughes to follow me outside.

"Found anything else," I asked Echo as we walked.

"Not much else. We couldn't get a match on any other faces we had on our intel. Must've been low-level operatives."

"Doesn't matter. The intel we got on the Bulgarian mafia was solid. There's a real chance we'll be able to undertake a rescue op. Nice work, Hughes. You were spot on with your Europol intel," I complemented him.

"Happy to help in any way I can. It's the least I can do. I can dig further if you get me on a phone," he offered.

"Thanks. We'll set you up on a secure line soon."

"Does that mean we're headed to Bulgaria for the op?" Echo asked.

"That's the plan. As to how in hell we're going to pull it off... I don't have a clue yet. We can't just get out of here and catch the next flight to Europe."

"That's what I was thinking. Planning to work your magic on the Lt. Colonel?" he asked.

"I don't know, Echo. Still trying to figure out the right way."

Flynn was the most supportive of bosses, but I didn't really want to put him in a tough spot. He couldn't simply say yes to every request just because we were on a personal mission.

When we entered the meeting room, we found Nate sitting with a thoughtful look on his face, his brows furrowed, as he stared intently on his laptop screen. Nate briefly glanced up, acknowledged my presence with a quick nod, then returned his attention to his screen without missing a beat. The presence of two new faces beside me didn't seem to have registered on him yet.

As we approached, we found him multitasking seamlessly. His right hand continued to tap on the keyboard while his left reached out to attach a lead to his laptop. With a swift, practiced motion, he connected the lead to the projector, causing a map to appear on the wall.

"Captain Blaze," he began, his eyes never leaving the screen, "I've figured out the likely route and timeframe from Kandahar to Sofia. My initial guess was spot on," he added, sounding satisfied with himself.

We gathered around him, focusing on the projected map. Nate, still typing, highlighted a path that snaked across the map, marking key points and potential detours.

"The kidnappers will have to avoid big cities and take a significant detour around Tehran. That pushes the distance well over 3,000 miles," Nate explained, his tone professional and concise. "They'll likely move at night when they cross Istanbul to avoid checkpoints. But the thing is, they'll keep on moving. They can't risk extended stops any place along the way."

He paused briefly to adjust the map, zooming in on key areas. "Factoring in all that and the mountainous terrain, it will take them about five days to reach Sofia. They would have had to set off immediately after the abduction to leave Afghanistan's borders as soon as possible. They've already been on the move for three days. Clock's ticking."

"Good work, Nate. This gives us a timeline to work with," I replied, before introducing him to Echo and Hughes.

At that point, Madison and Davis entered the room. Nothing on their faces gave me any indication on how their meeting had transpired.

But Madison's body language did look way more comfortable than it was when Davis hugged her.

"Do you have any intel on the Bulgarian mafia the Talis deal with," I asked Nate once he had gone through the route with Davis.

"How much do you know about Bulgaria?" Davis cut in before Nate could respond.

Beyond what I saw on the map, my intel was pretty limited. Bulgaria is positioned on the eastern flank of Europe by the Black Sea. To its east lies Turkey, with the bulk of it situated in Asia except for a small portion west of Istanbul. This makes Bulgaria a key waypoint on the main narcotics pipeline from Afghanistan to Western Europe. It is the first European stop for drugs and trafficked women—essentially a transit country. That's why our best shot at locating the girls was in Bulgaria.

"Well, not much," I replied, "Except that the mafia's deeply entrenched there, a legacy of the collapse of Communist regimes in the early nineties."

"Yeah, that's right. When Communism fell in Europe in 1989, Bulgaria began the transition to a parliamentary democracy. But as we've painfully learned in many countries, this shift isn't seamless. You can't suddenly shove democracy down the throats of people who aren't ready for it," Davis replied.

"Are you still talking about Bulgaria?" Madison asked with a slightly sharp tone.

"Yup. That wasn't a dig at our mission in Afghanistan. Madison's a fervent believer in her ability to change the world, something us seasoned vets can be a bit jaded about," Davis explained defensively. "But I do respect youthful enthusiasm. You know that, Maddie?"

"Yeah, sure, old man. Let's focus on Bulgaria, Dad."

She called him dad, and not James as she did ten minutes ago. Davis had clearly worked his charm on his daughter. I wondered what exactly he had promised her.

"Yeah, right. So, let's talk about transitions. That shift is what dumped all the missiles and hardware from Soviet states onto the black market. In Bulgaria, the period of weak governance and constant political changes created a breeding ground for organized crime to flourish. These guys thrived big time, dabbling in everything from cigarette smuggling to drugs, human trafficking, extortion, contract killing, arms trade... you name it. Getting the picture?" Davis asked me.

"Yup. Sounds like we're dealing with more than low-level street punks."

"Exactly. These aren't just thugs. These are well-organized syndicates operating with near impunity. There are two or three major rival groups, each with a legitimate front, usually in security and insurance. Most of them are ex-cops, ex-military. In the last 20 years, there have been at least 150 mafia-style contract killings of prominent figures, many in broad daylight in Sofia. No one's ever been convicted. These guys have powerful allies in the government, law enforcement, and judiciary. You see where I'm going with this?" Davis asked me.

"I guess I do. This needs to be off the books. An officially sanctioned mission will tip off the

Bulgarian authorities, and those girls will disappear for good."

"Exactly. This will have to be a black op. You get in under the radar and get out. But finding those girls won't be easy. There isn't enough time to land, infiltrate the gangs, locate the targets, and conduct raids."

"Infiltration wasn't exactly what I had in mind," I replied, my tone clearly conveying I was aiming for brute force.

"I figured as much. From what I've seen and heard, you guys are the best at kicking in doors."

"Well, we do enjoy taking down scum. Any more intel on who these guys are and where they operate from?"

"Nate, your turn," Davis said, looking at Nate.

"Right, sure. So, there are two main groups with ties to different Taliban factions. The Taliban seem to be playing both sides, often pitting one against the other. As Director Davis mentioned, these mafia groups hide behind seemingly respectable fronts, mainly security and insurance. One's called Black Eagles Security and the other's Crimson Security & Insurance. Sounds pretty legit, right?"

"You bet."

"Well, both started with extortion under the guise of their security and insurance services and then expanded their operations. I can't say for certain which one is dealing with your Sharia Righteous Brigade boys, but if I had to guess, I'd say it's Black Eagle. While both groups are into prostitution, Black Eagles has a broader network across Europe. Crimson's focus is more domestic."

"We'll take your guess as fact and proceed accordingly," I replied. "What else do you have on Black Eagles?"

"It's run by two brothers—Boris and Ivan Petrov. Boris is the head of the organization. They call him 'The Snake', and it's for a reason—he's cunning, ruthless, and always ten steps ahead. He's the brain behind the entire operation."

"And the other guy?"

"Ivan is Boris's right-hand man and specializes in contract killings and enforcement. If Boris is the brain, Ivan is the muscle. He ensures that all of their operations run smoothly and that anyone who crosses them pays the price."

"Nice little outfit," Echo commented.

"You bet. Black Eagles operates a nightclub in Sofia called Eclipse," Nate continued, pointing to the location on the map. "It's a known hotspot for sex trafficking. This might be a good place to get some leads on where they're holding the girls."

"Sounds good. That's where we'll start," I replied.

"Great, so when are we leaving for Sofia?" Madison, who had been quietly listening until then, suddenly spoke up.

"I think you meant when are 'we' leaving for Sofia, right?" I corrected her, knowing full well what she meant.

"Yes, I meant we, as in me and all of you guys."

I looked at Davis. He opened his mouth to say something, but changed his mind and simply shrugged.

"Let me explain," Madison began. "Hear me out before you begin to think I'm just being a spoiled brat who doesn't want to miss out. What I'm saying is logical."

"Go on. We're listening," I replied.

"OK. So, whatever your final plan is, it'll involve going into that nightclub called Eclipse and other seedy places where these guys operate. Once you're inside and you've done what you do best, like blowing things up and taking down every bad guy in sight—which, by the way, I don't dispute is the most crucial part of the mission," she conceded, before taking a breath and continuing. "Anyway, once that's done, there's the follow-up part where you need to rescue Zara and the girls. I'm sure that will be more complicated than hoping for a miracle and finding Zara conveniently waiting in some backroom, right?"

"Well, yeah, that won't be the plan, but we do get lucky sometimes. There have been times when we've stumbled onto something we weren't even looking for," I replied, referencing her own rescue, which was a matter of chance.

"Like when you found out we were being held hostage in that Taliban village? Believe me, that's one piece of good luck I won't forget, and I'm grateful to you guys every day for it," Madison said.

"I hear a 'but' coming."

"You're right," she laughed. "Let's say you come across a group of girls in there. How will you know if any of them are one of my girls? Only I can identify them. Surely you're not planning to click photos and send them to me out here for confirmation."

"Well, I guess that would be the plan..." I replied a bit weakly.

"But that might not work when you have to make quick decisions. And there might be the usual problems—poor connectivity, large image files... Echo, you're the comms expert. Don't you agree?"

"Uh, well, I guess..." Echo began a little hesitantly, but he never got a chance to finish.

"See. He agrees with me," Madison cut in, before continuing, "And suppose one of those girls you find is from that group, but it isn't Zara. How will you communicate? None of you speak Pashto beyond the basics. Am I right?"

"Well, you do have a point there, but..."

"Of course, I do, and I'm not finished yet. You need an interpreter, and someone the girls trust. Look, you guys are all good-looking hunks, I'll grant you that," she said with a cheeky smile, "but good looks alone won't cut it when it comes to building trust quickly, especially with bullets flying around," she said, pausing to look around with a challenging expression. "And now I'm done. Please tell me if anything I've said makes less than perfect sense."

There wasn't much left to say. We couldn't rely on luck to find Zara. We needed Madison to identify the other girls and talk to them. Her passion also confirmed the feeling I had that she was treating the loss of the girls as a personal failure. She would find it difficult to live with herself if they weren't brought back to safety.

I looked at Davis. He nodded.

"You made your point. But it's still a high-risk mission. We'll be going head-to-head against a ruthless mafia. You're in, but only if you understand it's a military mission. That means following orders."

"Absolutely," Madison replied with conviction.

"Um, am I included in this mission as well?" Hughes cut in nervously. "With the CIA involved, you might not need my assistance in gathering intel, but Europol does specialize in crime in Europe. I genuinely want to help find those girls. Besides, I was supposed to fly to Bulgaria yesterday until, well, the Taliban made me change my itinerary."

I was still trying to figure out a reply when Nate stepped in and helped me make up my mind.

"Access to a reliable source within Europol wouldn't hurt. It will only add to what we know," he said.

That settled it. We were all set to embark upon the mission to Sofia. The only thing left was getting the mission sanctioned so we could hop onto the first available bird.

CHAPTER 17

While Echo was tasked with connecting Hughes to his Europol contact, Raptor and Ninja Man escorted Madison to the secure apartment complex where she lived. We were on a tight schedule. She would make a quick stop to gather her things before they brought her back to KAF.

As I made my way across the KAF compound, my mind preoccupied with the upcoming mission, I suddenly heard a familiar voice call out, "Hey, Rockstar!"

The familiarity of the voice and the words was so unexpected that it made me freeze in my tracks. It was a nickname I had mostly left in the past. There was only one person in Afghanistan who would use that name—my big brother Ryan, older by two years, taller by an inch than my six foot two and outweighing my 200 pounds by 30 pounds of muscle.

Back when we were growing up, I had a phase of being a punk teenager, rocking long hair tamed by a badass bandana. Guns N' Roses were big and Axl Rose was the rage. My phase didn't last too long. But Ryan's nickname for me stuck for a while.

Before I could fully turn around, I felt the force of a large body tackling me from behind, nearly knocking the wind out of me. Instinctively, I tried to regain my balance as I recognized the strong grip and the hearty laugh that followed.

"Ryan, you big lug!" I shouted, half-laughing, half-grumbling as I tried to shake off my brother's hold. "Are you trying to break my ribs before I even get to the mission?"

Captain Ryan Blaze of the Marines finally let go and stood back, a wide grin on his face. His uniform was immaculate, and his posture spoke of the discipline and strength that had defined him since he joined the Corps after 9/11. But his eyes sparkled with the same mischief I remembered from back in the day on the ranch in Colorado.

"Well, if it isn't my little brother, the Ranger," Ryan said, his voice dripping with mock seriousness as he looked me up and down. "Still sporting that bandana under your helmet, Rockstar?"

"Nah, been too busy saving the world. Anyways, bandanas don't sit too well on short hair. What are you doing sneaking up on people?"

"Just making sure you haven't gone soft on me. I heard you Rangers need a little reminder of what real muscle looks like."

I rolled my eyes but couldn't suppress a smile. "Yeah, yeah, Marine. Just because you were a college football star doesn't mean you can tackle a Ranger and get away with it."

Ryan was the star quarterback for Colorado State University before he chucked it all and enlisted with the Marines after 9/11. I joined the Army a few months later. It took me that long to convince mom. Dad passed early, way before we even became teens.

"Can't have you Rangers thinking you're the only tough guys around here," Ryan quipped, grinning. "But good to see you, Ax," he added before grabbing me in a big hug.

"Yeah, Ryan. You really made my day, man," I replied, hugging him back big time. "What brings you to this neck of the woods?"

"About to head out on an op. Just dropped by to refuel and gear up," Ryan replied, his expression turning serious for a second before being replaced by a grin. "Heard through the grapevine you were around. Thought I'd drop by and see if you're still playing soldier."

"Still trying to keep up with you, big bro. And in case you were wondering, I still lug that ring around with me," I replied, digging into a pocket and taking out the ring Ryan had given me when I crushed RASP (Ranger Assessment and Selection Program) and made it to the Rangers. Ryan was kicked as hell about it. The ring had the Rangers' motto, *Sua Sponte*, inscribed on the top of the round face and "Rangers lead the way" on the bottom.

"You earned it. Better hang on to it if you don't want your ass kicked. But you're still a Rockstar, kid," Ryan said, taking the ring and examining it before handing it back.

"Yeah, right. How're you doing, big man? How's the football arm holding up? Haven't seen you throw a grenade yet."

Ryan laughed, a deep, hearty sound. "Still got the arm, but you know, Marines don't need to throw. We just charge right in."

"Yeah, because that always works out so well. How are things with the jarheads?"

"Same old, same old," Ryan replied, his eyes twinkling with amusement. "You know, dragging you Army boys out of trouble every now and then. Talking of which, how'd you manage to find the time to stroll around KAF with that blonde I saw you with earlier?"

"Oh, man. How long have you been keeping an eye on me?" I laughed. "It's nothing like that, you old dog, she's kind of a civilian consultant on a mission. Talis kidnapped her a couple of days back. We kind of landed in the middle of that and got her out."

"Good for you. But, man, why do us Marines get all the shitty missions. I wouldn't mind rescuing a babe every now and then."

"I'll ask her if she's got any friends that need rescuing," I replied, laughing.

"You do that, Ax. I've got to get moving now," Ryan replied, glancing back at a C-130 on the tarmac, looking like it was ready to depart. "Stay sharp out there. Mom needs us back on that ranch someday."

"You too, Ryan. We both need to make it back home. Stay safe out there. Don't go doing anything too crazy."

Ryan laughed. "You know me. Just the right amount of crazy. Catch you on the flip side. Hooah, Ranger," he said, pulling me into a quick, rough hug.

"Semper Fi, Marine."

With a final nod, Ryan turned and headed toward his waiting men, his broad shoulders carrying the weight of command with ease. I watched him go. It was a rare moment of connection in the midst of chaos.

CHAPTER 18

I turned and made my way toward Lt. Colonel Flynn's office. My mind was soon back on the brief I had given Flynn just minutes ago, explaining how Davis was eager to help cut through the red tape to send the Rangers' team on a covert mission to Sofia. Flynn knew about Zara's abduction and empathized with my sense of responsibility to save her from being sold into a sex ring in Sofia. Flynn was on board with getting Davis to sort out the mission, sparing him the endless administrative tasks required to pull it off.

As I approached Flynn's office, I nodded to his secretary, Staff Sergeant Jessica Collins. She was a no-nonsense NCO with short, sharp blonde hair and keen blue eyes that missed nothing. Her desk was immaculate, with neatly stacked files, a computer, and a framed picture of her family.

"Captain Blaze, you can go in. They're expecting you," she said, her voice crisp and professional.

I nodded and knocked on the door before stepping inside.

Flynn's office was utilitarian but organized. The walls were adorned with maps of Afghanistan, framed commendations, and photos of past deployments. Flynn's desk was a sturdy, well-used piece of furniture, cluttered with mission files, a computer, a landline phone, and a coffee mug emblazoned with the battalion insignia. Davis was seated across from Flynn, a tablet in his hands.

"Captain, come in," Flynn said, motioning for me to take a seat. "We've been discussing the logistics. Deputy Director Davis is already moving to get the necessary intel and clearance."

I took a seat, my posture straight and ready. Flynn leaned forward, his eyes serious.

"Captain, this mission is essentially a civilian operation from our perspective. You and your team will be on leave with a pass to leave the base for three days. Are you and the boys willing and ready for this?"

"Roger that, sir. The men are raring to go. We'll do whatever it takes."

Flynn nodded in approval. "Good. Then I wish you luck, Captain. Bring those girls home."

I stood up and exchanged firm handshakes with Flynn and Davis.

"Escort Director Davis to the meeting room, then report back here for a last-minute briefing," Flynn added.

"Yes, sir," I replied, turning to Davis. "Right this way, sir."

We exited Flynn's office and made our way back to the briefing room.

"I know I don't need to say it, but try to keep Maddie out of harm's way," Davis said as he entered the room.

"I will," I promised as I turned to head back to Flynn's room.

When I entered, I found Flynn leaning back in his chair with a thoughtful look on his face, his fingers steepled.

"Blaze, remember, you're not fighting the Taliban in Sofia. Be mindful of the body count.

We're not looking to start an international incident," Flynn said, his voice low but firm.

I knew exactly what he meant. If things went south, it would be his head on the line, black op or not.

"I understand, sir," I replied, meeting his gaze squarely. "I'll be mindful of the collateral damage. Although, with all due respect, anyone involved in sex trafficking is as much an enemy combatant as the Taliban who kidnapped those girls. But I'll be mindful. I know this is a covert op. We'll execute with precision and discretion. I'll ensure none of it traces back to the U.S. Army."

"Good. I know you will. We're counting on you to keep this clean and efficient," he replied, his expression softening slightly.

"Roger that, sir. We'll get it done."

"Good luck, Blaze," Flynn said, extending his hand.

"Thank you, sir," I replied, giving him a firm shake.

As I turned and exited the office, my mind was already working through the details of the mission ahead. This operation was going to be different, but we were ready for whatever Sofia had in store for us.

There was one more stop I needed to make before we departed. I walked through a secured facility and approached a makeshift lounge where Ayaan, Omar's teenage son, was sitting quietly and staring at the TV. Ayaan looked up as I approached, his eyes filled with a mixture of hope and apprehension.

"Hey, Ayaan. How are you doing, young man?" I greeted him before sitting down facing him.

"Captain Blaze!" Ayaan's face lit up with hope. "Any news about Zara?"

I gave him a reassuring nod. "I've got some specific intel, Ayaan. I'm heading out within an hour to locate and rescue her."

His expression shifted to one of intense focus. "Are you sure? I mean, do you think there's really a chance I'll see my sister again? Zara is all I have left, you know. The fear of never seeing her again is eating me alive."

I looked him in the eye, feeling the weight of his words.

"I won't lie to you, Ayaan. It's going to be tough. But I promise you this: I'll move heaven and earth to make it happen. Your sister will come back to you," I said, placing a firm hand on his shoulder.

Ayaan's eyes welled up, but he managed a small, determined nod. "Thank you, Captain sir. I trust you."

I gave his shoulder a squeeze before standing up. "Stay safe here. I'll be back with your sister."

As I walked away, I felt the weight of my promise settle into my bones. I knew I had to succeed—failure wasn't an option.

An hour later, our team of five Rangers and two civilians approached the waiting C-130 Hercules on the tarmac, its ramp lowered and ready for boarding. The aircraft, a hulking behemoth of metal, loomed large against the afternoon sky, its engines already humming with anticipation. We ascended the ramp at the rear of the plane, stepping into the cavernous interior.

The inside of the C-130 is a functional, no-nonsense space designed for utility over comfort. Rows of red webbed seats lined the walls, with cargo straps and equipment secured tightly along the floor. The hum of the aircraft's systems created a constant background noise, and the faint smell of oil and metal pervaded the air. Overhead, exposed wiring and ductwork added to the raw, utilitarian feel of the space.

The Rangers moved with practiced efficiency, helping Madison and Hughes strap into their seats. Echo secured Madison's harness, checking it to ensure it was tight enough but not uncomfortable.

"Comfortable?" Echo asked Madison.

"Not exactly first class, but it'll do," she replied.

Meanwhile, Hughes fumbled slightly with his straps, but Raptor stepped in to assist, his hands moving with the precision of someone who has done this countless times before. Once they were secured, we took our seats. I settled between Ninja Man and Raptor.

"How hard are we going on this mission?" Ninja Man asked, his voice low and serious.

"We're going after the worst kind of scum who prey upon young girls," I replied. "The mission is to rescue Zara. We'll do whatever it takes."

Raptor nodded. "So we hit them hard."

"Yes. When we hit, we do it hard and fast, make them regret ever thinking they could get away with this. No mercy."

The C-130 Hercules roared to life, its engines thundering across the tarmac of Kandahar Airfield. The giant aircraft surged forward, gaining speed as it thundered down the runway, lifting off with a shudder and soaring into the sky, leaving behind the dust and grit of the Afghan desert. It soon banked westward, carrying us toward the unknown.

CHAPTER 19

When the bird touched down at Sofia Airfield with a heavy thud at 1900 hours sharp, the city was already cloaked in the cool embrace of evening. Nestled at the base of Vitosha Mountain, Sofia's streets are a mix of commie-era relics, Ottoman mosques, and Byzantine churches, all haunted by the specters of past conflicts. The city's atmosphere is thick with the tension of a place that has witnessed the rise and fall of empires, now straddling the line between East and West. It's a place where the past is never truly gone, and where old grudges and new dangers intersect.

The flight from Kandahar had been a little over six hours long. As the cargo ramp lowered, the cool evening air of Sofia rushed in, mingling with the metallic scent of the plane. We disembarked swiftly and moved toward two unmarked black SUVs parked discreetly near a hangar.

Two figures stood in front of the SUVs, casually leaning against the hood of one, as they watched us disembark. I had their names from Nate's intel briefing before we took off, even though we hadn't met before.

CIA Agent Rick Brewer, a man in his early forties with a rugged build and a confident, knowing smile, sat in the driver's seat. His sandy hair was cropped short, and his blue eyes missed nothing as they scanned the surroundings with the alertness of someone always in the habit of checking for potential threats. Next to him was his

Bulgarian functionary, Niko, short for Nikolai Ivanov, a wiry man with a weathered face and an air of quiet competence. Rick waved at our group and approached us.

"Welcome to Sofia, Captain Blaze. Hope you had a smooth flight. I'm Rick," he said with a wry smile, extending a hand.

"Thanks, Rick. Blaze will do. The C-130's idea of a smooth flight is a bit like a high-speed chase in a tank. But it sure got us in the right mood for whatever Sofia has to offer."

"Well, I'm sure Sofia's ready for you. And by ready, I mean the usual chaos. This is Niko, our eyes and ears on the ground. He'll help you get acquainted with the city's finest that you guys have come all this way to meet."

After quickly going through the introductions, we loaded our gear into the SUVs and headed toward a secluded industrial area near the airport. The warehouse we arrived at looked rather unremarkable from the outside—a large, gray building with high walls and a reinforced metal door. It blended in perfectly with the surrounding structures, making it an ideal location for a clandestine operation.

Inside, the warehouse was a different story. The vast open space had been divided into several functional areas. One corner housed a living space with cots, a small kitchen, and a makeshift lounge with basic amenities like a table, chairs, and a portable heater. Another corner had a sturdy table laden with high-tech communication equipment, including encrypted satellite phones, secure laptops, signal jammers, and portable routers, all essential for maintaining secure lines with command.

"You've got everything you need here," Rick announced as he led us inside. "Food, water, and basic medical supplies are stocked. Echo, you'll find the comms gear set up and ready. Niko and I will be on standby if you need anything."

Rick seemed to have everything set up. It was time for us to hit the ground running.

"Alright team, let's get to work. Raptor, Ninja, Hawkeye, check the perimeter. Echo, start establishing our secure lines and get Madison and Hughes set up with phone lines. We'll have a briefing in twenty," I instructed.

"Roger that," their voices came in unison as each of them set about their tasks.

Rick led me and Niko to a spot that was set up as a meeting area, with a large, round desk surrounded by a few chairs. A tactical map of Sofia was pinned to a wall next to it.

"I take it Nate has already briefed you about the broad operations of Black Eagles and Crimson, so Niko and I'll get down to specifics. Makes sense?" Rick asked.

"Yeah, I'm all ears," I confirmed.

"Just to clarify, this operation is about rescuing a group of kidnapped Afghan girls, right?"

"Correct," I said, before giving him a quick account of our mission and how Madison had inadvertently become a part of that.

"Got it. So, this is as personal as it gets."

"Yes, it is."

"Alright, here's the deal: we've got a major problem here. We don't know jack about when or where that truck with the girls will show up. And once it does, we need to know the gang's exact playbook. How much do you know about how the sex trafficking racket operates?" Rick asked.

"Can't say I'm an expert on the subject. But one thing I do know for sure is that the scumbags running it don't deserve to breathe the same air as decent folks," I replied, my voice edged with anger.

"Damn straight. But what are the mission parameters?"

"This op is off the books. My CO said to keep the body count low, so that's the general plan. But let's be clear—we're five Rangers in peak shape, currently deployed on active war duty, trained to take down the enemy, and have worked together long enough to act like a well-oiled machine. Plus, we've got skin in this game. Omar was like a brother to us. If we can grab Zara quietly, great. But if we have to, we'll wreck these bastards to get her."

"And if it turns out she's already dead?"

"We'll cross that bridge when we get there," I replied, my voice getting a touch cold, before I shifted gears again. "But one thing's for sure— whatever we do, it won't come back to bite you guys or Uncle Sam in the ass. I get what 'off the record' means."

"Fair enough. That's the idea I got from Davis as well. He trusts you. And he must really like you. I know you saved his kid and he must be grateful and all, but he asked me to pull out all the stops to make sure you have everything you need for the mission. You know we're the CIA. Being nice and helpful isn't usually part of the job description," Rick said with a wry smile.

"Sure, pal, I do get that. That's nice of him, but I'm not sure it's got to do with liking me. I think it's more to do with the fact that he's scared of rubbing his daughter the wrong way. From what I've seen of her these last couple of days, she's got as much skin in this as us. Those girls mean the life to her. She feels responsible for them. The fact that they got taken from a place where she offered them safety is eating her up inside."

"I get it. But we'll need to plan this very carefully. Not be too visible with any moves we make until we're sure where and when the truck that's bringing the girls will arrive."

"I know. What did you have in mind?" I asked.

"We'll have to identify their main guys involved in this—specifically the ones involved in this sex trafficking business. Once we do that, it becomes way simpler."

"Agreed. Where do we start?"

"Niko's the local expert," Rick replied, looking at Niko. "Why don't you give us a backgrounder on the layout of the city?"

"Yeah, sure," Niko replied, taking over. "If you look at this map, both Black Eagles and Crimson operate in the center of Sofia. Black Eagles has a complete hold of the western part of the city while Crimson's solid in the northern part, mainly the district called Nadezhda. It's a remnant of the Soviet era, with rows upon rows of run-down apartment buildings. As for Black Eagles, they run most of their operations around the area called Fakulteta in the west. Not a place you'd find on a tourist map of Sofia—seedy alleys, unsavory characters, an entire landscape of dilapidated buildings and makeshift shacks... you get the picture?"

"Yup, you're quite the artist," I quipped.

"Well, the key to what we're looking for lies in those alleys. A couple of streets haunted by hookers with their pimps lurking around dark corners, a few dive bars, and a brothel run by Black Eagles."

"You know all these locations?" I asked.

"Pretty much, except for the brothel. They keep moving it every few months just to keep the heat off. There are these women's organizations that try to make a noise in the media about what's going on. The authorities never really used to care about them, but Bulgaria has been trying for some years to become a part of the European Union's free travel Schengen area. But the rest of Europe won't let them in because of their record on corruption and organized crime. The Bulgarian government is trying to show them they're serious about cleaning up their act."

"So whenever the mafia gets a little heat, it does stuff like moving the brothels and their drug dens, the government pats itself on the back, and sends its report to the EU. Not that those guys are buying it," Rick added.

"That's interesting info. Might come in handy when we're busting their operations. But the question still remains—where do we start?"

We were interrupted by Madison and Hughes who had walked over to join us. Both had grim looks on their faces.

CHAPTER 20

"I hope we're not interrupting," Madison said a little apologetically.

"Of course not. Rick and Niko were giving me the hang of things. Everything alright?" I asked.

"We made some calls and got some intel that might be of help," Madison started, her voice steady but with a hint of uncertainty.

"Sure. Go on."

"I'll go first. I just got off the phone with a contact here—a woman named Daniela. She runs a women's shelter in Sofia."

"Is that Daniela Karpova by any chance?" Niko cut in.

"Yeah," Madison replied, looking surprised. "You know her?"

"Only by reputation. I was just telling Blaze about her. Well, not exactly her, but some women's organizations that are giving Black Eagles some heat."

"But not very successfully, I think," Madison pointed out.

"Not yet. But things are changing. Daniela's a different breed. She's a real thorn in the side of both Black Eagles and Crimson. She gets threats constantly, but she doesn't back down. Last year, she took a bullet to the head and survived. No one knows who did it. But even that didn't shut her up. She's getting quite a fan following because of her guts. And enemies as well."

"No wonder," Madison muttered to herself before getting continuing. "Well, I didn't know any of that. I hadn't even heard of her until a few hours ago. I only got her contact from a friend back in the States this morning."

"Oh? So, what did she tell you?" Niko asked.

"She filled me in on the mafia, specifically their sex trafficking operations. What she said... it was chilling. I've been working with women in distress, it's not like I haven't heard horror stories before, but this... these men are monsters. It's modern-day slavery of the worst kind. The women face extreme violence daily. Most are trafficked from Eastern Europe, forced into the trade—some on the streets, others in clubs like Eclipse. The street girls get hooked on drugs, either forced or just to numb their reality. The ones too addicted or too rebellious are sent to brothels as punishment. Many just disappear—dead and forgotten," she finished in a whisper.

We stood in silence, the weight of her words sinking in. Madison was visibly shaken, but I could tell she had more to say. She took a deep breath and pressed on.

"Daniela thinks Zara and the other girls, all schoolgirls, none over fifteen... they're prime targets for these bastards. Fresh meat. Virgins. Daniela suspects that as soon as they arrive, they'll be cleaned up, dressed nice, and auctioned off. After that, they'll disappear, sold to the highest bidder. They could end up anywhere in the world, impossible to trace. Isn't that just fucking great? Oh, sorry," she cursed and quickly apologized, looking embarrassed.

162

"Does she have proof? Any details?" I asked, feeling Madison's anger fuel my own, as the precariousness of Zara's situation hit me again.

"Not concrete proof, but she's dealt with enough women who've been through this nightmare. Her own sister vanished, never found. And now Niko mentions she got shot, which she never even brought up. Dani knows how these guys operate, but she doesn't know where or when this auction's happening. That info's locked down tight, only for the gang's inner circle. It's going to be invitation only, for a selected clientele."

"That must be quite a list of scumbags," Rick pointed out.

"Yeah, sounds like it," Madison replied.

"That's very timely intel, Madison. Gives a whole new angle to this thing," I remarked.

"I wish I had some more info on locations. I'll keep digging."

Hughes looked like he was bursting to say something but was politely waiting for his turn.

"Hughes, you got something to add?" I asked him.

"As a matter of fact, I do. While Madison was making her calls, I touched base with my Europol contact at The Hague. He gave me some deeper insights into the mafia's operations. They've built a lot of connections, which has boosted their power, but they're starting to become a real thorn in the side of the authorities. He didn't specifically mention that remarkable woman Madison just talked about, but when I brought up sex trafficking, he noted that Bulgarian authorities are finding it harder to turn a blind eye to what's happening here. The EU is putting serious pressure on Bulgaria to clean up its act. Bulgaria is desperate to become a full member of the EU, but they're not going to get in unless they meet strict conditions on fighting crime and corruption."

"That's exactly what Rick and Niko were just talking about," I pointed out.

"Oh, were they? Well, here's the bottom line: the mafia isn't as untouchable now as they've been for years. What he was really getting at is that if we uncover a major sex trafficking ring, Europol can pressure the local cops to act. They won't be able to sweep it all under the rug."

"This Dutch contact at The Hague—did he give you any local Europol contacts?" Rick cut in.

"He did. You think that'll help?"

"It sure will. Gives us a lot more flexibility, Blaze," Rick said, looking at me. "If things escalate while we're rescuing the girls, these Europol guys can help manage the fallout. If local law enforcement can't hide it, they'll jump at the chance to take the credit. Makes them look good at the EU level. We just need to give Europol a heads-up if it looks like things are about to go sideways."

"That's true. And you know what? For the last few hours, I've been struggling to figure out a solid action plan. All this intel you guys have shared has helped clear things up," I said, looking at each one in turn.

"Care to elaborate?" Madison asked.

"Yeah, sure. I've got a good sense of our first steps. The thing is, even if we pinpoint the location and timing, we've gotta put a stop to this before it happens," I said.

"What exactly do you mean?" Rick asked.

"From what I've gathered, these mafia guys are connected to some serious power players. If this auction goes down, it'll be under the radar in a locked-down facility, probably with some high-profile locals involved. It's not the kind of place you just walk into with a wad of cash. The only way in would've been deep undercover, working the scene at places like Eclipse for weeks to build up credibility. But we don't have that kind of time."

"Yeah, those clubs are crawling with high-rollers, all throwing money around," Rick nodded.

"Exactly. So, we're looking at a hard entry. But if we go in guns blazing, we might step on some serious toes. Popping gangsters is one thing, but if some politician or bigwig gets hit, it could spiral into an international incident. We're aiming to avoid kicking that hornet's nest. What do you think?"

"You've got a point there. So what's your angle?"

"I've been soaking up intel on the Black Eagles all day. These guys aren't your average street-level crew—they're a well-organized syndicate posing as legit investment and security firms to keep their noses clean," I said, stepping up to the whiteboard and grabbing a marker. "Nate filled me in. The Black Eagles are run by two brothers—Boris and Ivan Petrov. Boris is the face of the operation, playing the part of a respectable businessman. He's involved in industry associations, which helps them launder their money. He's even planning to run for Mayor. Meanwhile, his brother Ivan handles the dirty work—contract kills and enforcement."

I started sketching out a flow chart, with Boris at the top, Ivan just below, and lines branching out to their different operations.

"Most of their top dogs are ex-cops or ex-military. Their operations are likely run with the same discipline, with a separate guy overseeing each racket—drugs, arms smuggling, sex trafficking... It's not just one boss running the whole show. What do you think?"

"Makes sense. But where are you going with this?"

"There's no point looking at the entire mafia. We need to fill in the blanks and zero in on this guy," I said, circling the "sex trafficking" section on the chart. "We've got to ID this guy who's running their trafficking op, track him down, grab him, and make him sing. Niko, think you can help us pull this off?"

"Sure, I'll help however I can. But what exactly are you getting at? Hang on, you mean start from the bottom... on the streets?" Niko asked.

"Damn right. We don't have time to play it safe. Whatever we do has to be done tonight. We hit those back alleys you mentioned, grab a pimp, squeeze him for intel on the brothels, and then we crash in and make those bastards talk. We work our way to the top."

"Well, that's a solid plan in theory, but just so you know, those brothels are going to be well guarded—tough guys with guns, very trigger-happy, who won't hesitate to use them."

I glanced over at my Rangers, then back to Niko. "And what do you think those guys over there are in the habit of doing?"

166

"Point taken," Niko said with a smile, holding up his hands. "So, what's the play? I know the shady alleys of Fakulteta, but are we going in blind? Grabbing the first pimp we see?"

"I wouldn't mind putting a scare into every pimp we see on the road, but maybe we should try to make it a little less random that that," I replied, trying to map out a plan on the fly.

"Dani could be a real asset here. Nobody knows those streets better than she does," Madison suggested.

"I don't doubt that..."

"I'm hearing a 'but' coming," Madison cut in.

"Well, yeah," I admitted, unable to restrain a smile.

"She's an unknown entity. I get that. But doesn't the fact that she survived a hit from Black Eagles count for something?"

"It sure does," I agreed. "You think she'd be up for this? We're short on time, and whatever we do, it has to happen now."

"I've got a feeling she'll jump at the chance. Let me get back on the phone with her. But before I do, let me confirm the plan so I know what to tell her. You Rangers plan to smash through every bad guy who comes in your way. All she needs to do is point out the bad guys. Right?"

"When you put it that way, it doesn't sound like much of a plan, but yeah, that's about it. Best to keep it simple."

"Roger that, Captain," she said with a smile, giving a mock salute before heading over to where Echo had set up the phone lines.

She was back five minutes later.

"As I thought, she's in. She'll meet us in half an hour near Alexander Nevsky Cathedral. It's about halfway between here and Fakulteta. She picked the place so we won't get lost—it's the most well-known landmark in Sofia, it seems," she said, looking at Rick and Niko for confirmation.

"Yup. That's true. You can't get lost trying to find it," Rick confirmed.

"That's what she figured too. She doesn't want us getting lost tonight. She was trying to play it cool, but I've got a feeling she's pretty excited about what we're planning. She's been fighting a mostly losing battle for too long."

"I get that. These guys are too powerful for her to make much of a dent on her own. But just so you know, Alexander Nevsky Cathedral is huge and in a very central area. She'll need to give us more specific instructions," Rick pointed out.

"Oh, she did. Dani's one meticulous woman. She gave me the exact map coordinates. She'll be in her car, which she says we'll recognize from a mile away. It's an olive green Fiat Panda with a roof rack, a huge dent on the driver's door—one of her battle scars from a run-in with a mafia thug's SUV—and a sticker on the rear windshield that makes it clear she doesn't back down."

"Well, she sounds like she's got it all figured out. That's what we needed," I said, before shouting out to the Rangers, "Time to hit the road, guys."

My words were met with a chorus of "Hooah!"

CHAPTER 21

Night had fallen and the time was just past 2000 hours when we left the warehouse and got into the two SUVs. The plan was for Madison to make the introduction, then head to Eclipse nightclub with Hughes and Echo, blending in as regular tourists to scope out the place. Given the chaos we were planning to stir up in Black Eagles' operations, it was better for Rick and Niko to avoid being seen with us around the city.

We drove through the dimly lit streets of Sofia, heading toward Fakulteta. The Cathedral was located almost dead center of the city, with the Parliament building behind it. It lay about halfway between the airport at the eastern edge and Fakulteta, which marked the western outskirts of the city.

About fifteen minutes later, we turned onto a wide avenue. The majestic silhouette of Alexander Nevsky Cathedral loomed ahead, bathed in floodlights. Its magnificent golden domes glowed against the night sky, a defining symbol of Sofia with its intricate architecture and solemn grandeur. We pulled up nearby, the towering structure casting long shadows over the square.

It didn't take us long to spot Daniela's car parked at the exact coordinates she had given us. It was a practical, unassuming European vehicle—an olive green Fiat Panda with a roof rack. A huge dent in the driver's door confirmed it. Any lingering doubts about the car's ownership were erased by the sticker on the rear windshield—it had a symbol of women's rights, a defiant fist rising over the white, green, and red colors of the Bulgarian flag. This car belonged to a woman who didn't believe in backing down.

As Madison and I exited the SUV and approached the car, a woman stepped out. Despite her petite frame, her presence was commanding. She wore a dark, no-nonsense jacket, jeans, and military boots. Her dark hair was pulled back, revealing a scar that traced the side of her head—a permanent reminder of her near-fatal encounter with the Black Eagles. Daniela's sharp eyes scanned the area with the caution of someone who had learned to be wary. Everything about her fit the description of a tough-as-nails woman who had no qualms about staring down the worst of Sofia's underworld.

Madison smiled and extended her hand as we approached. Daniela's expression softened slightly, though it was still far from a smile. Madison introduced me next.

"Captain Blaze, welcome to Sofia," Daniela said, gripping my hand with a firm shake, her expression serious, eyes sharp and unwavering.

"Thanks. Call me Axel. I'm just a tourist on vacation."

A brief flicker of confusion crossed her face before she gave a faint smile.

"Right. I get it. Madison filled me in. So, Axel it is. I'm Dani—your tourist guide for tonight. What you see here is the nice face of the city. But I'm here to give you a tour of the sewers, where the vermin thrive," she replied.

"That's exactly what we need. Good to have you with us, Dani. We need all the intel we can get."

"Before we begin, let me say this—what you're doing... I wish there were more men willing to go to such lengths to save these girls. I don't usually get the chance—or the support—to make these merciless bastards pay. There, I said it. Now, here's the plan. We're not traveling together. If they see me with the likes of you, the hyenas won't come out of the shadows. And the one we're after, his name's Borka—he's the one we need to draw out."

"What does Borka do?"

"What do any of them do? They're all pimps and gangsters. Borka runs a couple of streets where they force the girls to work. They act tough with the girls and any customer who steps out of line. They move in packs, so no normal guy stands a chance against them. But you and the men I see in that SUV across the street? You don't look like normal guys. If Borka sees that, he won't come out until he has called for more help. He'll stay hidden and send his men. But if he sees me alone, he'll come out to show me how tough he is. He'll just need a little incentive. I know exactly what to do."

I liked her. Direct. Straight to the point. No bullshit. Everything she said came from the heart.

"Alright, you're the boss. Whatever you say goes for us. So, do we follow you?" I asked.

"No, I'll follow you. I'll give you coordinates for a street in Fakulteta. Go there and park discreetly. We'll stay in touch over the phone. You'll see me arrive. I'll let you know when Borka shows up. That's when you step in."

"Sounds good," I replied, studying the coordinates she handed me on a piece of paper. "We'll get moving then."

"Sure thing. I'll give you a few minutes' head start. It's time these guys learned what it feels like to be hunted."

We headed back to our SUVs. Madison got into one with Hughes and Echo to make her way to the mafia's nightclub, Eclipse. I got into the other vehicle with the rest of the Rangers, and we set off westward, following the coordinates into the heart of Fakulteta.

As we navigated the narrow, winding streets, the city's atmosphere shifted, growing heavier with the weight of desperation and decay. The streets grew narrower, the buildings looked older and crumbling, and graffiti tagged every surface. Passing by the dark facades of old Soviet-era apartment blocks and dilapidated shops, the alleys became increasingly labyrinthine and foreboding. This was a place where the underworld thrived in the shadows.

The night was thick with tension as we rolled into the street Dani had directed us to. It was as grim as they come—a desolate stretch lined with low-end shops, half of them boarded up and forgotten, relics of a time when the area might have seen better days. Now, it was a hangout for prostitutes, with the dim glow of a few flickering streetlights casting long shadows over the cracked pavement, where a handful of women loitered.

The air was heavy with the scent of cheap perfume and despair, mingling with the distant hum of the city. The expressions on the faces of the women standing in front of the decaying shop facades were a mix of fatigue and resignation. Their hollow, tired eyes scanned the passing cars with a blend of hope and dread.

As we rolled down the dimly lit street in our black SUV with tinted windows, the scene before us was a harsh dose of reality.

Raptor was the first to break the silence, his voice tinged with anger. "Man, this is some twisted shit. Just look at them... These girls look like they've had the life sucked out of them."

Hawkeye shook his head, his jaw clenched. "Damn, they don't deserve this. It's like they're just... lost."

Ninja Man, usually quick with a quip but now deadly serious, muttered, "This ain't right. No one should have to live like this. Makes my blood boil."

"It's the bastards who put them here, who keep them here. We're gonna make sure these men get what's coming to them," I said, my voice carrying an edge of menace.

"That's what I needed to hear," Raptor replied.

I brought the vehicle to a stop a little way down from a seedy row of shops, careful not to draw attention. For a moment, we all just sat there, the weight of the scene before us sinking in. The quiet anger in the SUV was palpable. Finally, I turned to Raptor and Hawkeye.

"Raptor, Hawkeye, it's time. Take up position in the shadows near the shops. Stay low and be ready to move."

"Roger that. How hard are we going?" he asked.

"Non-lethal," I replied, then added, "For now. We need to stay under the radar of local law enforcement as long as possible. Too many dead bodies will complicate things."

"Copy. Leave them barely breathing, got it."

"Affirmative. When we leave this street, none of them should be able to walk unaided for months."

"Copy that," he said as he and Hawkeye silently exited the vehicle, disappearing into the darkness like shadows themselves.

Ninja Man and I stayed in the SUV, our eyes scanning the scene. Cars occasionally slowed as they passed, some drivers stopping to exchange a few words with the girls, haggling over prices or negotiating terms. The women looked like ghosts— figures trapped in an endless night with no dawn in sight.

One girl, in particular, caught our attention. She seemed out of it, her movements sluggish, her gaze distant as if she had long since given up on attracting attention from passing cars. She was young—too young—her thin frame barely filling out the oversized coat she wore. She leaned heavily against a shop window, her arms wrapped around her middle as if trying to hold herself together.

A pimp, a wiry man with a hard face, lurked around the corner, keeping an eye on the proceedings. Seeing the girl's lack of effort, he strode over with anger in his steps. He roughly shook her by the shoulders, snarling something in her ear that we couldn't hear but could easily imagine. The girl's shoulders hunched as she muttered a response, her eyes darting nervously to the ground.

A cold anger rose within me. The helplessness in the girl's posture, the way she shrank from the man and stumbled forward to catch the next car's attention, stoked a fire in my gut.

"Look at her, man. She's terrified. She can't be more than what, sixteen?" Ninja spoke up, his voice low and simmering with anger.

"If that. She's just a kid. Makes you wonder how the hell someone ends up in a place like this," I replied.

"It's like these guys think they're untouchable, like they can get away with anything. They're about to learn different."

"You bet. That guy's got a world of hurt coming his way."

The desperation of the women, the ruthless control of the pimps—it all spoke of a system as old as time, a system that chewed people up and spat them out. These girls were trapped in a brutal cycle of exploitation and violence, and time was running out for them.

A few minutes later, Daniela's Fiat Panda rolled into view and pulled to a stop nearby. She stayed inside, her silhouette barely visible behind the wheel. The car's arrival didn't go unnoticed by the women on the street—a ripple of unease spread through the area as they exchanged wary glances, sensing something was about to unfold. My phone buzzed a moment later.

"I'm here," Dani's voice came through the earpiece, steady and composed. "I'll approach the girls and draw the men out. Once they start coming for me, I'll lead them into the alley behind the shops—the one on the right. It's a dead-end. Your men can trap them there."

"Copy that," I replied. "Just be careful out there."

"Don't worry about me. I do this all the time," she replied with a hint of grim humor.

I relayed the instructions to Raptor and Hawkeye, telling them to move into position near the dead-end alley once Dani had drawn everyone's attention.

Dani soon stepped out of her car, drawing more uneasy glances from the women. It was clear she was known here, and not in a good way. Her boots thudded softly on the pavement as she walked toward the girls, her tough, no-nonsense demeanor evident with every step. Even from a distance, the scar on the side of her head was visible—a jagged line her hair couldn't fully conceal.

She approached one of the girls and started talking to her, her tone gentle. The woman responded hesitantly, her eyes darting nervously toward the nearby alley, as if expecting someone to emerge and punish her for speaking.

It didn't take long for trouble to find Dani. A man emerged from the shadows, his posture aggressive as he made a beeline for her. Simultaneously, the pimp who had been roughing up the girl earlier moved to block her path.

The man from the alley closed in on Dani, his intentions clear from the way he reached out to grab her. But she was ready, and the man surely wasn't expecting resistance. With a swift, powerful kick, Dani drove her boot into his crotch, making him double over in agony. He let out a choked cry, clutching himself with one hand while fumbling for a knife with the other.

But Dani was a step ahead. She stepped back, pulled out a canister of pepper spray and unleashed it in his face, sending him staggering back in agony. His screams echoed off the walls as he dropped the knife, clawing at his eyes before collapsing to his knees.

Her actions drew more attention. Three more men called out to her from the alley and began advancing with menace in their eyes. On the other side of the street, two more men appeared, cutting off her access to her car.

Dani took a few calculated steps toward the alley she had pointed out earlier, moving with a calm that belied the tension in the air, as if she was waiting for something. Then, as if on cue, two more men stepped out from the alley at the far end, their focus solely on her. She glanced in our direction, confirming with a look that Borka had just emerged from the shadows.

In an instant, Dani's demeanor shifted. She turned and bolted toward the alley, her sudden fear making the men laugh as they followed, confident in their control, certain she had nowhere to run. The three closest to her entered the dark alley first, followed by the pair from the other side, with the pimp blocking her escape route behind them.

Six men, sure of their dominance, pursued a lone woman into the shadows. Borka and his companion followed at a more leisurely pace, savoring the chase and the inevitability of their prey's capture.

It was time to hunt the hunters.

CHAPTER 22

Ninja Man and I slipped out of the SUV, moving swiftly and silently through the shadows. As Borka and his partner entered the alley, we sprinted after them, catching up just as they realized they were walking into an ambush and stopped short in confusion.

The sounds of an all-out brawl echoed through the narrow alley. Raptor and Hawkeye, both masters of Close Quarters Battle, were giving the six men a brutal lesson in the basics of CQB, using surprise, speed, and controlled but overwhelming force that does not stop until the threat is down.

Complete chaos reigned inside. The six men didn't know what hit them. Shadows danced with violent motion as Raptor and Hawkeye tore through them like a pair of predators unleashed. The sickening thud of fists meeting flesh echoed off the narrow walls, punctuated by grunts of pain and the crunch of bone against concrete.

Raptor grabbed one guy by the collar and slammed him against the brick wall, the impact reverberating through the confined space. Not wasting a second, he literally hurled another man to the ground, who landed with a bone-jarring thud that echoed in the confined space.

Hawkeye, moving with lethal precision, broke the arm of the nearest assailant, then smashed his head against a wall before hurling him at another guy, following close behind to violently take him out. The alley was filled with the sounds of groans, curses, and the dull thuds of bodies hitting the ground.

In the midst of the mayhem, Dani wasn't just standing by—she was in the thick of the fight. She was locked in a fierce struggle with one of the men, her hands grabbing his hair as she yanked his head back and drove her fist repeatedly into his face with relentless fury.

Borka and his partner froze for a moment, watching the carnage unfold as the two Rangers and Dani dismantled their crew with ruthless efficiency. Realizing they were trapped, the two men turned to flee but stopped short when they saw Ninja Man and me blocking the exit.

"Going somewhere, tough guy?" I asked, my voice cold as steel as I moved forward.

Ninja Man was already in motion, lunging toward Borka's partner with lethal precision. Borka, the classic bully, wasn't up for a fair fight. He needed an edge, and his right hand stealthily moved to his back, aiming to draw a gun. He threw a half-hearted punch with his left hand to distract me, but he didn't realize he had left himself wide open.

Taking him out wasn't a problem—there were a dozen different ways I could do it. I was more concerned with the "how" of it, given the constraints I had to observe while doing that. First was the use of non-lethal force—the scumbag needed to stay alive, at least for a while. So, punching him in the neck to crush his windpipe was out. I also needed him awake and talking. So, punches to the side of the neck or elbow strikes to his jaw or smashing his head against the wall were off the table as well. There was also the thought at the back of my mind that we might need him to escort us inside the brothel. So, keeping his face presentable enough wouldn't be a bad idea.

All that seriously limited my options. I needed to incapacitate and disarm him, causing enough pain to get him in a talkative mood without actually knocking him out. I liked the "causing pain" part of the plan. This guy deserved every bit of what was coming to him.

I moved forward and caught his loosely held left fist with my right hand, delivering a sharp jab just above his elbow on the inner side of his bicep. My knuckles smashed hard into his median nerve. That strike not only hurts like hell, it also paralyzes the hand. His fingers automatically loosened in my grip, and I pushed them back forcefully, breaking the middle three fingers.

His scream of agony filled the alley as he lost his grip on the gun he was still trying to draw. It clattered to the ground, and as his empty right hand swung forward, I shifted my focus. I drove my knee into his abdomen with just enough force to make him double over, then wrapped my right arm around his neck and pulled him down while grabbing his right wrist. With a quick, sharp jerk, I yanked his arm backward and upward, completely dislocating his shoulder.

I had to resist the urge to smash my boot into the side of his knee, remembering just in time that we might need him to walk later. I settled for simply hurling him into the wall. He slumped against it, howling in pain.

Mission accomplished—extreme pain inflicted while keeping him alive, conscious and presentable enough to take places. Almost at the same moment, the chaos inside the alley came to a halt. A tense calm settled in after the storm of violence.

As the dust settled and the last thug was knocked out, I glanced around and asked, "Everyone good?"

"Hell yeah," came the unanimous response from Raptor, Ninja Man, and Hawkeye, their voices charged with adrenaline and satisfaction.

Raptor grinned, flexing his fists. "Been a while since we got to put CQB into action like that."

"Damn, that felt good, didn't it?" Ninja Man chimed in.

"It was fuckin' awesome," Raptor replied with a wide grin, then quickly added, "Uh, sorry, ma'am—"

But Dani cut him off with a smirk, cracking her knuckles. "Fuck yeah, that was awesome."

The Rangers exchanged surprised looks before breaking into laughter, the tension of the fight melting away.

"Looks like you fit right in with this crew, Dani," I chuckled.

The woman who hardly ever smiled suddenly gave me a fierce grin, her eyes gleaming with adrenaline. "I'm just glad I could help wipe the floor with those scumbags."

"Speaking of which, it's time for a chat with our friend Borka," I said, glancing at the groaning man slumped against the wall.

Dani nodded and walked out to the street to talk with the girls. We had agreed earlier to conduct a parallel inquiry to find out the location of the brothel—Dani would gather intel from the girls while I pressed Borka for information. This way, we would be able to cross-check whatever he told us.

Ninja Man and Hawkeye followed Dani outside, keeping watch for any lookouts or reinforcements. I stood over Borka's squirming figure, with Raptor's hulking shadow behind me, looking like an angel of death. It was time to make Borka talk.

Borka was still slumped against the wall, but he had stopped groaning. His eyes were shut tight. Like he had passed out. But there was one problem. They were shut too tight, like he was putting real effort into it. It was clear he was pretending to be unconscious, too scared to face whatever was coming to him.

I decided to play along, leaning down and tapping his face lightly. His eyes squeezed shut even tighter.

Standing up, I turned to Raptor. "Looks like he's passed out. What do you think we should do?" I asked, frisking Borka and grabbing his phone.

Raptor caught on quickly and played along. "Don't know, boss. We've got to get moving. He ain't worth shit if we can't get him talking. I say we just put a bullet in his head and get moving."

"Guess you're right," I sighed, pulling a SIG from my back holster, racking the slide, and pressing the muzzle against Borka's forehead.

That suddenly brought him back to the land of the living. He groaned, opened his eyes, and looked around, disoriented like someone just waking from a deep sleep.

"Oh, look, he's awake," I said with mock surprise, then my tone turned cold. "Now listen up, tough guy. I need your full attention."

"No English," he muttered sullenly.

I turned to Raptor, feigning frustration. "He says he doesn't understand English."

Turning back to Borka, I asked, "Is that what you meant?"

He nodded, too thick to carry on his charade for long. I grabbed his left wrist and held his hand in front of his eyes. The middle three fingers were horribly twisted out of shape, sticking out to the back and almost touching the back of his palm. I lightly tapped one of his broken fingers. He let out a howl of pain, which I cut short by shoving the barrel of the SIG into his open mouth.

"We're done playing games. You want a bullet in your brain? I don't have a problem with that?"

Borka frantically shook his head, trying to speak through the gun in his mouth.

"Ready to talk?"

He rapidly nodded his head. I pulled back the gun but kept a firm grip on his hand.

"I need to hear it," I said.

"Yes, yes, ask me anything," Borka gasped.

"Good. Let's have a chat."

CHAPTER 23

"I don't know much. I'm just a small man running a small business," Borka insisted in a thick accent.

"Alright, businessman. Let's start with the code to unlock your phone."

"Uh..." He hesitated, trying to stall, but when I tightened my grip on his hand, he quickly blurted, "9475."

I released his hand, giving him a brief respite. After unlocking the phone, I noticed everything was in Bulgarian. I switched the language to English, and the menu and contact list instantly became readable. Scrolling through recent calls and messages, one name kept coming up: Viktor.

"Who's Viktor?"

"Uh, my friend."

"What does the friend do?" I asked, continuing to scroll through the messages. It was clear from their tone that Viktor wasn't his buddy—he was Borka's boss.

"He's a businessman."

"Really? Just another honest businessman like you?"

I grabbed his left hand again, this time clutching his palm. Fresh jolts of pain shot through his broken fingers. When he opened his mouth to scream, he found the muzzle of the SIG inside his mouth again.

"You were saying?" I asked, pulling the gun away slightly.

"Sorry, sorry, he's my boss," Borka gasped.

"Lie again and I'll get to work on the remaining fingers. Got it?"

"Yes."

"What does Viktor do?"

"He's my boss. He controls all the girls in Fakulteta."

That sounded promising. We were finally climbing up the ladder. Viktor sounded like a guy who would have access to the mafia's top guy.

"Where can we find Viktor?"

"He'll kill me if I tell you."

"And what do you think's going to happen if you don't?"

"I know I'm dead either way."

I could see that this was the time to offer him a sliver of hope. Borka wasn't one of the Taliban fanatics ready to endure a shit amount of pain. Weasels like him were in it for the easy money. Loyalty and sacrifice were concepts as alien to him as compassion to a rattlesnake. While I could force the information out of him through threats and pain, I would be limited by the questions I could ask. If I wanted him to volunteer extra information on his own, I would have to show him a realistic path to staying alive.

"Here's the deal. You've seen what we're capable of," I said, glancing toward the dark alley where his men lay broken and unconscious. "We're all ex-military specialists, hired to save the girls you've got hidden. If we wanted to kill you all, you'd already be dead. Understand?"

"Yes," he replied, not a trace of doubt in his voice.

"But make no mistake, if killing every one of you is what it takes to get to those girls, we'll do it without hesitation. The only reason you're not lying back there half-dead is because I wanted to question you. Lead us to the girls, and I'll let you live. If not, I won't waste time with you. I'll put a bullet in you and wake up one of your guys back there. I'll keep going until I get what I need. Do you doubt that?"

"No."

"Good. I have Viktor's number; tracking him down won't be hard. We've got people who can pinpoint his location, but it might take about an hour. Your life is only worth something to us if you can save us that hour. If we save the girls, we have no reason to kill you. After seeing what you do to those poor girls, we wouldn't hesitate, but we're not on a mission to clean up the streets. Understand?"

"Yes," Borka confirmed, nodding repeatedly.

"Now, think carefully about what you say next. If I don't like your answer, I'll pull the trigger," I warned him, pressing the SIG hard into his intact left shoulder.

"Viktor will be at the brothel," Borka blurted out.

My words had the desired effect. We were in business.

"Good. Now give me the location."

Borka was quick to provide the details.

"Who's the top man controlling Black Eagle's prostitution business?"

"Top man? I don't know. I'm just a small guy on the street, running a small business. I only know this street," Borka replied, trying to deflect.

"Wrong answer," I said, reaching for his hand.

"No, no, wait, I can only tell you what I've heard. I've never talked to him. He's a big man, doesn't even know I exist."

"I need names."

"Sergei. Sergei Volkov. He's boss number three after Boris and Ivan," he blurted out.

"You've got their numbers here?" I asked, holding up his phone.

"Me? Have their numbers? I wish. I don't think they even know I exist. I told you, I'm just a small..."

"Yeah, yeah, I know, you're a small businessman. Now, cut the crap and tell me where we can find Sergei."

"I don't know, really. It's like you're asking me where to find some movie stars. I know their faces and names, but I don't know where to find them. They're way out of my league."

I believed him. From what I knew about how these gangs operated, the top guys wouldn't associate with small-time pimps like Borka.

"If you want to live, you'll have to figure out a way to lead us to Sergei."

"Viktor will have his number. I know he called him once when I was there. Viktor was showing off, trying to look important."

"What does Viktor look like? Do you have his photo?" I asked, flipping through the photos on the phone, most of which were of women.

"I don't have his photo. He's just my boss, not a friend. I only have photos of people I like."

"All these women—these are the people you like?"

"Yes. They all work the streets for me."

"Past tense. They worked the streets for you. Depending on whether you survive the night, you're going to have to find a different profession somewhere far off from this place."

"Thank you."

"For what?"

"I can now see you were serious about not killing me."

"Let's not jump the gun. This whole deal depends on if we manage to rescue the girls."

"What girls?" Borka asked, suddenly more interested now that he knew his life was tied to theirs.

"Kidnapped Afghan girls, being smuggled into Sofia in a truck. If we save them, we let you walk. If not, we don't. That's how it's going to play out. Whatever you know about the girls, you'd better tell me now before something happens to them."

"Afghan girls? We don't have any Afghan girls on the street."

"What about at the brothel?"

"I can't be sure, but I don't think so. I mean, I don't know every girl in there. Viktor handles all of that. Most of the girls here are Bulgarian, some Romanian, Serbian, Ukrainian, Russian, but no Afghan."

"Then start praying Viktor knows more than you."

"He will, but he's a very dangerous man. I don't think he'll tell you."

"He will, if I ask him nicely. Didn't you suddenly become talkative? A few minutes ago, you didn't even understand English. And we'll have you with us—surely he'll be happy to talk."

"Wait, what? I've given you the location. I can't go there. He'll kill me if he finds out I brought you."

"He'll be too busy dealing with me to worry about you. You should be more concerned about what happens if we don't find the girls. Your best bet is to figure out how to get us to Viktor without too many bullets flying. You're going to be right in the line of fire if they do."

"Uh, alright."

"Don't move until I come get you," I ordered him, not that there was any risk of Borka running away—it was a dead-end alley.

"Think he was telling the truth?" Raptor asked as we moved outside.

"I think so. The guy's convinced I wasn't bluffing about killing him. He didn't have anything to gain by lying."

"I guess. You think this Sergei character holds the key to the girls?"

"I'm positive. We just need to figure out how to get to him."

The intel Dani obtained from the women in the street confirmed the location of the brothel. Not just that, but also the fact that it was run by Viktor, who outdid everyone else in being cruel to keep the girls in line. I was especially intrigued by one detail Dani shared—the possibility of finding an ally inside the brothel.

"The girls were too scared to talk at first, but once they knew we had you on our side and saw what we did to those guys in the alley, they opened up," Dani said. "There's something that could help you once you're inside. One of the girls, Yana, told me she has a distant cousin named Tanya who

189

works in the brothel's bar. Yana was sent to the brothel as punishment last year. It's a horrible place, but Tanya helped convince Viktor to let Yana back out on the streets. Imagine, life on the streets working for these heartless bastards is actually a step up for these girls."

"But why don't they just run away?" I asked.

"They're too scared. These guys have eyes everywhere. They threaten to hunt them down, and if one runs, they'll chase them just to make an example," Dani explained.

"Well, tell them it's their lucky day. None of these guys are going to come looking for them. And by the time we're done with the rest, chasing these girls will be the last thing on their minds."

"That's what I thought. You have no idea how long I've waited for something like this to happen. I always believed it would, just didn't know when."

"We'll do our best. What else can you tell me about Tanya and Yana?"

"Right. Tanya's kind of Viktor's girl. Not because she likes him, but it's her way to avoid being treated like the other girls, like a piece of meat who's fair game for everyone. Still, she's just as trapped. If she gets the chance, she wants out. If you mention Yana and that you're after Viktor, she'll help however she can."

"An insider will be useful. Can Yana call Tanya before we head there?"

"No, none of the girls inside are allowed to have phones. It's how they keep them trapped—no contact with the outside world."

"That bad, huh?"

"Afraid so. Yana's the same. No phones. But she described Tanya for me—sharp features, blue eyes, and flowing, curly, platinum blonde hair. Also, her tattoos are very distinctive. On her right arm, she has a tattoo of a dandelion being blown, with its seeds turning into birds as they drift up her arm. On her left wrist, she has an image of broken shackles."

"Sounds like someone more than ready to break free," I commented.

"Exactly. If you need to gain her trust, mention the dandelion tattoo. Tanya's grandma used to tell her that story. Only Yana would know that."

"It'll be good to have an ally inside. And it might just be her lucky night. We don't have a clear plan for what exactly we'll do at the brothel, but it'll likely involve taking out most of Viktor's men before we get our hands on him. Tanya and the women trapped there can get out after that. Will they have somewhere to go? We can set them free, but that's about all we can do."

"I get it. I'm sure Tanya can take charge. From what Yana tells me, Tanya's a survivor, even in this mess. Just get her on a phone with me, and we'll sort out the rest."

"Sounds good. One more thing—are you familiar with the name Sergei Volkov?"

"Yes, he's part of Black Eagles. Among their top men."

"He's the mafia's top guy for sex trafficking," I informed Dani.

"Oh, I didn't know that."

"He's the one we need to get our hands on tonight. He's our ticket to the girls we've come all this way to rescue."

"I hope you do."

"Me too. We'll move on the brothel. We need to get Viktor and Sergei while we still have the element of surprise. If they get wind of us, they'll disappear, and we'll lose our chance."

"That's true. I'll take care of these girls. They're glad to be rid of these men. I'll make sure they all get out of the city to safety tonight. They can decide tomorrow what they want to do with their lives. They're lucky that they can even consider the question of a future."

"Do you need any help with that?" I asked.

"No, I've got the people for this. This is what we do—help women like them. We've got ways to get them to safe places. What you've done today, you've no idea how many lives you've saved."

"Don't mention it. The night isn't over yet. We're taking down Black Eagles' trafficking operations tonight."

"Amen to that. But let me warn you, when you see the plight of the girls inside that brothel, you won't be able to unsee it. It sticks to your mind, like a shadow that clings to your soul," Dani cautioned.

I didn't realize at the time how true her words were going to turn out.

"Thanks. It all ends tonight. We can't get every lowlife on the planet, but the one's we can, we certainly will," I promised.

"I'll keep my phone close. Let me know if you need anything. Good luck, Axel."

"Good luck, Dani."

I sent Viktor's number to Rick to start tracking it and confirm the location. We were ready to move. As we walked back to the alley to pick up

Borka, I thought about how to patch up the broken man slumped against the wall.

The guy was a wreck. His left hand hung uselessly, three fingers broken, his right shoulder dislocated. I didn't feel any sympathy for someone who had likely done the same to countless women, but we needed him to get inside the brothel without raising suspicion. We were bound to sound alarms with him walking in there like a scarecrow. That meant patching him up, at least temporarily.

"Alright, Borka," I said. "Time to get you field-ready. I'm going to fix your fingers and shoulder. It'll hurt like hell, but you'll be in better shape after that."

Borka's eyes widened as I crouched down and grabbed his mangled hand. "You're not a doctor—" he started to protest.

"Relax, he's done this a thousand times," Ninja Man cut in. "Ever heard of tough love?"

"Hold still," I muttered, more out of habit than actual advice.

With a quick, sharp motion, I snapped the fingers back into place, one by one. The sound was like twigs breaking underfoot. Borka let out a strangled yell, his eyes squeezed shut from the pain, but almost immediately, a wave of relief washed over him as the pressure eased.

"See? Just like popping bubble wrap," I said dryly, giving the fingers a test wiggle. "You'll live."

Next, I moved to his shoulder. I gripped his arm as if I was going to check it, then without warning, I jerked the shoulder back into its socket with a sickening pop. Borka screamed, but I held him steady.

"It's not a permanent fix, but it'll do," I said. "You won't be stumbling around like a zombie."

"Just don't start any arm wrestling contests," Ninja Man chuckled.

Borka panted, sweat dripping from his face, but he nodded. The pain was still there, but it had become manageable. He could move without drawing too much attention.

"Alright, get your shit together," I said, hauling him to his feet. "We've got a party to crash. We need you to walk in there like nothing's wrong. Mess it up, and you're the first one to go down."

We got inside the SUV and hit the road. It was time to get our hands on Viktor and shut down his evil empire.

CHAPTER 24

The low growl of the SUV's engine was the only sound in the otherwise still night as we rolled further west toward the outskirts of Fakulteta. The area was an urban wasteland, where crumbling warehouses, overgrown lots, and graffiti-covered walls told the tale of a once-thriving industrial zone now rotting from within. Streetlights flickered sporadically, casting long shadows over the abandoned buildings, adding an eerie quality to the scene.

A few stragglers shuffled along the sidewalks, their faces gaunt and eyes hollow—people used to looking the other way. Here and there, huddled figures gathered around makeshift fires in old oil drums, their low murmurings barely audible in the cold night air.

The city's underbelly had a different pulse—darker, meaner, a place where shadows concealed more than just the night. It was the kind of place where the law dared not tread, where danger and desperation reeked from every corner. This was the Wild West—where might made right and the strong preyed on the weak in a place forgotten by time.

"This place is a damn ghost town," Ninja Man muttered.

"No kidding," I replied.

"Feels like we're driving through a warzone," Raptor observed.

"Perfect spot for these scumbags to operate," Hawkeye joined in.

In the rearview mirror, I saw Borka squirming, his face etched with an expression of impending doom.

As we drove deeper into the district, the streets grew narrower and more twisted, as if the city itself was trying to trap us. We passed sites lined with rusted metal fences topped with barbed wire—makeshift barriers that spoke of a neighborhood on edge, constantly defending itself against the decay it was drowning in. The air was thick with the stench of burnt plastic and the acrid tang of fear.

We finally halted about half a block away from our target—a decrepit three-story building that stood like a forgotten monument to everything rotten in this part of town. The building had once been part of a factory complex, but now it was a haven for scum. It loomed in the darkness, its windows boarded up, the walls stained with grime and time.

A chain-link fence surrounded the property, more symbolic than functional—holes had been cut through the wire, and the gate hung crookedly on its hinges. The surrounding area was a graveyard of abandoned warehouses and overgrown lots, nature reclaiming what people had left behind. The only signs of life were the rats scurrying through the trash and the distant, echoing bark of a stray dog.

"This place looks like it's seen better days," Ninja Man observed.

"Yeah, about a hundred years ago," Hawkeye added.

A few men loitered outside the entrance, their expressions a mix of desperation and dull resolve. Some were likely customers, but most looked like they had hit rock bottom. Their clothes were worn and dirty, their eyes avoiding contact with anyone who might be watching. This was the kind of place where the worst of humanity hid in plain sight—a black hole where people disappeared without a trace.

"Looks like the kind of place you go into but don't come out of," Hawkeye commented, his eyes locked on the thugs at the door.

"Not tonight," I replied.

The front entrance had three men standing guard. One large guy stood with his big arms folded across his chest, glaring at anyone who passed by. The shotgun slung across the back of a second, smaller guy was as clear a deterrent as the biceps of his partner. The third guy didn't have a visible firearm, but it was almost certain he was armed.

We had received detailed intel from Borka on the way, which matched what Dani had found out from Yana. The building had three floors, packed with makeshift rooms where the mafia ran their sordid business. The ground floor was where the muscle hung out, keeping an eye on who came and went. The second floor had rows of makeshift cubicles for "clients". The top floor was being converted into a VIP area, where you paid extra and got whatever twisted kicks you were looking for. That night, we planned to tear the place apart, room by room if necessary, to find Viktor.

"How hard we hitting this op? Full throttle or playing it cool?" Raptor asked before we exited the vehicle.

"We've got multiple armed adversaries inside. Plan A is a covert op—we sneak in, grab Viktor, and get out without raising too much hell."

"And if Plan A goes sideways?" Ninja Man asked.

"Then we go with Plan B—lethal force. Take them down fast before it turns into a shootout. We want them down before they know what hit them. Minimize collateral damage. Clear?"

"Crystal. Quiet if we can, loud if we must," Hawkeye nodded, checking his weapon.

"Exactly. We're here to get the job done. Any which way. Let's move, Rangers."

"Hooah," they echoed in unison, ready to move.

I signaled Raptor and Hawkeye to circle around and take position in the shadows behind the main entrance. They would wait for my signal before taking out the three guards. Ninja Man and I moved with Borka toward the entrance without making any attempt to conceal ourselves.

"Just remember, Borka—don't get any ideas. This time it's serious business. I won't be breaking any bones. It's going to be a bullet for you if you try to play smart," I warned him, pressing my SIG into his back. To reinforce the message, Ninja Man pressed his gun on the other side of his back.

"I know," he replied in a resigned tone.

Borka led the way with a tense, almost reluctant stride, trying to mask his discomfort. But the pain in his freshly snapped-back fingers and shoulder was evident in his stiff movements. The guards' eyes were on us as we approached the entrance, but Borka's presence seemed to put them at ease.

"Borka, who're the new guys?" one of them grunted, his voice rough from years of smoking.

"New muscle," Borka replied, his voice strained but steady. "Viktor's orders. They are here to help with a... delivery."

The guards exchanged glances but eventually shrugged and stepped aside to let us pass. A security camera hung above the entrance, though it looked as if it hadn't worked in years. Even if it was functional, I doubted anyone was monitoring it. And even if they were, it wasn't like anyone could recognize us.

As we stepped inside, we were immediately hit by the dim, smoky atmosphere typical of a seedy dive. The inside of the brothel was a grim reflection of its exterior—dark, dirty, and oppressive. The air was thick with the stale scent of sweat, cheap alcohol, and the faint undertone of desperation. The low hum of conversation mingled with the tinny sound of a radio playing in the background, giving the place a gritty, unsettling vibe.

The layout was simple—a small, rundown bar sat against the far wall, its wooden counter scarred and stained from years of neglect. Behind it, bottles of mostly low-grade liquor were lined up alongside mismatched glasses. The bar stools were old and wobbly, their once-padded seats now torn and frayed.

Behind the counter stood a woman with platinum blonde hair that caught the dim light. Her striking features were set in a neutral expression, but there was a hardness in her eyes—a look that spoke of a woman who had seen more than her share of trouble. She was still too far off for me to identify her by her tattoos. But even from a distance, I was already sure the woman was Tanya.

A few rickety tables were scattered across the floor, surrounded by mismatched chairs. A handful of burly, hard-faced men sat at these tables, their eyes flicking toward us with wary interest. These were the muscle—guys paid to watch and, if necessary, act. Their presence gave the place a tense, charged atmosphere. Some were nursing drinks, while others engaged in low conversations, their attention constantly scanning the room.

Two young women, dressed in revealing outfits, moved between the tables, flirting with the men and laughing at jokes that, judging by their forced smiles, were far from funny. One perched on a thug's lap, playing with his hair while he held her close with a possessive grip. Another girl, barely out of her teens, stood by a table, refilling glasses and trying to avoid the wandering hands of a drunk patron.

Tanya was alone at the bar, and I decided to seize the opportunity to talk to her before anyone else approached. I nodded to Ninja Man to grab a table with Borka while I headed toward the bar.

Tanya watched me closely, trying to assess me as I approached the bar. As I got closer, I noticed the tattoos on her arms—the delicate dandelion seeds floating up her right forearm, turning into birds, and the broken shackles wrapped around her left wrist. This was definitely Tanya.

She was wiping down the bar, her expression hard and unreadable. The crackling radio's music was just loud enough to mask our conversation from the rest of the room. I leaned in casually and gave her a nod. She raised an eyebrow in acknowledgment.

"Three beers, please," I said loudly enough for others to hear.

"Which ones?" Tanya asked, pointing at three different options on the rack behind her.

"Whatever you recommend. You're Tanya, right?" I continued, keeping my tone casual. "Yana sent me."

Her hand paused mid-wipe, but she didn't look up. "Yana?" she murmured, barely above the music.

I nodded, keeping my eyes on the bottles behind the bar. "We got her and the others out. Safe. Yana said you could help us handle things here."

Tanya's hard eyes studied me briefly, searching for any sign of deception. Her expression didn't indicate she was ready to trust me. At least not yet.

I knew I had to establish trust quickly. "Yana told me about the dandelion. How your grandma used to say those seeds were like wishes, drifting free. She said to tell you the birds are going to get free tonight."

For a split second, a flash of emotion broke through Tanya's tough exterior. "Yana's safe?" she asked, her voice cracking slightly.

I nodded. "Safe with Dani. Yana mentioned you know her."

Tanya gave a small nod, her voice barely a whisper. "Yes, most of the girls have heard about her."

"We're here to shut this place down. For good."

Tanya looked conflicted, like she wanted to believe me but was wary. Her eyes flicked to where

Borka was seated with Ninja Man. A hint of suspicion crept into her voice again. "Why is Borka with you?"

"We needed a way in without getting frisked. We're armed, and we're going to need those guns in about two minutes." I leaned in closer, speaking just above the hum of the radio. "You must've noticed Borka's strange walk. His right shoulder's messed up. If you look closely, he can barely move his left hand. That's because we broke all his fingers. We beat the hell out of him and his boys before freeing Yana and the others."

Tanya's lips twitched into a faint smile. "Serves him right. But listen, this place is crawling with Viktor's men. It's not going to be easy."

"I know. We're ready. We've got the layout of the building from Borka, but I don't trust him. Can you confirm what's on the floors above?"

"The second floor is nothing but hell for the girls trapped there," she said, shuddering involuntarily. "It's a large hall divided into small spaces... you can't even call them rooms. Just spaces made out of sheets and curtains with a bed inside... and a woman, like an object in the room that men use and then leave."

"Dani hinted at that—told me I wouldn't be able to forget what I'd see."

"Yes. It gives you an idea of how sick the world can be. You don't have to die to see hell," she said, her voice trembling before she took a deep breath and continued. "The top floor used to be the same, but it's been renovated. Viktor has come up with a plan of earning more money. Better rooms, so more money for Viktor, not that it makes any difference to the girls."

"There'll be a difference tonight. That's a promise. How many men does Viktor have in here?"

"There are seven on this floor. You must've seen the three at the entrance," Tanya replied, taking out three bottles from a cooler and slowly beginning to wipe each one with a dishcloth.

"Yes," I confirmed.

"The three men at the table to the right of your friends are Viktor's men," she said without glancing in their direction. "The seventh man is by the stairs leading up. There are four more on the second and third floors. I can't say exactly where, but they'll be spread out across the two floors. And then there's Viktor. His office is on the third floor—the renovated one. It's at the end of the hallway when you enter from the stairs. So, including Viktor, there are twelve men."

"That's great intel. And the rest of the men? Are they just... I don't know what the right word for them would be."

"Scum of the earth?" Tanya asked. "But we call them customers for the sake of simplicity. That's who the others at the tables are, and some are in the cubicles on the second floor. They haven't started business on the third floor yet."

"That's all I need. What does Viktor look like?"

"He's big. As tall as you, maybe taller, and much heavier. He's got a beard and a scar on his right cheek—a lucky escape from a bullet. Lucky for him, but unlucky for all of us."

"It's not his lucky night. We're going to take him out. Keep your head down when things go down. I'll need you to keep the girls safe until we can get them out."

"Yes, I will. But... who are you? Why are you doing this? I don't understand," Tanya asked, her voice filled with confusion.

"We're soldiers. Made a promise to a dying friend. It's a long story, but his little girl was kidnapped and is on her way to Sofia. You know anything about kidnapped Afghan girls being brought here?"

"No, I haven't heard anything," she said regretfully. "I can try to find out."

"No, that's fine. Do you know a guy called Sergei Volkov?"

"I've seen him once, but I've heard Viktor talk about him a lot. He's big in the Black Eagles. I think he's the one who ordered the hit on Dani. Viktor's man did it. Did you know that?"

"No, I didn't. But I know Viktor and Sergei are the ones who can lead me to the girls."

"I hope you find them," Tanya said with all the conviction she could muster, though it remained tinged with disbelief. "I can't believe this is happening."

"It is. Just be ready for it," I said, grabbing the three beers off the counter. "Bulgarian brand?" I asked loudly.

"Yes. It's called Kamenitza."

I nodded, then turned and headed back to the table. Sitting down, I leaned in close to Ninja Man, keeping my voice just above a whisper, ensuring Borka couldn't overhear.

"Here's the plan," I began. "I've got confirmation Viktor's on the third floor. I'm heading up with Borka. I'll clear the second floor quietly—no noise, no mess. Once it's secure, we move to the third and grab Viktor."

"Sure you want to go solo?" Ninja Man asked.

"Affirmative. You've got enough to handle down here. There are seven hostiles on this floor—the three we passed at the entrance, three at the table on the right, and one by the stairs. When you get my signal, hit them hard, but with precision—no collateral, no stray shots. We keep it tight."

"Copy that," Ninja Man replied, all business.

"Once it kicks off, you take out the four inside. Raptor and Hawkeye will handle the three at the door. Quick and clean—no one gets a chance to yell."

"Roger that. We'll drop them before they know what hit them."

CHAPTER 25

I stood up and locked eyes with Borka. "Let's move," I ordered.

Borka reluctantly rose to his feet. I stayed behind him as we approached the stairs. I relaxed slightly when I saw there were no security cameras in sight. Once we passed the guard, we could proceed unnoticed.

The guard gave Borka a look but let us pass without incident. As we ascended, I stayed mostly hidden behind Borka, pulling out my handgun. Without breaking stride, I retrieved a suppressor from my tactical pants pocket and screwed it on. I pressed the gun against Borka's back briefly—a reminder not to try anything foolish.

My senses were on high alert as we reached the second floor. The doorway opened into a large hall divided into cramped, makeshift rooms. Each "room" was barely more than a small space enclosed by dirty, threadbare curtains, offering only the illusion of privacy. Inside each one, a bed and a woman. The scene was grim, the air thick with desperation and despair.

Some of the women lay passed out, their bodies limp and lifeless, victims of whatever drugs had been forced into them. Others were awake, their hollow eyes and twitching limbs showing they were in deep, struggling to maintain any grip on reality. Tanya had been right—hell couldn't be much worse than what these girls endured daily. Some cubicles had men inside, engaging in their vile business, cursing at the intrusion when I peeked in.

Dani's parting words echoed in my mind: "When you see the plight of the girls inside the brothel, you won't be able to unsee it. It sticks to your mind, like a shadow that clings to your soul."

With each step, my anger grew—a burning rage at the men who had reduced these women to such a sub-human existence. The men who profited from this suffering were beyond redemption. And all the while, a voice in the back of my mind kept reminding me that this would be Zara's fate if I didn't reach her in time.

I scanned the area as I moved, making sure no threats were lurking. As I neared the end of the hall, I took a quick look around the corner, ensuring no guards were posted there. The coast seemed clear, but something felt off.

My heart skipped a beat as a sudden realization hit me—Borka was no longer beside me. I whipped around, scanning the area as I cursed myself for momentarily losing focus. That was all it had taken for Borka to slip away. My mind raced as I sprinted back toward the stairs, cursing under my breath. Borka had likely ducked into one of the cubicles and escaped out the back. The sudden sound of shouting in Bulgarian confirmed my fears, followed by more voices responding with urgency.

I drew my gun as I reached the stairwell entrance, holding it in a high-ready position, my finger hovering just above the trigger. Two guards at the entrance were already armed, their eyes darting around in confusion as they tried to figure out where the threat was coming from. They were too slow. I squeezed the trigger four times, blasting two controlled shots into each guard before they could react. They dropped instantly, their weapons clattering to the floor.

My instincts screamed at me that the danger wasn't over. My sixth sense kicked in—Borka had to be close, probably hiding in one of the cubicles and likely armed. I didn't waste a second. Diving to the floor, I rolled across the dirty, splintered wood. As I came out of the roll, I caught sight of Borka, AK-47 in hand, charging around a corner.

I didn't hesitate. Two bullets, center mass. Borka staggered, eyes wide in shock, before collapsing in a heap. I exhaled, my mind already shifting gears, knowing I had to move quickly before the entire building came down on us. I had cleared the second floor, but the mission was far from over. Viktor was up on the third floor, and I couldn't afford any slip-ups. My gun had been as silent as it could be, but the guards' shouts could have been heard by the guys on the top floor.

I spoke into my mic, my voice low and steady. "All units, this is Blaze. Execute now. Engage and neutralize all tangos. Ground floor's a go—secure it ASAP. Second floor clear, I'm moving up to the third to bag Viktor. Full control downstairs, no tangos left standing. Over."

A series of quiet affirmatives came back over the comms.

I moved to the stairway and took a quick peek up. I knew the guard at the bottom would already have been neutralized by Ninja Man. The stairway was clear. I was mindful of a security camera perched above and held the suppressed gun hidden behind me as I began rushing up.

Before I had covered half the steps, I was caught off guard when a gunman suddenly appeared at the top of the stairs. He had a gun in his hand, though not aimed directly at me. One of Viktor's guards, he had likely just come around for a look. The situation was delicate—if I tried to swing my gun around, there was a chance I would take a bullet before I could get off a shot. My best option was to act as if I were one of Borka's men.

"Hey," I called out, putting on an air of urgency while still moving toward him at a slower pace. "Something's wrong on the second floor. Borka sent me up to get Viktor to send some guys."

The gunman hesitated, his eyes narrowing as he tried to assess me. But before he could make a decision, a voice called out from deeper inside the third floor hall. My act had been good enough to create a passable deception. Distracted, the gunman turned his head to look over his shoulder.

That was my cue. I didn't waste a second. I swung my gun around, the suppressed weapon barely making a sound as I put two rounds into the gunman's chest at almost point blank range. The man's body jolted with the impact, his gun clattering to the floor. As he started to slump forward, I stepped up, catching him under the arms and using the dead weight as a shield.

I stepped into the third-floor doorway and peered down the passage. The renovated top floor of the brothel was a stark contrast to the squalor below. A narrow passage ran the length of the floor. The walls, though still cheap, were painted in a dark hue, trying to mask the decay underneath. Dim, red-tinted lights lined the ceiling, casting an ominous glow that barely illuminated the way ahead.

On either side of the passage, was a row of rooms. Unlike the lower floors, these rooms had actual wooden walls and doors, providing a semblance of privacy. Each door had a small, frosted glass window. These rooms were where the real money would be made, a place for Viktor's "elite" clientele.

At the far end of the passage was Viktor's office. Though it wasn't visible from my current position, Tanya had briefed me on its exact location. It was the last door on the right.

I took all this in within a second. But there were more pressing matters to deal with—like the second gunman moving toward me, already reaching for the AK-47 slung across his body. I didn't give him the chance. Two quick shots dropped him before he could even unsling his weapon.

As the second body hit the ground, a large figure emerged from a room at the far end of the hall. From his size, I had no doubt the bear of a man was Viktor. Our eyes met for a brief second, and I saw fear flash across his face. Without a moment's hesitation, he spun around and rushed back into the room.

I knew what was coming next—Viktor wasn't retreating; he was rearming. He would be back out with some heavy firepower, ready to spray the entire hallway with bullets. I had to decide fast— charge in and risk getting cut down by automatic fire or find a way to even the odds.

I chose the second option. Dropping the gunman's body, I sprinted forward, covering the distance to the second gunman's body, which lay about halfway between the stairwell door and Viktor's room. Diving down, I used the body as a shield, my SIG drawn and ready. I knew Viktor would be coming out guns blazing any moment.

A second later, Viktor's right arm came into view, an Uzi gripped tightly in his hand. He fired wildly down the passageway, spraying 9mm rounds everywhere. The bullets zinged above me, ricocheting off the walls and ceiling. I knew Viktor was just clearing the area, creating chaos before making his move.

But I realized that once he fully emerged, he would likely have another weapon ready in his left hand. Facing dual automatic fire in this tight space would be a death sentence. I couldn't let it happen.

Before Viktor could step out fully and spot me, I squeezed the trigger, sending rounds down the passage. The bullets tore into Viktor's right arm and shoulder, shattering bone and muscle, sending the Uzi clattering to the floor. But Viktor, driven by sheer fury and adrenaline, kept coming, his face twisted in rage.

Our eyes locked again for a brief, tense moment. I didn't hesitate. My aim was steady, my mind clear. I fired again, the rounds finding their mark. Multiple bullets punched into Viktor's face, tearing through flesh and bone. The force of the impacts sent Viktor crashing back against the doorframe, his body crumpling to the floor in a lifeless heap.

I kept my gun trained on Viktor's body, making sure he was down for good. The echo of gunfire faded, leaving a heavy silence in its wake. I slowly got to my feet, my eyes scanning the hallway, ready for anything. But it was over. Viktor was down.

CHAPTER 26

"All units, this is Blaze. Second and third floors are clear," I radioed in a low tone. "Viktor's down. Secure the ground floor. Stay sharp."

"Ninja Man to Blaze. Copy that. Ground floor secure. I'm on my way up," Ninja Man's voice came through the earpiece.

I knelt beside Viktor's lifeless body, quickly frisking his pockets. I found a cell phone, but not surprisingly, it was locked. This was 2012—fingerprints and face scan unlocks hadn't made an appearance in the world of cell phone technology yet. There was no option but to punch in a code. And I had no clue about that.

"Any luck with the phone?" Ninja Man asked as he walked in through the doorway at the other end.

"Nope. Needs a code. Let's see what he's got in there," I replied, as I pocketed the phone and we moved into Viktor's office.

The room was more organized than I expected, with a sleek desk and a computer sitting atop it. Viktor had been using it when I surprised him, so the screen was still unlocked. I began rifling through the computer, searching for anything that could lead me to Sergei. I scanned through files, trying to find something, anything, that could give me a clue. But I couldn't find anything useful. Then, a thought struck me.

"Ninja, get Tanya up here. Let's give the phone another shot."

"You think she might know the code?"

"Dani said Viktor was sweet on her. It's worth a try."

"Right. On it," he said, walking out.

A few minutes later, Ninja Man returned with Tanya in tow. Her eyes lingered on Viktor's body as she walked in, but she quickly snapped out of it.

"Still finding it hard to believe, huh?" I asked.

"Yes. You have no idea what this means to us," she replied.

"I saw what was happening on the floor below. You were right—those girls were in hell."

"Thanks for getting them out."

"I was happy to do it. Scum like Viktor don't deserve to breathe the same air as the rest of us."

"What about Borka?"

"He too got what was coming to him."

"Good," she said, a slight smile of relief crossing her face. "Is there anything else I can do?"

"Actually, yeah. Do you know Viktor's phone code?"

"I think I do. I've seen him punch it in a few times," she said, holding out her hand for the phone.

She tapped in the digits, and the phone unlocked.

"There you go," Tanya said, a smile brightening her face for the first time since I met her.

"As simple as that?"

"Yeah," she beamed.

My own eyes lit up as well when, flipping through the contacts, I found what I was desperately looking for—Sergei's number.

"Bingo," I muttered, quickly texting the number to Rick.

"On it. I'll get back to you in ten," Rick texted back immediately.

As I looked up, I saw Tanya looking at me like she wanted to say something.

"Something on your mind?" I asked.

"That computer is the only thing that still hangs like a shadow over the girls," she said, looking at me with urgency in her eyes.

"What do you mean?"

"That's where Viktor kept all the information about the girls—their families, where they came from. He used it to make sure they wouldn't dream of running away. The girls were trapped because they were too scared of Viktor's men coming after them if they escaped. If you wipe out that information, the mafia has no way to track them down when they go home, away from this sick place."

"You have my word. I'm checking it for any intel that might help us in our search, and then I'll wipe it clean. This will never come back to haunt these girls."

"Thank you. I'll go check on the girls," she said quietly.

I dialed Dani next. The line buzzed for a moment before Dani's voice came through, sharp and alert. "Blaze, what's the status?"

"Viktor's down, along with all his men. Tanya's taking care of the girls. They're shaken, but they'll be okay."

A sigh of relief echoed through the line. "Thank God! I'm on my way. I've got an extra vehicle to get the girls to safety. I'll be there in ten minutes max," Dani confirmed before hanging up.

Next, I called Madison. She, Hughes and Echo had gone to the mafia's Eclipse nightclub after we met Dani. I hadn't heard from them since.

"Hey, Axel," Madison kind of shouted into the phone, trying to keep her voice from being drowned out by the loud music in the background.

"Madison, we're almost done here, waiting for some intel to come in. How's it going at the nightclub?"

There was a pause on the other end, and I could hear the tension in Madison's voice when she spoke. "Something weird happened a minute ago. I'm not sure how to put it, but something's off. I'm getting a bad feeling."

"What do you mean? What happened?"

"There's this guy who's been eyeing me for a while. At first, I thought he was just hitting on me, but it felt like he was trying to figure out who I was. He came over and started asking questions—if I'm a tourist, where I'm from, when I got here, my name..."

"That doesn't sound like pick up lines."

"I know. He was too focused on establishing my timeline and trying to somehow identify me."

"Is that so?" I asked, puzzled.

"Yes. I don't know how, but I'm getting the strong feeling he knows me somehow."

"What did you tell him? Did you give him your name?"

"No, I just came up with a random name. Told him my name was Kelly. And that I was a New Yorker and landed with my boyfriend yesterday."

"That was quick thinking."

"It wasn't difficult—not the first time I've been hit on," she pointed out, before adding, "but somehow, I don't think it's the end of the story. He walked off looking unsure as hell—the look on his face definitely wasn't that of a convinced man. And he's still lurking around close by. I'm sending you his photo. Maybe Rick or Niko or Dani knows who he is?"

"You took a photo? You're getting pretty good at this," I replied. "Where are Hughes and Echo?"

"Echo is close by, keeping an eye on me and stuff going on around us. He said it would be better if we aren't all seen together, just in case. At that time, I was wondering what the hell he meant by 'just in case', but now I get it. He set us all up with radios, so we can be in constant touch. I just spoke to him and told him what's going on. That was his idea again, you know, to create the impression that I'm here only with Hughes."

"That was smart. Echo's a sharp guy," I remarked. "Is Hughes with you?"

"No. He wasn't feeling too well. Not exactly the nightclub type—there's too much flashing lights, smoke and over-the-top loud music in here. He went out for a breather."

"Alright. Send me the photo. I'll have a word with Echo. Stay alert."

"I will. Sending it now," she said, ending the call.

I immediately called Echo. I realized there wasn't enough time to go through the contents of the computer. While the call went out, I unplugged Viktor's computer and removed the hard drive. If the guy eyeing Madison was with the Black Eagles, Tanya might be able to identify him. Echo came on the line as I headed downstairs.

"Hey boss, how's the party on your end? You all done, or should I come over and help clean up? All I've got here is bad music. This babysitting gig is really cramping my style," Echo complained.

I couldn't help laughing. "You're missing out, Echo. Just took down the whole crew at the brothel. You'd have had a blast."

"Yeah, yeah, you always get the good gigs. And here I am, playing guardian angel. Seriously, dude, you owe me one."

"Yeah, sure. But what's going on with Madison? She just called saying there's a guy eyeing her and giving her the creeps."

"Yeah, I clocked him. Sharply dressed, not part of the usual crowd. Looks more like he might be Black Eagle. He's been hovering, giving weird vibes. Don't worry, I've got eyes on him. If he makes a move, I'll be all over it."

"Good. Keep your eyes peeled. This guy might be trouble. We've got enough on our plate without a wild card in the mix. Madison's sending me a photo of the guy. I'll see if anyone here recognizes him. Just stay alert, Echo."

"Roger that. Babysitting with a side of throat-punching, if needed. You just keep having fun without me."

"I'll try," I chuckled. "Stay sharp."

"Copy that. Echo out."

Madison's message had landed on my phone by the time I ended the call and reached the ground floor. I opened the message to find the photo of a man in a tailored black suit, paired with a white shirt and a black tie. The hair was jet black, slicked back neatly, not a single strand out of place.

The face was in a side profile—Madison must have clicked him when he was looking elsewhere. It was a sharp, angular face with high cheekbones, a carved jawline, and a hooked nose. The man radiated menace.

I walked over to Tanya, who was quietly tending to the shaken women we had freed.

"Hey, Tanya," I said, pulling her aside and showing her the photo on my phone. "Do you know this guy?"

Her eyes widened instantly. "Yes. That's the man you've been looking for. That's Sergei Volkov."

I suddenly felt a cold chill run down my spine.

CHAPTER 27

"Are you sure?" I pressed Tanya, needing absolute certainty.

"Positive. That's him," she confirmed without hesitation.

I felt my stomach tighten. Suddenly, it all became clear as the pieces fell into place with an almost audible click. Sergei was the linchpin between the Black Eagles and the Taliban, the guy running the flesh trade. If he was eyeing Madison, it wasn't because he was interested in a dance. He must have received photos of the kidnapped girls from Afghanistan—and Madison's face must have been among them. If Sergei recognized her, she and Echo were in serious trouble.

I didn't waste another second. "All units, this is Blaze! We're moving out, now!" I barked into my radio, the urgency in my voice leaving no room for questions. "Madison and Echo are in the red zone. We're heading to Eclipse."

As I turned, Dani walked in. I rushed over to her.

"This is your scene now. Madison's in danger. We've got to rush."

"Go on. I've got this covered," Dani replied. "Good luck."

"Thanks," I replied as I sprinted out with the team.

We raced toward the SUV, urgency pumping through our veins. Ninja Man jumped into the driver's seat. I rode shotgun while the others piled into the back. As soon as the doors slammed shut, I dialed Echo's number. The line rang once, twice, then he picked up.

"Echo, listen up," I almost shouted into the phone in my urgency, my tone leaving no room for doubt. "The guy eyeing Madison is Sergei Volkov. He's the Black Eagles' head of sex trafficking and the Taliban's contact man. He might've recognized her as the woman the Talis captured with the girls. You need to exfil now."

There was a brief pause on the other end, and I could practically hear Echo shifting into high alert. "Copy that," he replied, his voice calm but edged with urgency. "Hughes just walked in too, and joined Madison at the table."

Damn it! I clenched my jaw. "That's bad news. If Sergei sees them together, it'll confirm who she is."

"Yeah," Echo replied, "he's already looking at them and comparing something on his phone. I gotta move, Cowboy. Can't talk."

"Do what you have to," I responded. "We're ten minutes out. Hang tight until we get there."

"Roger that," Echo replied before hanging up.

Ninja Man floored the gas pedal, the engine roaring as we tore down the streets. Every second counted.

I gripped the door handle tightly, my mind racing. This mission had just taken a hard left turn into dangerous territory. In my gut, I knew this was about to go down fast and dirty. Sergei wasn't the kind of guy to leave loose ends, and neither were we. But first, we had to get to him before he made his move.

A call from Rick broke the tension as we raced through the streets.

"Blaze here. We're en route to Eclipse," I said as I took the call.

"Well, that's where Sergei's phone pinged," Rick replied, sounding surprised.

I gave him a quick account of what happened.

"Damn, you think he's clocked Madison?" Rick asked.

"I'm sure of it, especially with Hughes joining her. What do you have on Eclipse? You've got the schematics?"

"Yeah, I do. We dug up intel on all known Black Eagles locations. Give me a few seconds while I bring it up. What exactly are you looking for?"

"We need the layout and all entry and exit points. Four of us walking through the front door will set off alarms. We need to get in quietly and avoid triggering the bouncers. Neutralizing them is a last resort. We need the flexibility to search inside without anyone breathing down our necks."

"Got it. Pulling up the schematics now. Eclipse is on the nineteenth floor of the Star of Sofia hotel. Five-star joint. Only the penthouse floor above the nightclub. And restaurants on the floor below. The main entrance to the club is from the hotel's elevator lobby, with a reception area leading into a large dance floor. The bar is set against the far wall, and there's a VIP section off to the right. Behind that, there's a hallway that leads to private rooms."

"Good," I said, mentally mapping it out. "What about entry points?"

"The most obvious one is the hotel's main elevators, which open directly into the club's reception area. There's also a service elevator that runs from the basement parking to the kitchen area behind the bar—staff only, so it's low traffic. Fire escape is another option, but it's alarmed on the club's floor, so you'd need to disable it."

"Service elevator sounds like our best bet. Do Black Eagles own the whole hotel or just the club?"

"They started with just the club, but they're getting their claws into the whole hotel now—typical playbook, starting off with security and extortion, before they start squeezing. They've got the security detail locked down and partial ownership. Full takeover is just a matter of time."

"Right. I get the picture. We'll take it from here. Keep you posted," I said, ending the call as lights of the towering Star of Sofia hotel loomed ahead.

We tore through the cobblestone streets of Oborishte, the historic heart of Sofia. The hotel was close, not far from the cathedral where we had met Dani just a couple of hours earlier. This district was a mix of chic cafes, trendy boutiques, and centuries-old buildings.

"Alright, Rangers, gear check," I ordered, instinctively tapping the retractable baton holstered on my combat pants. "We go in silent—fists and batons first. Stealth is the name of the game. Move fast, move quiet. If we do this right, they won't even know what hit them until it's too late."

The team nodded. They all knew the drill. The SIG P320s and the KA-Bars were for emergencies—last-resort measures when stealth and silence failed.

Just then, my phone buzzed again with another call from Rick.

Rick's voice crackled through the phone, urgent and to the point. "Blaze, it's Rick. I've got some more intel that might come in handy."

"Go ahead, what've you got?" I asked.

"First off, there's a private elevator behind the VIP booths. It goes straight from the nightclub to the penthouse and the roof. Likely the Black Eagles' escape route."

I nodded, "Good to know. What's the other thing?"

"There's usually a Black Eagles helicopter parked on the roof. It's part of their cover as a security firm. If you need a fast exit, that could be your way out."

"A chopper, huh? It just might be a life saver. Can you confirm if it's there right now? Use a drone if you have to. Text me if I can't pick up."

"On it. I'll get back to you ASAP."

"Thanks. I'll be standing by for your update."

I hung up, already planning the next steps. The rooftop chopper might be our ticket out if things went sideways. A few moments later, Rick's message pinged on my phone: the Black Eagles' helicopter was indeed parked on the roof. The pieces were falling into place, and a clear plan was forming in my mind.

My phone buzzed again just before we reached the hotel's entrance. It was Echo.

"How's it looking?" I asked as I answered.

"Madison and Hughes are safe for now," Echo replied, his voice low and tense.

"What's the situation?" I asked, my grip tightening on the phone.

"Sergei's out cold. Knocked him and a couple of his goons out. Got them stashed away."

"You've got Sergei?" I asked, surprised. That was an unexpected bonus. "Good work, Ranger,"

"Thanks, but the place is crawling with his guys, and they're on the hunt for Madison and Hughes. No one's noticed Sergei's gone missing yet, but it's only a matter of time," Echo replied, his voice strained.

"We're a minute out from the hotel. We'll be up there inside the nightclub within five minutes max. Any of you hurt?"

"Madison and Hughes are fine," Echo answered, then added with a wry chuckle, "But I got slashed. One of Sergei's guys had a knife. Couldn't dodge in time."

"How bad is it?"

Echo shrugged it off. "Just a flesh wound. Not like I'm dying or anything. Just a little extra ventilation in my side."

"Keep that ventilation under control. We need you in one piece."

"I'll do my best, boss," Echo quipped, though I could hear the fatigue in his voice. "Now get your ass up here."

"We're almost there. Are Madison and Hughes with you?"

"Nope. I stashed them someplace safe."

"Where?"

"On top of the DJ booth. Long story—don't ask. But they're secure."

I held back from pressing for details. If Echo said they were safe, then there was nothing to worry about. The priority was getting his location first. "What about you? Where are you?"

"I'm inside the disabled restroom. Got Sergei and two of his guys in here with me. Out cold."

"Nicely done, Ranger."

"Well, there's a reason they call us badass," Echo replied, sounding a bit more upbeat. "I couldn't use the gun; shit would've really hit the fan. But the baton came in handy to knock their daylights out. They're down, but I'm ready to drop them again if they start waking up. Can't leave Sergei—he's the key to getting Zara, right?"

"Exactly. We need him alive and talking. Just hold on a few more minutes."

"Copy that. I'll give you the layout of this place. This disabled restroom is tucked into an alcove off to the side of the main restrooms. There's a small utility room next to it—tiny, more like a walk-in closet. I reconned the area when we first got to the nightclub, just in case. That's where I set up, lured Sergei and his two bodyguards in, and took them down. But I couldn't hole up there—the damn lock was busted. Barely had time to drag them into the restroom and secure the door."

"Smart move. Just keep Sergei out cold and out of sight. We're on our way."

"Copy that. Someone already banging on the door. I yelled that I'm taking a dump and need a few minutes, but I'm running out of time here. You guys need to hurry."

"Hang tight. We're almost there."

By then, we were pulling into the basement parking of the Star of Sofia hotel.

"Echo's got the situation under control for now, but he's hurt," I informed the others.

"How bad?" Raptor asked.

"Got slashed. He's lost some blood. This place is swarming with tangos. Move fast and watch your corners."

"Roger. How're we going up?"

"Service elevators."

We cruised toward a spot out of the direct line of sight of the service elevators and stopped. Before we got out, we spotted a man standing guard by the entrance. His jacket and cap marked him as a Black Eagles man. The emblem—a fierce golden eagle with outstretched wings gripping a blood-red banner—on both sides of his jacket and his cap was unmistakable. This security business was the so-called respectable face of the mafia.

"Elevators have a guard. If we all approach at once, he might get twitchy and call for backup. Spread out, stay casual. I'll handle the guard. Converge when I give the signal," I instructed.

We exited the SUV smoothly, each of us heading in a different direction as if we had no connection to one another. Hawkeye wandered toward a row of parked cars, pretending to check out a luxury sedan. Ninja Man moved briskly toward the stairwell, as if heading to the main lobby. Raptor hung back by the SUV, appearing to rummage through the trunk.

I walked straight toward the guard, my eyes glued to my phone, thumbs tapping the keypad as if texting. I didn't glance at the guard, playing the role of a distracted hotel guest. Only when I was within a few feet did I look up.

"Where do you think you're going?" the guard asked, his voice gruff, hand hovering near his sidearm, as he stepped forward, blocking my path.

I put on an apologetic smile, holding up the phone to show him the screen. "Hey, sorry, man. I'm supposed to meet a friend down here. Just trying to figure out where he is."

The guard instinctively leaned in to glance at the phone, giving me the opening I needed. I struck him with a precise jab to his neck, hitting a nerve that sent shockwaves of pain through the man's body. Before he could react, I followed up with a swift, powerful elbow smash to the jaw. The man's head snapped back, and he crumpled to the ground, unconscious.

"Move in," I muttered into my comm, pressing the button for the service elevator.

The other Rangers converged on my location. Once I stripped the unconscious man of his Black Eagles jacket and cap, Raptor dragged him to the fire exit and hid him beneath the stairs.

The elevator soon arrived, its doors sliding open with a soft ding. We immediately stepped inside, and I pressed the button for the nineteenth floor. Another soft ding less than a minute later announced our arrival. When the doors slid open, we stepped into a narrow corridor behind the bar. The scent of alcohol and cigarette smoke wafted toward us, mingling with the faint thrum of bass-heavy music that vibrated through the walls.

As we stepped out, a bar worker glanced at us with some curiosity. But seeing my Black Eagles jacket and cap, he quickly lost interest and went back to wiping down the counters. We walked toward a door at the end of the corridor. The bass grew louder with every step, a relentless reminder of what lay ahead. Beyond that door, Madison lay hidden in the labyrinth of flashing lights, and Echo, a lone wolf in a den of predators, faced off against Sergei.

CHAPTER 28

When we pushed through the door into the nightclub, we were hit with a sensory overload. The pulsing beats of electronic music slammed into us like a physical force, making it hard to think straight. The air was thick with the haze of smoke machines, swirling under the flashing strobe lights that bathed the room in alternating shades of neon blue, red, and violet. The scent of sweat, perfume, and spilled drinks hung heavy in the air.

To our left, a massive bar stretched along the wall, its black marble counter underlit with shifting colors. Behind it, shelves of spirits were softly backlit. Bartenders, dressed in sharp, all-black outfits, move with practiced efficiency, mixing drinks for a crowd three-deep, their movements a blur of practiced efficiency. Glasses clinked, laughter and shouts mingled with the music.

Directly ahead of us, the dance floor was packed—about 300 bodies moving in sync with the pulsing beat. The crowd ebbed and flowed like a living organism, faces illuminated briefly by the strobe lights before fading into the darkness. The energy was electric. The crowd was a mix of locals and tourists, all lost in the rhythm.

Beyond the dance floor, on a raised platform, stood the DJ booth— the heart of the club's rhythm. I scanned the area, squinting through the dim lighting, trying to cut through the fog and flashing lights. Echo had stashed Madison and Hughes above the booth, but from this distance, with the dim light and constant movement, it was nearly impossible to see anything clearly. Then, a white strobe flashed, turning the area to daylight for a split second. It was enough to spot two shadowy figures huddled above the booth.

I leaned toward Hawkeye, shouting over the music. "Get over there. Position yourself by the DJ booth. Anyone tries to get to them, they go through you first," I instructed.

Hawkeye nodded and moved off, slipping through the crowd with practiced ease, his tall frame cutting through the sea of dancers. As I watched him go, I called Echo.

"Hey, Cowboy. Are you guys here?" Echo's voice came through, strained and tired, making me worry.

"Yeah, we're in the club now. Be with you in a minute. How're you holding up?"

"Man, you have no idea how glad I am. Got a guy outside this door, banging like he's gonna break it down. I've got half a mind to open the door and knock him out, but I'm blind in here —no clue how many guys he's got with him."

"Just hang in there, pal. On my way."

"Roger."

I felt Ninja Man nudge my arm. "Four Black Eagles guys, 10 o'clock," he said, nodding left. I followed his gaze and spotted the group, easily identifiable by their matching jackets, weaving through the crowd with a purpose. They were heading toward the private booths laid out along the periphery, past the bar.

"They're heading for the private booths. Echo's holed up in a restroom behind those booths," I informed Ninja Man and Raptor. "You two head straight for them and block their path. Stall, knock them out, whatever it takes. And if you do knock them out, grab their jackets. I'll make a beeline for Echo."

"Copy that," they replied.

We split up and moved swiftly, making our way through the pulsating crowd. As I approached the alcove, the noise and chaos of the nightclub dimmed slightly, replaced by the quieter hum of the restroom area. The alcove was set back from the main flow of traffic, creating a shadowy nook. The walls were a deep, muted gray, illuminated by soft, recessed lighting that cast long shadows across the floor.

The restroom door was plain but sturdy, with a dark wood finish contrasting with the sleek modern design of the club. A polished metal plaque at eye level displayed the wheelchair symbol, indicating it was an accessible restroom. Below the symbol, "Accessible Restroom" was etched in a clean, simple font. The door had a handle with a thumb-turn lock, and just above it, a small sign read "Occupied."

But my focus was on the two men in Black Eagles jackets, banging persistently on the door. I stepped up casually, drawing their attention.

"The restroom's out of order, guys," I called out, my tone authoritative. "Got a repairman working inside."

One of the men turned, eyeing me suspiciously. "Who are you? I've never seen you before."

I arched an eyebrow, gesturing to the Black Eagles emblem on my jacket. "Look at the jacket, genius. What do you think?"

The man hesitated, confusion on his face. I pressed on, not giving him a chance to think. "Didn't Sergei tell you about the rich American group coming in tonight? He hired me and a couple of American security guys to schmooze them into spending all their dough."

The men exchanged knowing laughs, their suspicion disarmed. I seized the moment. "Hey, grab one of those Out-of-Order signs from the utility area and hang it outside the door, would you?"

One of the men nodded and walked into the utility room nearby. My hand was already on the retractable baton, and the second the man turned his back, I snapped it open. The metallic click echoed in the alcove, and before the other guard could react, I swung the baton in a swift arc, catching him at the base of the skull. The man crumpled, unconscious before he even hit the ground.

Without missing a beat, I darted into the utility room. The second guard was rummaging inside a shelf and was turning around after grabbing the Out-of-Order sign. Before he realized what was up, my baton connected with his chin in a powerful upward swing. The impact lifted the man off his feet, and he collapsed in a heap, knocked out cold.

I grabbed the sign from his hands and stepped back into the hallway, only to be met by the shocked gazes of two women who had wandered in from the main club area. One was on the verge of screaming, her hand already halfway to her mouth.

In an instant, I switched to damage control. "Ladies, it's a security situation," I said, my tone firm and official as I pointed to the Black Eagles emblem on my jacket. "My team's bringing in a doctor. I need you to clear the area immediately."

The women nodded quickly and retreated toward the main restrooms. As they disappeared, I turned back to the restroom door and called out, "Echo, all clear. Unlock the door."

The door opened and I stepped inside, quickly taking in the scene. Three men lay sprawled on the floor, out cold. Echo was leaning against the wall, looking pale, with a wad of bloody tissue pressed tightly against his side.

"Let me see that cut," I said, kneeling beside him, quickly checking the wound.

"It's just a scratch, boss. I've had worse shaving," Echo muttered through gritted teeth.

"Yeah? You shave with a chainsaw?"

"What can I say? I'm a real tough guy."

"Yeah, you're a regular superhero. How about we patch you up before you start leaking all over the floor?"

"Fine by me. I'm not big on redecorating anyway," Echo replied, wincing as I examined his wound.

It was still bleeding, but not too badly, which was a small relief.

"You're gonna be fine. But we need to get you out of here and patched up. You're in no shape for anything active."

Just then, Hawkeye's voice came through my earpiece: "Hawkeye to Cowboy. Three Black Eagles heading your way."

"Cowboy here. Copy that." I replied, before looking at Echo. "You're out of luck, pal. We've got three more Black Eagles incoming. Looks like you'll have to lock yourself in the restroom again."

"Back to my luxury suite, huh? Do I at least get room service?"

"Sure. I'll tell one of the guys to bring you the menu. I'll be back in a minute. Don't get too comfy."

"Oh, I'll be fine. Just another day in paradise," Echo replied, trying to sound perkier than he looked.

"Lock it from inside. I'll hang the sign outside so no one disturbs your peace," I said, holding up the Out-of-order sign.

I hung the sign outside the door before slipping back into the hallway and spotting the approaching men. They were still a little distance away, but I knew I couldn't take all three without drawing attention. My eyes scanned the area, landing on a private booth with heavy curtains drawn and a "Reserved" sign displayed in front.

I guessed the booth would be empty. I didn't have time to check to be sure. I simply walked over purposefully, in full view of the approaching men, and slipped inside the curtains, acting like the place belonged to me. I breathed a sigh of relief when I found it empty.

All private booths, even the ones that were occupied, were shrouded in semi-darkness. The domain of VIP guests and those willing to spend big, they offered a semblance of privacy, with plush seating and low tables. The heavy drapes could be drawn for privacy, without cutting out the music from the dance floor. That worked out well for me.

As the three men drew closer, I called out, "Hey, you guys. Sergei wants a word with everyone in here."

"Who are you? I've never seen you before," one of the men called out as they came closer.

I was getting a sense of déjà vu. I had heard the same words from another guy just minutes ago. I gave them the same bullshit answer I had given to the other guy: "Look at the jacket, genius. What do you think?" I retorted, gesturing to the Black Eagles emblem on my jacket.

The men glanced at each other, then moved toward the booth, their suspicion momentarily clouded by the jacket and the idea of a direct order from Sergei.

Two men stepped into the booth. I held back, waiting for the third guy to enter. The two men scanned the booth warily. I stood at the back, leaning casually against the wall, my hand resting on the baton concealed inside my jacket.

The third man was still outside, a problem I needed to solve without raising the alarm. I couldn't risk taking those two out while the other one was still out there. One wrong move, and the man could alert the rest of the gang. Stealth was the name of the game—if this turned into an all-out firefight, things would get messy fast.

"Why aren't you looking around for that American woman Sergei was talking about? Have they found her?" one of the men asked.

I nodded casually, keeping my voice steady. "Yeah, she's been found. That's why Sergei wants everyone to gather here."

The second guy narrowed his eyes. "And you're supposed to be...?"

I smirked, trying to defuse the tension. "I'm the guy Sergei hired to make sure you don't screw it up. You know, quality control."

They exchange confused glances, not getting the joke, keeping their serious expressions, like I had just suggested a mandatory performance review. Just then, Ninja Man's voice came through my ear piece: "Ninja Man to Cowboy. Taken out the four Black Eagles. Heading to the restroom."

"Copy that," I replied, making no effort to hide that I was talking to someone on the radio. "Meet me in the private booth next to the restrooms. It's got a 'Reserved' sign."

The two men were starting to get suspicious. One of them squinted at me. "Who are you again? I've never seen any Americans in the Black Eagles."

"Yeah, and where's Sergei?" the other one added, his hand moving inside his jacket.

I could feel the tension ratcheting up. The room was about to blow. I couldn't stall any longer. I looked past them, pretending to see someone at the entrance. "There he is," I said loudly.

Both turned instinctively. That's when I made my move. I flicked open the baton and slammed it on the side of the first guy's head. He crumpled like a sack of bricks. The second guy barely had time to react before I nailed him below the jaw in an upward swing, sending him crashing into the table. They both hit the floor, unconscious.

I rushed to the entrance, almost bumping into the third guy as he stepped inside. He was too startled to react as I grabbed his jacket and hauled him into the booth, throwing him to the floor. He struggled for a split second before I silenced him with a quick, decisive strike to the back of his head.

Before I could catch my breath, Ninja Man poked his head into the booth. "Having fun?"

CHAPTER 29

"Just a regular night out, Ninja," I replied, sheathing my baton. "How about you?"

Ninja Man grinned as he stepped inside, followed by Raptor, who was lugging a bundle of Black Eagles jackets and caps in his arms. "Got these off the guys we took out. Guess we could've just pulled them from these fellas."

I chuckled, shaking my head. "Well, at least now we have options. Where did you leave the guys whose jackets you brought?"

Ninja Man cut in, "This isn't the only 'Reserved' booth in the nightclub. There's another one at the other end. They're tucked away in there—out of sight, out of mind."

"Good. That should buy us some time."

"So, what's the next play? And how's Echo holding up?" Raptor asked as we dragged all the knocked out men and hid them behind couches.

"Echo got slashed. Lost some blood, but he's still kicking. Problem is, we're on the clock. Once the Black Eagles realize what's going on, they'll lock this place down tighter than a drum. We need to get out, and fast. You head to the DJ booth and join Hawkeye, get Madison and Hughes down, and escort them down and out of here. Same route we came in—service elevator straight down to the basement, then into the SUV. Those Black Eagles jackets and caps should help keep them from sticking out."

"What about you and Ninja?"

"We'll grab Echo from the restroom and bring him to the service elevator from the other direction. We'll meet you there. Then you, Hawkeye and Ninja take Madison, Hughes, and Echo down to the basement."

"But what about that Sergei fella? He's the only one who knows where Zara and the other girls are. We need to take him too and get him talking, right?" Raptor asked.

"Yeah. But we can't risk taking Sergei out with the others. The guy owns this place. Everyone in this club knows him. If his men spot him, they'll try to block our escape. Even if we hold Sergei at gunpoint, the risks will skyrocket with a group this big. And with Madison and the others in tow, the risk goes through the roof. We can't afford to have Madison taken again. Worse, if Sergei's bosses find out we're here to rescue those girls, they'll divert the truck and make them vanish for good."

"So what's the play? We're gonna interrogate Sergei right here in the club?" Ninja Man asked.

"Yeah. But just me. The only safe play is for me to question Sergei inside the club, get the location, and start the rescue operation before getting out of this place."

Raptor and Ninja Man looked unconvinced.

"You sure about this, Cowboy? Sounds risky," Raptor commented.

"And after you're done playing 20 Questions with Sergei, how exactly are you planning on making this grand exit? Walk out the front door with Sergei as your plus one?" Ninja Man shot back.

"No, smartass. I'll use the service elevator, same as you guys. If things get hairy, there's a chopper on the roof. I'll convince the Black Eagles' pilot to give me a lift."

"That sounds great, boss. Just one little thing. Remember that night in Kandahar? The one with the harebrained plan to take out the Tali's MANPADs?"

I knew what was coming. "Oh yeah, what about it?"

"Back then, I thought you were totally winging it. But now, compared to stealing a chopper, that plan sounds like it was cooked up by Einstein."

"Well, what can I say? Some of us are born to wing it. Guess it's time to see if that applies to stealing a chopper too," I replied, chuckling.

"Great. But you're gonna need a proper wingman either way—someone to keep an eye out while you're having a heart-to-heart with Sergei. Also, it wouldn't hurt if that wingman knew a thing or two about choppers, just in case the pilot tries to pull the old 'whoops, it won't start' trick. Know anyone with that skill set?"

Despite the tense situation, I couldn't help chuckling at Ninja Man's attempts to sell himself. Ninja had initially enlisted in the U.S. Army with vague aspirations of becoming a helicopter pilot. He went through WOCS (Warrant Officer Candidate School) and had even started IERW (Initial Entry Rotary Wing) training at Fort Rucker. But he soon realized that spinning rotors couldn't compare to the thrill of Ranger life on the ground, where he could be in the thick of action. Ninja Man voluntarily left the aviation track, cracked RASP (Ranger Assessment and Selection Program), and earned his place in the 75th Ranger Regiment.

"You've got a point," I replied, smirking and shaking my head. "It just so happens I know someone who's dabbled in that field. Not a certified pilot, but he did start out with some training before deciding he liked the ground game better. If it came to a life or death situation, he could still maybe kind of fly a chopper, but I wouldn't bet my life on it."

"Oh, you've got no idea. You surely need this guy as your wingman. He's got a lot more to offer here than babysitting a couple of civilians. Raptor and Hawkeye can any day handle that. And Echo won't need babysitting. He might be banged up, but he's still more of a badass than half the guys we've faced. These guys don't need me, but you might."

"Ninja's right. We've got the extraction covered. He's better off with you, Cowboy," Raptor put in his weight behind Ninja.

"Alright," I gave in. "Ninja can stay back with me. But you know what you're signing up for, right? Things can get ugly fast."

"Oh, man, I'm quaking in my boots. Maybe after we're done, we can all sit down for a nice cup of tea and talk about our feelings?"

"I'm serious, Ninja. It's going to be risky."

"Risky is my middle name. Well, actually, it's Carl, but you get the point."

"I surely do," Raptor chimed in. "So, that's settled, Cowboy. And honestly, I don't want to deal with this guy's wisecracks all the way to the safe house."

"You know what, Raptor? That really hurt," Ninja Man shot back.

"We'll talk about your feelings later," I intervened. "Raptor, time to get moving. Catch you at the service elevator."

"Roger that," Raptor turned and headed toward the DJ booth.

I turned to Ninja Man. "Let's go get Echo."

"Yup, let's go," Ninja Man said, falling in step beside me.

I knocked on the restroom door. "Echo, it's time to hit the road."

Echo opened the door, looking pale but determined. "About time. Thought you guys forgot about me."

Ninja Man chimed in, "Forgot you? Nah, we just took the scenic route. How're you doing, Ranger?"

"I'm alright, not like I'm about to die."

"You're a tough cookie, Echo. C'mon, let's get you all dressed up," I replied, handing Echo a Black Eagles jacket.

Echo managed a weak smile. "Great, just what I always wanted, a gang jacket. Matches my new collection of stab wounds."

"Hold tight, Echo," I said, helping him into the jacket. "Ninja, stay here and keep an eye on Sergei. We can't have him waking up and throwing a party while we're gone."

Ninja Man gave a mock salute. "Aye aye, captain. I'll make sure Sergei here gets his beauty sleep."

With Echo leaning on me, we maneuvered through the crowd on the dance floor, making our way to the service elevator. We reached it just as Raptor and Hawkeye arrived with Madison and Hughes. Madison, swimming in an oversized jacket, looked almost comical.

I couldn't help but grin. "I bet you've never looked more undercover in your life."

Madison rolled her eyes but managed a small smile. But then her eyes widened in concern as she noticed the blood seeping through Echo's jacket. "Echo, you're hurt," she cried out.

"It's not that bad," Echo replied, a little unconvincingly.

"You saved us again today," Hughes broke in, before looking at me and adding, "When Echo realized Sergei had recognized us, he didn't hesitate. He got us through that dance floor and up to the DJ booth before we even knew what was happening."

Madison chimed in, "Yeah, and by the time Sergei and his men arrived, we were already hidden. He got them to follow him to the restrooms without a second thought." She paused, looking at Echo with gratitude. "Thank you."

Echo gave her a reassuring grin. "No problem, ma'am. It isn't as bad as it looks."

"Ma'am? Really? And here I was thinking Axel was the Cowboy in the group."

"We're all cowboys, Madison. You don't need to be riding a horse to be one," I chimed in.

Echo smirked, wincing as he shifted his weight. "Yeah, someone's got to lasso the troublemakers."

"Alright, folks, we're running out of time. Let's hurry it up. You and Hughes will be safe with these guys. Ninja Man and I will follow later."

The urgency in my voice was clear, and they quickly moved into the service elevator. The elevator doors closed, and as they descended, I turned back toward the restroom, ready to finish what we started.

CHAPTER 30

I knocked on the restroom door, and it opened almost immediately. Ninja Man stood there, a grin playing at the corners of his mouth.

"Sergei's still out," Ninja said, stepping aside to let me in. "One of the other guys started coming around, but I gave him a little love tap. He's back in dreamland."

I stepped inside, finally getting a good look at Sergei. He was a big guy. A jagged scar ran down his cheek, and a sneer seemed etched permanently into his features. His jet-black hair was slicked back with military precision, not a single strand out of place—it screamed obsessive control freak. Even knocked out, the dude radiated pure menace.

I shot a glance at Ninja Man. "Time to drag this dirtbag to the roof, scare the living crap out of him, and get him talking."

"Sounds like a party. What's the game plan?" Ninja Man asked.

"I reconned the area behind the booths. There's a private elevator with a guard parked in front. No way to neutralize him quietly— too much open space, too many eyes. Our best bet is to wake Sleeping Beauty here, shove a muzzle into his ribs, and have him escort us up like we're his loyal lapdogs. With these Black Eagles threads, nobody'll think twice."

Ninja Man gave a sharp nod. "Works for me. Let's wake the beast."

He moved over to the sink, filling his cupped hands with cold water before unceremoniously splashing it onto Sergei's face. Sergei sputtered, coughing as he jerked back to consciousness. His eyes blinked rapidly, darting around as he tried to piece together what the hell was happening.

Before he could fully process the situation, I leaned in, pressing my SIG firmly into his ribcage. Ninja Man mirrored my move on the other side, his gaze icy.

"Rise and shine, princess," Ninja drawled. "Time for a little field trip."

Sergei's eyes narrowed into slits, his voice gravelly and laced with venom. "You have no idea who you're messing with. My men will skin you alive."

Sergei tried to shift, testing our grip, but I dug the muzzle deeper into his ribs, eliciting a grunt. "Let's skip the threats. You're going to walk us to that private elevator nice and easy. No sudden moves, no funny business. You cooperate, maybe you get to see tomorrow."

Sergei sneered, but a slight flicker in his eyes betrayed a hint of uncertainty. "You think you can waltz out of here? This place is crawling with my soldiers. One word from me and you're dead men."

I leaned in closer, my voice dropping to a lethal whisper. "The only word you're gonna be saying is 'yes'. Now, on your feet."

With a frustrated growl, Sergei complied, struggling up as we kept our weapons trained on him, hidden beneath the folds of our jackets. Leaving the two unconscious lackeys sprawled on the restroom floor, I quietly closed the door behind us. Using my knife, I manipulated the thumb-turn lock from the outside, ensuring no unexpected guests would stumble upon our handiwork too soon. I slapped the "Out of Order" sign back onto the door for good measure.

I gave Sergei a firm nudge between the shoulder blades. "Alright, big guy, lead the way. And remember, any heroics and you'll be breathing through new holes."

We moved down the dimly lit corridor, the thumping bass of the nightclub muffled but persistent, like a heartbeat underscoring the tension. As we approached the private elevator, a burly guard stood at attention, his eyes scanning the crowd lazily until he noticed us approaching with Sergei at the helm. He looked a little wary at first, his eyes flicking between Ninja and me before settling on Sergei. But then, recognizing Sergei, he nodded.

"Boss," the guard said, his voice cautious. "Want me to call the elevator?"

Sergei hesitated for a fraction of a second, clearly uncomfortable. I could feel the tension radiating off the man. I pressed the barrel of my gun harder into Sergei's back, a silent command.

"Yes, call it," Sergei finally replied, his face impassive but his tone a little strained, reflecting the tension simmering beneath the surface.

The guard complied, pressing the button without hesitation. As we waited, the guard glanced back at Sergei, curiosity creeping into his voice. "Did you find that American woman?" he asked.

Sergei hesitated, his mind racing for the right answer. He could feel the cold metal of my gun dig deeper into his back, urging him to speak. "Yeah,"

Sergei finally said, his voice a little strained. "We found her. Everything's under control."

The seconds dragged on as we waited for the elevator to arrive. That was one part of the plan we hadn't thought through—waiting in an uncomfortable silence. I decided against saying something to break the tension as the guard could become even more suspicious with my American accent.

I could feel the unease growing, not just in Sergei but in the guard as well. Something wasn't sitting right with him. The guard's eyes kept darting to Sergei, and I sensed that the man was picking up on the tension, realizing that something was off. I remembered Nate telling me that many Black Eagles members were ex-cops. This guy surely must have been one.

Suspicion had started to creep into his gaze. Sergei's unease was palpable, and the longer we waited, the more likely the guard was to piece together that something was off.

When the elevator finally arrived with a soft ding, the doors slid open with a soft chime, revealing a polished interior lined with dark wood and mirrored panels. Despite Sergei tending to drag his feet a little, we didn't waste any time in stepping inside and hitting the button for the rooftop. But by then, the guard had sensed that something wasn't right. And he had also guessed that we weren't local.

Just as the doors began to close, the guard called out to Sergei in Bulgarian, his tone carrying an edge that I didn't like. He was taking a chance that I wouldn't understand what he was saying. The guy was smart that way. I couldn't understand the words, but I caught the look in the guard's eyes—sharp, assessing. His ploy would have worked, had my own senses not been on hyperalert for the slightest discrepancy.

Sergei's response to the guard's words was immediate. He nodded, his expression tightening, before switching to English. "Keep up the good work," he said, his voice casual, almost too casual.

But I wasn't fooled. I had caught the quick exchange, noticed the flicker of understanding in the guard's eyes as Sergei nodded. The sudden shift in the guard's expression, the way his face tightened for a split second before resuming a neutral look—it all screamed that something was wrong.

As the elevator doors began to close, I reacted on instinct. I jammed my foot between the closing doors, forcing them back open. In one swift motion, I turned, pointing my gun directly at the guard. "Inside. Now," I ordered.

The guard moved fast. His hand was already on his gun, the other shooting up, radio in hand, ready to call for backup. I had no choice. I stepped forward, my suppressed gun spitting out a round before the guard could raise his weapon. The bullet went through his heart. Before the man could collapse, I caught him and stepped back into the elevator, dragging his body inside as the doors finally closed.

The entire encounter lasted only a few seconds, but in that time, Sergei made his move. While I was occupied with the guard and Ninja Man's attention was momentarily diverted, Sergei tried to wrestle the gun from him. But Ninja was faster. He sidestepped Sergei's grasp and, with a cold precision, fired a round straight through Sergei's hand, the bullet tearing through flesh and bone.

Sergei let out a guttural scream, clutching his shattered right hand as blood spilled between his fingers and dripped onto the elevator floor.

"You think we're playing fuckin' games here?" Ninja snarled, his eyes cold as ice.

The elevator began its ascent, a soft jazz tune playing overhead—a stark contrast to the pounding music in the club below and the tension inside the enclosed space.

I turned my attention back to Sergei, my gaze hard and unforgiving. "One more wrong move, and you'll get another bullet. Don't try us," I warned.

Sergei glared back at me, his face twisted in agony, his breath coming in ragged gasps as he cradled his ruined hand. But he said nothing. The agony in his hand was enough to keep him silent.

It turned out to be a good thing that Sergei made the move. The speed with which we neutralized the guard and dealt with Sergei left no doubt in his mind—we weren't playing games. We weren't there to negotiate. We were there to take whatever we needed, by any means necessary.

CHAPTER 31

The elevator passed the penthouse floor before coming to a smooth stop at the roof level. We stayed alert. It was easy to keep Sergei under tight control by grabbing his right wrist, a small twist of which sent shock waves through his shattered hand.

The doors slid open with a soft ding, revealing the sprawling rooftop of the five-star hotel. The night air was cool, and the city lights stretched out in every direction, giving the rooftop a surreal, almost otherworldly feel. To our right was a helipad, its circular markings distinct against the flat surface. On it sat a sleek Bell 407 helicopter, its rotors still and the cabin door closed.

The roof itself was mostly open space, with a few air conditioning units, communication arrays, and a couple of small, locked storage sheds. The helipad dominated one side, while the other side featured a low, sturdy barrier that ran around the perimeter of the building. There were no other visible personnel on the roof. Night had fallen a while back and the roof was mostly dark. But once our eyes adjusted, the perimeter lights were bright enough for us to scan the area.

While Ninja Man led Sergei out of the elevator, I dragged the dead guard and left him lying in the doorway. I didn't want the elevator going down and then having to deal with unexpected intruders when it came back up. With the man lying in the doorway acting as a door stopper, that elevator wasn't going anywhere. Every few seconds, the doors closed in on the man, met resistance, and opened up again.

I covered Sergei while Ninja Man moved out, his SIG drawn and ready, scanning the area around before moving out, checking behind every vent and structure. The rooftop looked mostly clear, but we weren't taking any chances. Sergei looked around, trying to find some kind of escape or backup.

"You don't know who you're messing with," Sergei spat, trying to sound menacing. "You're making a big mistake. I've got powerful friends. Whatever you're after, it's not worth—"

I cut him off with a sharp jab of my gun into his side, keeping my focus on the rooftop. Ninja Man continued his sweep, silent as a shadow, while Sergei tried a different approach. "What is it you want? Money? Drugs? Women? Just name it. I can make that happen."

I didn't respond, just kept my grip tight on the man. Our silence was beginning to unnerve Sergei. He was used to barking orders and having men scramble to follow them. But with us acting like stone-cold professionals, he was getting nothing to latch onto. Our plan was to keep increasing the pressure on him until he became terrified out of his mind and became compliant like a lamb.

"On the ground, face down. Hands behind your back," I barked out an order, my voice ice cold.

Sergei hesitated, his pride warring with his sense of self-preservation. "You think I'm just going to lie down like some—"

I didn't wait for him to finish. I drew back my right leg and drove the hard toe of my tactical boot into Sergei's shin. As he yelped in pain, I swept his legs out from under him with a brutal efficiency. Sergei fell on his back, hitting the rooftop hard, the impact knocking the wind out of him. I immediately rolled him over face down and pressed my boot into his back, pinning him down.

"Hands behind your back," I repeated calmly.

Sergei's defiance flickered one last time, and he tried to resist. I knew what I needed to do—the guy needed to be taught a quick lesson that he absolutely didn't have any control on the situation. Without a word, I fired a round into the back of Sergei's left shoulder, but angling it so that it wasn't more than a flesh wound. The shot was precise, the sound barely more than a muffled pop. But flesh wound or not, getting shot hurts like hell. Sergei's scream echoed across the rooftop, raw and filled with agony.

"Now," I said, my voice calm but deadly. "Hands behind your back."

Sergei, shaking from the pain, immediately complied. I quickly secured his arms behind him with a flex cuff. Finally, Ninja Man reappeared from around a corner, giving me a curt nod.

"All clear. That way," Ninja Man said, gesturing toward a section of the rooftop with his gun.

I caught Sergei by his collar and intact right shoulder, hauled him to his feet, and shoved him toward the roof's edge in the direction Ninja indicated. The man was breathing hard, his face slick with sweat and contorted in pain. When we reached the perimeter, I yanked him forward, landing a brutal punch to his abdomen that made him double over. With a quick, calculated movement, I shoved Sergei to the very edge, holding him by the collar and the belt, so that he was suspended over the void, nothing but open air beneath him. The cityscape below was a dizzying drop, and Sergei's eyes went wide with terror as he realized how close he was to a deadly fall.

"Please! What do you want?!" Sergei screamed, his voice cracking as he stared down at the nothingness beneath him.

I tightened my grip on Sergei and held him there for a few seconds, leaving him teetering on the brink, letting the fear sink in. Finally, I leaned in, my voice low. "Now it's time to talk. Where's the truck carrying the Afghan girls?"

Sergei's first instinct was to stall. "What Afghan girls? I don't know what—" he started.

But the words died in his throat when I nudged him a little further over the edge, his feet leaving the ground for a second. The man's scream was pure panic.

"No! No! The truck—it's on its way to Sofia. A few hours out!" Sergei babbled, desperation in his tone.

My grip was unyielding as I pressed further. "I need exact details and location. We get the girls and you get to live. It's as simple as that."

"It's in my laptop! In my office below. The truck's headed to a parking lot outside the city. I will get the exact location once the truck's there. All the information's on my laptop, I swear!" Sergei was almost sobbing, the fear evident in his voice.

I eyed him critically, weighing the truth of his words. "You're telling me you don't remember the location of this parking lot? You think I'm stupid? You're just trying to get us down there."

"No! No, I'm telling the truth!" Sergei babbled, desperate now. "I'm not saying I don't know the

251

location of the lot. I know it, but it's a huge place, spread over many miles, thousands of trucks. The driver will park only where it's safe. Then he'll turn on a tracker we've given him and send me the location coordinates. The tracker and the coordinates and the license plate number, that's how we'll locate the truck. All that's on my laptop."

What he said made sense. My gut told me that Sergei was telling the truth—there was no way the man could have fabricated such precise details under the pressure of almost being tossed off the roof. The size of the parking lot, the exact coordinates, and the specifics of the truck's tracker— these were details that couldn't be made up on the fly. Even though I knew Sergei was a snake and would try his best to turn the tables once we were back down in the nightclub, I was convinced it wasn't just a ruse to trap us in a place filled with his men. I posed him a few more questions just to be doubly sure.

"How will the driver send you the coordinates?" I asked.

"He'll text it to me on my cellphone. You can check that on my phone. You can check the conversation. Just pull me back. Please!"

"Keep answering my questions and I might. What's the plan after you get the coordinates?" I asked.

"The girls will be transferred to smaller vehicles and taken to a warehouse," Sergei replied, without wasting a second. "And then there's an auction. That's all I know! Please!"

"Keep talking. Why the auction? Why these girls?"

"They're young, untouched. People are willing to pay a lot for that. Once they're sold... they just disappear, not my problem anymore," Sergei panted, his words tumbling out in a rush. "Why do you care? They're worthless, no one will miss them."

My jaw tightened, the urge to let go and let him get smashed into pulp almost overwhelming. But I reined it in and held on. "I need the girls' names. Now."

"I don't know any names! It's all in the laptop!" Sergei cried out, sensing how close he was to going over the edge.

"When's the auction?"

"Tomorrow night."

"Who are the buyers at the auction?"

"They're from everywhere... Europe, Middle East, different countries."

I knew there was no other option. We needed that laptop. I pulled Sergei back from the edge, tossing him onto the roof like a ragdoll. He hugged the ground, panting, glad to be back on solid ground after hanging in space for what must have seemed like an eternity to him.

"Show me the conversation with the driver. If you tell me now that you don't have it, you're going over the top," I threatened him.

"Yes, sure," he said, reaching into his inner pocket carefully, pulling out the phone, opening the message, and handing it to me. "It's in Bulgarian. But if you show it to anyone who can read Bulgarian..."

"Never mind that," I said, before going into the settings and switching the language to English. Sergei was speaking the truth. There was a text exchange with the truck driver, who gave him an update every time he reached a certain destination on the way. The last update came in a few minutes ago. The truck had reached a city called Haskovo.

"Where's Haskovo?" I asked Sergei.

"About 150 miles south-east of here, kind of midway between Istanbul and Sofia."

I figured the truck would arrive in Sofia in about three hours. That gave us more than enough time to stage a rescue, provided we got our hands on the details in Sergei's laptop.

"Where's the chopper pilot?" I asked my final question.

"He hangs around the club until he's needed to fly," Sergei replied, giving me an odd look.

"Stay here. You try to move and the only place you'll end up is on the ground 20 floors below," I said, walking off to consult Ninja.

I didn't need to fill Ninja in. He had heard every word that Sergei had screamed out in desperation. Both of us knew we didn't have much of a choice—we needed that laptop. If we moved quickly, we might have some surprise on our side, before the entire nightclub was alerted to our presence. The only question was whether or not to have Sergei tag along.

"If we try to do this without him, the place will go hot in seconds. We'll be swimming in Black Eagles. Our best shot is to keep him under tight control and use him to open doors," I pointed out.

Ninja nodded, his expression grim.

I walked back to Sergei and hauled him up. "You're coming with us. Give me the key to your office."

"Uh, can I ask what's so special about those girls?" Sergei asked as he handed me the key without fuss. "You can have the best women in the nightclub. Just take your pick."

"Listen carefully so you know the lengths we're willing to go to tonight," I said to Sergei, moving real close, boring holes in his eyes. "One of those kidnapped girls is family. We're soldiers, we've been trained really well, and there are more than just the two of us. We've already destroyed your entire street operation and brothel in Fakulteta. Viktor and his entire gang are dead," I said, pausing to let it sink in. "If we get the girls, we're willing to leave it at that and take them away from you sickos. But if we don't, we'll tear apart the city and all your operations. But you won't be around to see it as you'll be dead long before that. Understand?"

"Yes," he whispered. "You can have them. I'll give you that information if you guys walk away and don't look back."

"That's the idea. But you so much as breathe wrong, you're getting the first bullet," Ninja Man warned him.

Sergei's face was pale, a sheen of sweat on his forehead, but he nodded frantically. He knew he was out of options.

It was time to get the dead guard's body out of the elevator doorway. He was a heavy guy, and death hadn't lightened the load. I hauled him behind the elevator shaft, out of sight of anyone who might stumble across the scene.

I signaled Sergei to get inside the elevator. He complied immediately, no longer resisting any command. I could feel the tension in his body, the nervous energy that comes from knowing your life is hanging by a thread. Ninja Man and I stepped inside behind him, getting on each side of Sergei. He stood a little hunched over, his shattered hand cradled close to his chest.

The elevator doors, now free to close, slid shut with a soft ding. The elevator was functional again. I exchanged a quick, wordless glance with Ninja Man. His face was unreadable, but his eyes told me he was ready. No words were necessary. We were about to walk right into the wolf's lair, and both of us knew what that meant.

CHAPTER 32

The elevator began its descent, the hum of the machinery almost calming. I kept my SIG ready, eyes locked on the digital display counting down the floors. Sergei's face was pale, a mixture of fear and pain from his shattered hand, but there was also a flicker of calculation in his eyes. I kept my gun pressed into his ribs, a silent reminder of the consequences if he tried anything.

When the doors finally slid open on the nineteenth floor, we were hit with a wave of the nightclub's sounds once again—pounding bass, muffled voices, the hum of a crowd enjoying their night, blissfully unaware of the violence simmering just beneath the surface.

But the hallway outside the elevator was empty. The private elevator was only for the mafia's top brass, so it didn't see much traffic. Lucky for us, no one had noticed the missing guard, and no one had tried calling the elevator in the ten minutes we had been gone.

I leaned in close to Sergei, my voice low and threatening. "Don't try anything smart if you want to live through the night."

He nodded quickly, sweat dripping down his temple. "I don't have a death wish," he muttered. "I just want you to get what you came for and leave me the hell alone."

"Smart man," I said, giving him a shove.

We stepped out of the elevator and moved fast, keeping close to the walls. Ninja Man and I kept close to Sergei, not giving him an inch of breathing room. Our senses were on high alert, every shadow a potential threat. We were deep in enemy territory—the place was crawling with Black Eagles. One wrong move could turn this quiet march into a firefight. We just needed to keep moving fast and stay under the radar.

The entrance to the private booths loomed ahead, and behind them, Sergei's office—our destination. Every instinct screamed that we were walking straight into a trap, but we didn't have a choice. The intel we needed was in that office, and we were going to get it, no matter the cost. Finally, we reached the office door.

"Ninja, take up a position inside one of the booths," I said. "Keep an eye out and let me know if there's any movement."

Ninja gave a curt nod and melted into the shadows of a nearby booth, finding a vantage point with a clear view of the area. I already had the key. I quickly unlocked the door, pushed Sergei into the office, and closed the door behind us.

The office was small, but opulent—dark wood paneling, leather chairs, and a heavy mahogany desk. I ignored the luxury, my focus zeroing in on the laptop sitting on the desk. I walked over, grabbed the laptop, and turned it on.

"Password," I demanded, my tone leaving no room for negotiation.

Sergei hesitated for a fraction of a second, but the hardening in my eyes made him think better of it. "It's Sophia. Capital 'S'," he muttered, his voice strained.

I entered the password, and the laptop unlocked. "Show me the files," I ordered.

Sergei moved over, his good hand trembling slightly as he navigated through the folders. He opened one labeled "Special Cargo". Inside were photos of the girls. My stomach tightened when I saw Zara's face, and then Madison's. The reality of the situation hit me hard, but I pushed the emotion down, focusing on the task at hand.

"Truck's license plate, the driver's photo, and the tracker details," Sergei said, pointing to a series of files. I opened them, confirming the information. It was all there—everything we needed.

I took out my phone and snapped photos of the laptop screen, ensuring I had backups. Then I spotted a laptop protective case on a nearby shelf. I placed the laptop inside, zipped it up, and shoved it into a crossbody bag lying on the table.

"Let's go," I said, slipping the bag across my back before turning toward the door.

Sergei's face had gone ashen, and he looked like he was about to collapse. "I... I need to splash some water on my face. Please... just let me—"

I considered it for a moment. We needed Sergei functional. He would be useless to us if he passed out. "Fine," I said, casting a quick look inside the attached restroom before signaling him to go inside.

Just as he reached the door, he turned back to me. "There's a medicine bottle in that drawer," he said, pointing to a table near the door. It'll help with the pain. Could you—"

I couldn't believe I fell for it. Still kick myself over it. But all I did was get momentarily distracted as I looked toward the drawer. In that second, Sergei bolted into the restroom and slammed the door shut.

I reacted instantly, rushing toward the door, but the unmistakable sound of a magazine being loaded into a gun made me freeze. Sergei must have had it hidden behind some easily accessible panel. The man must have practiced for such a situation—I couldn't believe how fast he was in bolting the door, grabbing a hidden Uzi, and slipping in the magazine. He was armed, loaded, and ready to shoot me full of holes. Had I not immediately recognized the sound, I would have been drilled with a 20-round burst of 9 mm fire.

Thinking fast, I grabbed a nearby chair and hurled it at the door. The impact was loud, making Sergei panic, and he opened fire, the bullets ripping through the door and embedding themselves into the opposite wall. Sergei had let loose a full magazine, thinking I was trying to break in.

I waited for the gunfire to stop, and the moment I heard the click of an empty magazine being ejected, I moved in. Without hesitation, I fired several rounds through the door with my suppressed SIG. The gunfire was followed by the clatter of something metallic hitting the floor, followed by the heavy thud of a body collapsing.

I kicked open the ruined door, my gun trained on the figure slumped on the bathroom floor. Sergei was dead, a pool of blood beginning to spread out from beneath him.

But I didn't have time to process the situation. As I inserted a new magazine in my gun, my earpiece crackled to life and Ninja Man's voice came through, calm but laced with urgency. "Ninja to Cowboy, we've got company. Eight gunmen, serious firepower, heading our way."

"How serious?" I asked, already knowing I wouldn't like the answer.

"AKs, Uzis, and a couple of shotguns," he replied without missing a beat.

"Damn," I muttered. My eyes darted around the office. Sergei had somehow managed to trigger an alarm, and now we were trapped.

Ninja went into what I called "Ranger mode", his tone steady, reassuring. "Take up a defensive position. I'll cover them from the back, move in when I can. Got enough extra cartridges to keep them pinned down."

But we both knew the score. Two handguns against eight heavily armed men wasn't a fair fight—it was a death sentence. Ninja was just saying what he needed to say to keep our spirits up, but I wasn't buying into false hope.

While Ninja talked, I scanned the room, looking for an escape or a place to hide. The office wasn't large, and there weren't any hiding places that a determined crew wouldn't find in a heartbeat. And then my eyes settled on the window.

I moved quickly, crossing the room to get a closer look. It was a heavy sliding window, secured with a flimsy lock that wasn't going to stand up to what I had in mind. I pulled out my SIG, aimed, and fired a single shot, shattering the lock. The window slid open with a low groan, revealing the cold night air. I leaned out, assessing the situation.

It was a sheer drop from the nineteenth floor to the ground. Anyone else might have seen it as a death wish. But I saw options. There was a narrow ledge just below the window, extending across the building's exterior. Narrow grooves in the wall—enough to offer some basic friction for fingers and toes. Most importantly, the wind was almost non-existent. A gust would have been a killer, but the night was on my side.

My mind was made up in an instant. Trying to hold off eight heavily armed men wasn't just suicide—it was irresponsible. The chances of winning a shootout were slim, more like skinny, and the risk of a firefight spilling over into the nightclub was too high. Innocent people could die. The risk of sidestepping along the ledge, however insane it seemed, was lower than that of a bloody shootout. And if I made it to the next room, we could figure out a way of getting the hell out of that place without a firefight.

It was a long shot, but it was our only shot. I radioed back to Ninja Man. "Ninja, stay put. Don't engage," I said firmly. "We can't outgun them. I'm taking an alternate route out."

"What are you thinking?" he came back, sounding unsure.

"I'm going out the window," I told him. "There's a ledge outside, pretty wide, enough to cross over to the next room."

Ninja's voice came through after a brief pause, a mix of disbelief and caution in it. "Blaze, I don't want to scare you, but we're on the fucking nineteenth floor. You wanna rethink your Spiderman routine?"

I let out a laugh, more to keep the mood light than anything else. "Man, you really know how to pump a guy up. Ever considered a career in motivational speaking?"

"Yeah, sure, I'll work on my TED Talk about how not to die doing stupid shit," he replied wryly.

While I talked, I moved to the heavy mahogany desk, planted my feet firmly on the ground, and with a grunt, shoved the desk across the polished wooden floor, the legs screeching in protest. It was a solid piece, old and weighty, but my adrenaline gave me the strength to push it against the door. The desk thudded into place, blocking the only entrance. It wouldn't hold forever, but it would buy me many crucial seconds.

It was time to move out the window. Someone outside the door had begun to knock quite insistently. I walked to the window, gripping the frame tightly. The cool night air hit my face as I prepared myself mentally. I gave Ninja a final feel good message before heading out.

"It's not as bad as it looks. The ledge out there's practically a sidewalk. I've had morning jogs on worse. And remember the ledges back in the Rockies? Barely wider than our feet, with a sheer drop on one side and nothing but a wall on the other. This is a damn cakewalk," I said, trying to pump myself while making Ninja feel better.

There was a pause, and I could almost picture him shaking his head. Then, with just a hint of resignation, Ninja said, "Just don't get cocky. Be careful, brother."

"I will. Stay low, keep out of sight. If it goes south, bail out and meet me outside. I'll see you on the other side, brother."

Without waiting for a response, I stepped out onto the ledge, pressing myself flat against the wall. Outside, the night was eerily still. The wind was light, barely a whisper, carrying the distant hum of the city below. Nothing but the cold, hard wall to keep me company, with the ledge as my lifeline. One wrong move, one slip, and I knew I would be a red smear on the pavement far below.

The world seemed to shrink as I began to sidestep along the narrow ledge, the drop below me a constant reminder of what a single misstep could mean. The key was to block it out completely and stay focused on one step at a time. That's all it took. One step at a time.

The ledge was barely wide enough for my feet, and the grooves in the wall were shallow, but I kept moving, inch by inch. Each movement was deliberate, slow. I kept my body close to the wall, almost hugging it, as I shuffled sideways. The wind, thankfully, was gentle—just a whisper against my skin. The only thing that mattered was reaching the next window.

When I finally made it to the next room's window, I let out a breath I hadn't realized I had been holding. I clung to a small protrusion on the window frame, kind of a big bolt, drawing my SIG with my free hand. I fired two shots, shattering the glass. The sound of breaking glass was loud in the night, but there wasn't anyone around I needed to worry about. I reached inside, unlocked the window, and slipped into the room, landing on the floor with a soft thud.

For a moment, I just sat there, breathing heavily, letting the adrenaline settle. I was alive. That was what mattered. But I knew the night was far from over. I had to regroup with Ninja and get the hell out of there.

CHAPTER 33

The room was dark and empty, which was exactly how I wanted it. No surprises. I crossed to the door, gun drawn, and cracked it open just enough to get eyes on the hallway.

The gunmen were right where I expected them to be, crowded around the door to Sergei's office, breaking it down. The heavy desk I had barricaded it with was about to give way. One look at the guys' hardware confirmed what Ninja had already told me—these guys were loaded for bear, packing AKs, Uzis, and shotguns. Not the kind of gear you want pointed your way when you're outgunned and outnumbered.

I scanned the area quickly. The men had blocked off access to the dancefloor. No way we were getting back to the dancefloor or the service elevator without drawing some serious heat. That couldn't be the plan, not with the firepower they had. There would be too much collateral damage.

But off to the side, I spotted a secluded corner next to a private booth. It was as good a place as any to set up shop and figure out our next move. I slipped out of the room and made my way to the corner, staying low and moving fast. Once I was tucked in, I keyed up Ninja on the radio.

"Cowboy to Ninja, I'm done playing Spiderman. It's time to move."

Ninja's voice came back almost immediately, a hint of relief cutting through his usual deadpan.

"Man, good to know you made it across in one piece. I'd hate to lose my favorite pain in the ass."

"Flattery will get you nowhere, Ninja. Time to earn your keep. Head toward the private elevator. We'll link up there," I replied, moving stealthily along the wall.

"Roger that. On my way. But just so we're clear, we're still on the nineteenth floor, right?"

"Last I checked," I replied, as I moved toward the elevator. "Why?"

"Just making sure. You were talking about that 'broad ledge' earlier like it was a goddamn runway."

"Wasn't my first rodeo, Ninja. Though I gotta say, I wouldn't do it again for a million bucks."

"That's what I figured."

"Hey, quick question— you don't need a key to start a chopper, do you?" I asked, keeping my tone casual.

Ninja's reply was quick. "Nah, no key needed. Just need to flip a few switches. But what's with the sudden urge to increase your general knowledge?" he asked suspiciously.

"It's time to start brushing up on those flying lessons, pal. We're taking the scenic route outta here. We're gonna need that chopper hot and ready."

There was a pause, then Ninja's voice came through, this time with a mix of disbelief. "With all due respect, Captain sir, but are you fuckin kidding me?"

"Dead serious, Ninja. It's our best way out. Now move your ass. I'll explain when we meet."

"Copy that," he said, a touch of resignation in his tone. "See you at the elevator."

We converged on the elevator at the same time from different directions. Two men holding AK-47s were guarding it. Before they could register our presence and raise their guns, we drew our suppressed SIGs and dropped them both. It was an unspoken understanding. This was our final getaway from this place. It had to be quick and clean.

We dragged the bodies inside the elevator and hit the button for the roof. As the elevator hummed up, Ninja Man glanced at me. "You really weren't kidding about the chopper, huh?"

"Nope. It's the best shot we've got. The nightclub's swarming with Black Eagles. We can't have bullets flying on that packed dancefloor. And even if we make it to the service elevator, I'm sure all exits would be the same. They might even have cops helping them out. Best to avoid that screw up."

"Copy that. We'll make it happen."

When the doors slid open, we found two more armed men standing guard outside. We took them out just as smoothly as the first two, their bodies hitting the ground before they even knew what hit them. We dragged them across the elevator doorway, making sure the sensors would pick up the obstruction and keep the doors open. No one was coming up from below—not unless they wanted to climb.

"Ninja, get that chopper running. I'll take care of the service elevator."

Ninja didn't need to be told twice. He bolted for the chopper while I made a beeline for the service elevator at the other end of the roof. One more obstacle to clear. Another guard was posted at the entrance, but he didn't last long. One suppressed shot and he was down.

I blocked the service elevator the same way, ensuring no surprises from below. Once that was done, I sprinted to the helipad where the chopper blades were starting to spin. Ninja Man was in the cockpit, flipping switches like he had done it a hundred times before. The rotors were picking up speed, and I could already feel the rush of air from the blades cutting through the night.

As I slid into the cockpit, Ninja shot me a sidelong glance as he fiddled with the controls. "I gotta be straight with you, Cowboy—it's been five years since I last sat in the cockpit of one of these birds. You sure you wanna put your life in the hands of my rusty skills?"

I looked at him, letting a grin slip. "Ninja, I've heard enough of your war stories about flying through hell in an AH-64 Apache during IERW training. It's about time you put those skills on display. Besides, if you could handle that beast, you can damn well fly a Bell 407. I'm no expert but I think this thing's a walk in the park for an army pilot—lower payload, simpler controls."

"I never finished the course, Cowboy," Ninja chuckled, shaking his head as he focused on the instrument panel. "Guess we'll find out if those few lessons stuck, huh? But don't say I didn't warn you if we end up riding this thing into the ground."

"Remember our motto, Ninja, if we don't have a clear plan, we just wing it. Now, let's see you fly this thing like you've been doing it your whole life."

The rotors were spinning faster, kicking up dust and gravel around the helipad. Ninja adjusted the collective, flicked a few switches, and gave the gauges a quick scan.

"Alright, here goes nothing," Ninja muttered, easing the chopper into a hover. It wobbled at first, dipping slightly to one side. My hand instinctively gripped the door handle, but Ninja quickly found his rhythm. He steadied it with a deft hand on the cyclic. Within moments, we were airborne, slicing through the night sky as Ninja guided us east, toward the airport.

It was time to call Rick to get us emergency landing clearance. I called him using the helicopter's radio.

"Rick, we're coming in hot. Need emergency clearance to land. And just so you know, we've borrowed Black Eagles' helicopter. We're heading your way as we speak."

There was a pause before Rick's voice crackled back, "You gotta be shitting me. You hijacked the damn chopper?"

"More like borrowed without asking," I quipped. "Now, you gonna get us that clearance or do we have to knock on the tower's door ourselves?"

"Alright, alright, I'm on it," Rick grumbled, but I could hear the grin in his voice. "Hold tight, I'll have you sorted in a minute."

Ninja shot me a glance, his grin matching mine. "Sounded like he almost choked on his coffee when you told him."

"Can't say I blame him. Not every day you hear about someone jacking a mob helicopter."

A couple of minutes later, Rick's voice crackled back through the radio. "Alright, you're cleared. Sending you coordinates now. ATC's expecting you, so just don't crash into anything, okay?"

"Copy that," I replied, relaying the coordinates to Ninja. "Rick says hi, and try not to wreck the bird."

Ninja smirked, adjusting our course as we neared the landing zone. "No promises, boss. But I'll do my best."

I settled back in my seat as Ninja brought us in smoothly toward the designated landing area. He brought the chopper down smoothly, the skids touching the ground near the warehouses with only a slight bump, no wobble this time.

"Not bad for a guy who hasn't flown in five years," I said, clapping Ninja on the shoulder.

Ninja grinned. "Well, what do you know? Turns out I wasn't that rusty. But, man, that was fun."

As Ninja Man and I stepped out of the chopper, the night air hit us like a cool breeze after the heat of the action. The whirring of the helicopter blades was still dying down when we noticed headlights cutting through the darkness. An SUV was barreling toward us, tires crunching on the gravel, and for a split second, we both tensed, hands instinctively hovering over our sidearms.

"Friendlies?" Ninja Man muttered, his eyes narrowing as the vehicle drew closer.

"Hope so," I replied.

As the SUV drew nearer, we realized it was our own guys.

"Looks like our ride's here," Ninja declared.

The SUV skidded to a halt a few yards away, and the doors swung open. Rick, Niko, and Hawkeye hopped out, grinning like they were just back from a joyride.

Rick shot me a look, one eyebrow arched. "Blaze, wasn't this supposed to be a clandestine black op? You know, the kind where we're ghosts, not jacking helicopters?"

I gave a wry smile. "Affirmative. That's exactly why we flew in under the radar—no witnesses, no trail."

Niko chuckled. "Except for the stolen chopper parked right here."

Rick rolled his eyes, smirking. "Yeah, that's one hell of a calling card. But you sure know how to keep things interesting. We'll just leave it here for now. I'll pull some strings later to make it disappear."

We nodded and piled into the SUV, heading back to the warehouse where the rest of the team was waiting. The tension that had been knotting my shoulders began to ease as we stepped inside. The familiar faces of my Rangers brought a sense of calm.

First thing I noticed was Echo half-reclining on a makeshift bed, patched up by the medic. He was pale, bandaged, and hooked up to an IV drip. He looked like hell, but he was alive, and would be back on his feet in a few days.

I crouched beside him, giving him a once-over. "How are you holding up, Ranger?"

He grinned weakly. "Just a scratch, Cap. I told you I've had worse shaving."

"Right. When you used a chainsaw," Ninja quipped.

"I'll be back on my feet in no time, Ninja."

Rick gave us a quick rundown. "Echo needed multiple stitches and a blood transfusion. Doc says he'll be fine, but he's gotta rest for a few days."

"Glad to hear it," I replied, gently grabbing Echo's shoulder.

Madison hurried over, her face etched with concern. "Did you find the location of the girls?"

I nodded, glancing at the team. "Everyone, gather up. We've got a briefing to get through."

As the team assembled around the map spread out on a table, I marked the location of the truck parking lot. "Here's where we'll find the truck. Sergei's phone should ping with the exact coordinates within the next hour. The tracker will lead us right to them."

Madison's eyes widened when I turned on Sergei's laptop and showed her the photos of the girls and herself. "This is how Sergei recognized you, Madison. They had you pegged from the start. But that threat's over—Sergei went down in a firefight."

Turning to Rick, I said, "Rick, you gotta see this. There's a trove of intel on the Black Eagles on this laptop—enough to bring down their entire operation. Once we're done here, pass it on to Hughes' contact in Europol. Also, get it to some trusted sources in the Bulgarian administration."

Rick leaned in and went through some of the folders in the laptop. "If this intel gets into the right hands, it's going to shake them to their core. But you know these bastards will do everything they can to bury it."

"Exactly why we need to act fast. With the heat Bulgaria's under to join the EU, they can't afford to sweep this under the rug. This'll cripple the mafia's trafficking operation."

Hughes nodded, stepping closer. "My contact's ready and waiting. They've been itching for a chance like this to take down these men. Once this gets out, it'll blow up in the mafia's face. They won't have anywhere to hide."

"I'll leave this to you guys," I said. "This isn't about bringing the entire mafia down. It's about making sure they can't bounce back from it. We need to hit them where it hurts."

As I handed the laptop to Rick, I felt the weight of the mission settle even deeper on my shoulders. The job wasn't done, not by a long shot. The real mission was still out there—getting Zara and the other girls out of the hellhole.

CHAPTER 34

I looked around at the eager faces, all of them ready and waiting.

"Alright, team, it's go-time. We're taking both SUVs and a van. We'll move out to the truck terminal and take up position. The truck arrives, we hit fast and hard. This is it—time to bring the girls home."

Ninja Man grinned, his usual cocky confidence shining through. "About damn time. Let's bring them home."

Hawkeye checked his gear, a steady calm about him. "Locked and loaded. Let's roll."

The room fell into a focused silence as everyone prepared for what was to come. This was it—the moment we had been waiting for.

We moved out into the night, our convoy cutting through the stillness of Sofia's streets. The city, with all its hidden darkness, was a far cry from the mountains and deserts we had fought through in the past. But the mission was the same—find the enemy, and bring the innocent home.

When we reached the truck terminal, I couldn't help but take a moment to absorb the sheer scale of it. The place was massive, a sprawling labyrinth of steel and rubber. Rows upon rows of container trucks, hundreds of them, all packed in tight. The security lights cast long shadows, and the place was eerily quiet, like it was holding its breath, waiting for something to happen.

I immediately understood why we needed those exact coordinates. We would be out here for hours if we were looking for a needle in this haystack. Even if we had the license plate, it wouldn't be enough. Spending hours looking for the right truck would surely alert the driver. The tracker was literally going to be a lifesaver.

We hunkered down, waiting, every minute feeling like an hour. My mind was on overdrive—thinking about the girls, about Zara, about the promise I made to Omar. The air was thick with anticipation, the kind that wraps around your chest and squeezes until you can barely breathe. Then, finally, Sergei's phone buzzed. The driver had sent the message we were waiting for. The truck was in the lot, and the tracker was live.

I quickly logged into the tracker's software on Sergei's laptop and pinpointed the truck. There it was—sitting in the middle of the maze.

I motioned to Ninja Man and Hawkeye. "We move now. Madison, you stay put with Raptor. We'll signal when it's clear."

Madison gave me a firm nod, eyes full of determination. She knew what was at stake. We moved in, cutting through the rows of trucks, our steps barely making a sound. In ten minutes, we had eyes on the truck. Three men stood leaning against the back of the truck, casually chatting, oblivious to the storm about to hit them.

I whispered to the team, "We take them down hard and fast. Let's go."

We moved as one, like a well-oiled machine. The takedown was swift and brutal. We struck like lightning, the three of us moving in perfect sync. The first two men never knew what hit them, out cold before they could draw breath. The third barely had time to react before he found himself staring down the barrel of my SIG, his face drained of all color.

"Where are the keys?" I growled, keeping my voice low but threatening.

The man, shaking like a leaf, fumbled them out and handed them over without a fuss. I grabbed the keys from him and wasted no time unlocking the massive padlock that secured the truck's rear doors.

When the doors swung open, what I saw made my blood boil and my heart break at the same time. Ten girls, huddled together in the darkness, their eyes wide with terror, their bodies trembling. My heart clenched at the sight of them. They were so young—too young to have seen what they had seen, to have endured what they had endured. This was the ugly truth of the world, the reason we fought, the reason we risked everything.

I stepped inside, keeping my voice low, gentle, trying to cut through their fear. "Do any of you understand English? We're American soldiers, and we're here to take you home."

For a moment, there was nothing. Just blank stares. Then, one girl stood up hesitantly and took a step forward. Her voice was barely a whisper, but it hit me like a freight train.

"Captain Axel Blaze?"

My breath caught in my throat. I recognized her immediately—Zara. The girl we had come all this way to save. The girl Omar had spoken of with so much hope, the one I had promised him I would find.

Zara looked up at me, her eyes full of a mixture of disbelief and desperate hope. Without another word, she stepped into my arms, clinging to me like a lifeline. I wrapped her in a protective hug, feeling the weight of the mission, the responsibility, the promise I made to Omar.

"You're safe now, Zara," I whispered. "We're getting you out of here, and we're taking you back to Ayaan. He's waiting for you."

She didn't say anything, just held on tighter, as if letting go would make this nightmare start all over again. I could feel her trembling start to subside, just a little, as if she was starting to believe that maybe, just maybe, this was real. That she was safe.

We stood there for a moment, the world outside the truck forgotten. My mind drifted back to Omar, to the promise I made as he bled out in my arms. Ayaan was already free of the Taliban's grip, and now, we had Zara. But there was one last loose end to tie up in this nightmare.

As the other Rangers radioed Raptor to bring Madison and the van around, I felt a cold, hard resolve settle in. The mission wasn't over. There was one last piece of unfinished business—Bilal. The man who kicked off all this hell. The one who shattered Omar's family and set off this entire chain of horror. It was time to end him.

"It's almost over, Omar," I thought, holding Zara just a little bit tighter. "I got your girl. Now it's time to finish this."

The time for reckoning was coming. And when it did, there would be no mercy—just cold, hard justice.

CHAPTER 35

The sun was sinking behind the jagged peaks, casting long shadows over the barren landscape as we dug into position. The mountains around us were dead silent—the kind of place where even the wind seemed too scared to hang around. Up here, the air was thin and biting, cutting through the rocky terrain like a blade.

I crouched low behind a jagged outcrop, eyes glued to the unpaved road winding through the valley below. It was a rough, twisted stretch of dirt and gravel, a snake slithering between the mountains—unforgiving, just like this terrain.

That road wasn't much to look at, just a backwater dirt trail cutting through no man's land, linking Quetta in Pakistan to Kandahar in Afghanistan. Smugglers' highway. Insurgents, weapons, dope—everything illegal moved through here. No law, no order, just a corridor for the worst of the worst.

Perfect spot for an ambush. That's why we were here. Eyes on the prize—Bilal Mustafa.

Raptor was about 20 yards to my right, cradling his RPG-7 like it was part of him, eyes glued to the road, sharp and locked in. He had that deadly calm about him—the kind you only get from being in the shit too many times. On my left, Ninja Man was about the same distance away, tapping the stock of his HK416 like a drummer in a slow rhythm, face calm but ready. We were spaced out just right, close enough to cover each other but spread enough to create a hell of a kill zone. This was our playground—waiting, watching, and gearing up for the hit.

Up top, on the ridge, Hawkeye was lying flat, his body nearly invisible against the rocky outcrop. He was the overwatch, the angel of death with his Barrett M107A1—the kind of rifle that didn't just kill, it erased targets. That beast could punch through anything with its 50-cal BMG armor-piercing rounds, good for nearly 2,000 yards. The guy was an executioner from a mile out.

Right next to Hawkeye was Echo, eyes glued to the spotter scope, fresh stitches running down his side like a brutal zipper. He should have been back at base, healing up, but no way he would sit this one out. We came into this mission together, and Echo wasn't about to miss the finish line. None of us were. This wasn't just a mission—it was personal.

Time moved differently up here, stretched out and compressed all at once. We could sit for hours, barely moving, just watching. Patience was part of the job. We were trained for it. Every breath, every twitch was controlled, calculated. The tension hung thick in the air, but we had been here before. This was the calm before the storm, the last quiet moment before things went loud and violent.

"You ever wonder why we do this, Captain?" Raptor's voice came through the comms, low and gritty. He wasn't looking at me, his gaze still locked on the road.

"Not really," I answered, keeping it just as low. "I'm just here for the view."

Ninja Man let out a quiet laugh. "Yeah, I hear this place is lovely in the spring. Nothing like a little desert bloom to get the blood pumping."

Hawkeye chimed in, voice cool as ever. "This kinda waiting's what separates the men from the boys."

Ninja Man grinned, not taking his eyes off the road. "Ain't that the truth. Lucky for us, we're all grown-ass men here. Even Echo."

"Ha ha. Funny guy. I'm up here freezing my ass off, and you clowns are down there having a damn picnic," Echo shot back.

Raptor chuckled softly. "Hell, I missed this. Just the quiet, the build up... and then the sweet, sweet sound of chaos when it all kicks off."

"Focus, boys," I said, but there was no edge to my tone. This was our ritual. Dark humor to keep the edge sharp, to drown out the tension of waiting for the storm to hit. It kept us wired in, ready to flip the switch when the time came.

We were here for one reason: to drop Bilal Mustafa and his crew. Sure, we could have just lit him up with a drone strike, a Hellfire missile turning him into a smoking crater. But that wasn't the play this time. You need exact coordinates for a drone to be useful, and all we had was a rumor—Bilal was set to meet an arms dealer in some crowded Quetta market. No way we could ID him from the sky. We needed boots on the ground, eyes in the shadows, and the flexibility to adapt the plan on the fly. This wasn't about dropping a bomb and hoping for the best. It was about making sure the job got done up close, no loose ends.

That's why I hadn't kicked this up to HQ, and why my CO, Lt. Col. Flynn, was still in the dark.

Looping him in meant more red tape, more hands on the steering wheel, and more chances for this to get screwed up. We had one shot. Miss it, and Bilal would melt into the mountains, and we would be chasing his ghost for months. Flynn was solid—good leader—but he played by the book. And this? This op wasn't in any damn manual. I would brief him once we got it done, but until then, the mission was ours alone.

Luckily, we had a silent backer—James Davis, Deputy Director at the CIA, and Madison's old man. He was the kind of guy who understood that sometimes, the rules needed bending. He had given us the intel off the books, making sure it didn't hit any official channels. Davis knew this wasn't just another sanctioned op. He was in it with us until the very end, whatever it took.

Before we set off for Sofia, we had got the initial intel from Hamid Gul. Before he got blown up by his own device, he tipped us off that Bilal would be hitting up a "dry fruits" shop in Quetta. That shop wasn't just slinging pistachios and apricots—it was a front for Arif Khan, one of Pakistan's biggest arms dealers. Running an op on Pakistani turf without clearance would have kicked off a political firestorm, the kind we wanted no part of.

So, Davis flipped the switch on one of his deep-cover assets. This guy had been embedded in Quetta for years, a seasoned pro who knew every shadow and back alley. He tailed Arif Khan the whole day, eyes on him like a hawk. When Bilal finally showed up at the shop, our asset was ready, camera in hand. He snapped off a few covert shots, grainy as hell, but clear enough. Nate, the CIA's top guy on Taliban intel, took one look and confirmed it—it was Bilal, in the flesh. We had our target.

The asset didn't stop there. He managed to slip a tracker on Bilal's vehicle—a risky move, but the guy had nerves of steel. After that, it was just a waiting game. Once Bilal's convoy pulled out of Quetta, the tracker lit up, feeding us their route in real-time. They were coming right toward the kill box we had set up in this no-man's land.

Nate's voice buzzed through my earpiece, cutting through the silence. "Blaze, you've got movement. Convoy's about a mile out, closing in. Two pickups and a truck, twenty fighters, give or take. ETA, two minutes."

I relayed it to the team. "Alright, boys, target's a mile out. Two pickups and a truck, twenty hostiles. We've got two minutes to get ready."

We hunkered down, eyes locked on that road. Every second stretched, the calm before the chaos. This is the part that always got the adrenaline pumping—the quiet, knowing the enemy was closing in, knowing it was about to get real loud, real fast.

The dust cloud appeared first, rising from the winding road like a signal flare. Two pickups leading, the truck trailing. They were cruising like they owned the place, not a care in the world. Little did they know, they were driving right into the lion's den.

"There they are," I whispered, my voice carrying through the comms. "Hawkeye, Echo, you got eyes on them?"

Hawkeye's reply came back, calm and cold. "Got them in my sights. Bilal's in the lead truck, riding shotgun. I've got the driver locked."

I could practically see the crosshairs dancing over that driver's chest. Hawkeye wasn't the kind of guy who missed. And when it went loud, that first shot would set the whole thing in motion.

"Raptor, have that RPG ready. As soon as Hawkeye drops the lead driver, you light up the second pickup. We need both vehicles disabled before they know what hit them."

"Affirmative, Cowboy," Raptor responded, his voice steady with that lethal edge. He was built for this—delivering chaos with a well-aimed shot. "RPG's primed and ready."

The convoy kept creeping closer, two pickups up front with a truck lagging fifty yards behind. My eyes locked on the men riding in the beds of the pickups—six in each, AK-47s slung over their shoulders, relaxed like they were on a Sunday drive. They didn't think anyone would dare ambush them on this road. Big mistake.

The first pickup rolled right into the kill zone. The low growl of its engine bounced off the mountains, cutting through the silence. I tightened my grip on my rifle, the tension thick enough to cut with a knife.

"Hawkeye, now," I whispered into the comms.

There was no hesitation. The crack of the Barrett's .50 caliber round echoed through the mountains like a thunderclap. The driver of the lead pickup never knew what hit him. The bullet punched through his chest, severing his head from his shoulders in a grisly spray of blood and bone. The round kept going, smashing clean through the pickup's body. The vehicle swerved violently, the lifeless driver slumping against the door, before coming to a halt in the middle of the road.

"Raptor, hit it!" I ordered.

A split second later, the whoosh of Raptor's RPG firing filled the air. The grenade flew true, slamming into the second pickup. The explosion lit up the mountainside, turning the vehicle into a ball of fire. The pickup was launched into the air before crashing down in a twisted heap, flames licking at the wreckage.

The guys in the bed of the lead pickup never had a chance. Before they could even blink, Ninja Man and I opened up with our HK416s, cutting them down where they sat. Rounds tore through flesh and bone, the six men jerking like ragdolls before hitting the dirt in a bloody mess.

The truck in the rear skidded to a stop, the driver and passenger frozen for a heartbeat too long. Hawkeye put a round through the driver's skull, while Raptor, now armed with his rifle, took out the passenger with a double tap to the chest. Clean, precise.

Two guys in the back of the truck made a desperate run for it, spraying rounds from their AKs as they bolted for the rocks. They didn't get far. Ninja Man and Raptor took them down with controlled bursts, the sound of gunfire echoing through the mountains like a death knell.

And then, just as suddenly as it had begun, everything went still. The only sounds were the crackling of flames from the wrecked pickup and the faint whistle of the wind through the valley. The ambush went down exactly like we planned—fast, brutal, and final.

I scanned the area, finger still on the trigger, but there was no movement. Just bodies and burning wreckage. But one man was still alive, and I knew exactly where he was.

I spotted Bilal in the passenger seat of the lead pickup, frozen like a deer in the headlights. His gaunt face framed by a thick, unruly beard no longer had a menacing quality about it. His eyes were wide, mouth slightly open, as if his brain hadn't yet processed what had just happened. His AK-47 rested uselessly across his lap. For a moment, he looked like he might have accepted his fate, but then survival instincts kicked in.

As I stepped out from cover, rifle ready, Bilal snapped to life. He scrambled out of the truck, raising his AK with a frantic desperation. But he was too slow, and I was too close. I could have put one right between his eyes and ended it quick. But I wanted him to see his end coming, to feel the weight of his sins bearing down on him. He had killed Omar and his family, sent us on this mission of vengeance, and he needed to know that retribution was coming toward him, one step at a time.

I took a deep breath, steadied my aim, and squeezed the trigger. The shot was clean—his AK went flying, along with a few fingers from his left hand, exploding in a mist of blood and bone.

Bilal screamed in agony, his hand a mess of blood and torn flesh, but he wasn't done. He reached into his coat and whipped out a Glock, cursing in Pashto as he tried to bring it to bear on me. I could see it in his eyes—he wanted me to end it quickly, to put a bullet in his head and spare him the pain. But that wasn't happening. Not that day.

After firing, I had slung my rifle and pulled out a SIG. I advanced with measured steps, each one

285

bringing me closer to him. I aimed low, my finger squeezing the trigger almost gently, and the SIG barked once. His right hand, the one holding the Glock, exploded in a mess of blood and broken fingers. The gun tumbled to the ground as Bilal let out another guttural scream.

"You're in Taliban territory!" he spat, clutching his ruined hands to his chest, fear and rage mingling in his voice. "My men will be here any minute, and they'll skin you alive!"

I didn't bother replying. I wanted him to experience the terror he had dealt out on Omar, his family, and countless others. I aimed and fired again, this time putting a bullet through his right knee. The bullet tore through his kneecap, sending him crashing down onto one knee. The fear in his eyes now was unmistakable.

His bravado crumbled. "What do you want?" Bilal gasped, his voice trembling.

I didn't answer. Instead, I brought the butt of my SIG down hard on his temple. His head snapped to the side, and he crumpled to the ground, unconscious. I quickly cuffed his hands and feet, tying him further to the truck's front grille, then gagged him with a strip of cloth. He wasn't going anywhere.

Ninja Man and Raptor moved past me, rifles at the ready as they pulled apart the tarp at its back and checked inside. It was filled with stacks of crates, packed full of AK-47s, rocket launchers, grenades, and enough ammunition to start a small war. This was Bilal's stockpile, the tools of his trade, and soon, it would all be reduced to ash.

Ninja Man pulled out the C-4 from his pack and began setting the charges with practiced precision.

"Five-minute timer," he said, giving me a thumbs-up.

I walked back to Bilal, who was beginning to stir. Grabbing a canteen, I splashed cold water over his face, waking him with a start. His eyes darted around wildly, then locked onto mine, wide with panic.

"This is for Omar Haq and his family," I said, my voice cutting through the crackle of the fire like a blade. "We saved his children—his blood, his legacy. They'll live to honor his name. But you..."

Bilal's eyes darted around, frantic, searching for some shred of hope. But there was none. He was done, and he knew it. I leaned in closer, letting my words sink deep into the pit of his gut.

"You think this place, these mountains, will remember you? They won't. In five minutes, you'll be gone. No one to mourn you. All you'll be remembered as is a drug-dealing, pedophile piece of trash."

Bilal's muffled cries grew more frantic, but I was already turning away, walking back up the hill with the Rangers. There was nothing left to say. We walked away in silence, making our way up the hill without looking back. The only sound was the crunch of gravel under our boots. The wind had picked up, carrying the scent of diesel and blood.

As we reached the top, the C-4 detonated with a thunderous roar. The truck erupted in a fireball, the blast wave washing over us as we watched from our vantage point. Secondary explosions rattled the valley as the munitions cooked off, sending shards of metal and debris into the sky.

We stopped for a moment, watching the fire rage below. There was no cheering, no high-fives. Just the grim satisfaction of a job well done.

I thought about Omar Haq, about the promise we had made to him. Bilal had been a monster, a man who thrived on the misery of others, and now he was gone—erased from the world as if he had never existed. Zara and Ayaan were safe under Madison's care. They were in good hands, protected and cared for, just as we had vowed.

The mission was over, another chapter closed. We were ready to head home, knowing we had done what needed to be done. Nothing more, nothing less.

As we stood there, gazing at the sun dipping below the horizon, a speck appeared in the distance, growing larger until the silhouette of a Black Hawk helicopter came into view.

"Well, look who's here to give us a lift," Raptor broke the silence. "Guess we don't have to hump it back through Taliban country after all."

Ninja Man smirked, shouldering his rifle. "Damn shame. I was just starting to enjoy the mountain air. Nothing like the fresh scent of explosives in the evening."

Echo, still wincing slightly from his injuries but not missing a beat, chimed in, "Can't wait to see what's for dinner back at base. Hopefully, something that doesn't taste like cardboard for once."

Hawkeye chuckled, clapping Echo on the shoulder. "Don't get your hopes up, Echo. But hey, at least we won't have to eat it on a mountainside."

For once, I didn't have anything to say. Just stood there, watching my team, the silent bond between us speaking louder than any words could. As the Black Hawk's rotors hammered the air, I took in the moment—the grim satisfaction of a job done right. Justice had been done the way we knew best—not pretty, not quick—but final.

The mission was wrapped, just one more in a long list. Tomorrow, there would be another fight. But for now, this would do.

— THE END —

BLAZE RETURNS
(Book One)

Deputy US Marshal Carter has gone missing in Little Butte, Nevada. The Dawsons own the town. A Mexican cartel is moving in. A gang war is coming to town. Blaze returns for one last assignment to find Carter before all hell breaks loose.

LETHAL FORCE
(Book Two)

When Blaze takes out a Mexican cartel's operations in Nevada, the cartel sends hitmen after him and everyone he cares about. Bad move. What the cartel doesn't realize is, it has messed with a Lethal Force.

HARD TARGET
(Book Three)

When Blaze stops at an isolated gas station, he stumbles upon an execution about to go down. Blaze's intervention gets a pack of mercenaries after him. What they don't realize: when it comes to deadly sport, Blaze is a master of the game.

MEAN STREETS
(Book Four)

Midnight in New York City. A car stops at an intersection. A girl in the back gives Blaze a distress hand signal. The chase that begins in Manhattan takes Blaze on a treacherous chase through the city that never sleeps.

UNCHAINED FURY
(Book Five)

There is a contract out on Blaze and his old team. Floated by the Cady brothers—ruthless arms dealers who will stop at nothing to get revenge. But when the game becomes no holds barred, there's nothing to hold back Blaze's fury.

NO ESCAPE
(Book Six)

Chaos erupts in Bison Creek, Wyoming. Two slain officers. Blood-soaked ex-Marine Logan on the scene. A sinister link between a cult and a pharma company. But one man will move heaven and earth to dig out the truth—Blaze.

FEAR CITY
(Book Seven)

Blaze heads to Boston after a shadowy group of investors—rich, powerful, and ready to bulldoze anything in their way. Blaze is up against these ruthless players who would sooner bury the truth than face it. They play dirty.
But so does Blaze.

NO MERCY
(Book Nine)

CIA agents in the Middle East are turning up dead. Blaze must save trapped agents and stop a rogue analyst from blowing their covers. With the Italian mafia and terror outfits in the picture, Blaze has only one rule: No Mercy.

WARPATH
(Book Ten)

Blaze and his Delta team head to Mexico to dismantle a powerful drug cartel. They take it apart piece by piece. But when the cartel brings the fight to US soil and targets Americans, Blaze makes it personal and goes on the warpath.

CROSSFIRE
(Book Eleven – July '25)

Americans are caught in the inferno as Yemen's going up in flames.. Blaze is sent to extract an Al-Qaeda informant, who is the key to saving lives. He faces betrayals and deadly odds. But Blaze won't just hold the line—he'll obliterate the enemy.

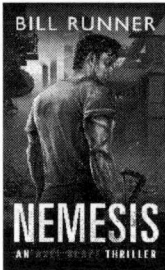

NEMESIS
(Book Twelve – Nov '25)

They killed his brother. They buried the truth. They thought it was over. But Blaze won't stop until the men responsible pay in blood. No rules. No mercy. Just a one-man war from the battlefield to the streets of America. The nemesis is coming.

ABOUT REVIEWS AND NEWSLETTERS

Thank you for reading my book. If you could take a moment to leave a review on Amazon, even just a sentence, it would help a lot. Should you wish to share any feedback, my email is billrunnerauthor@gmail.com.

You can join my mailing list on my website: https://bill-runner.com. You will receive updates on new releases and special offers.

Made in the USA
Columbia, SC
27 April 2025

57203148R00176